All the Impossible Things

lindsay lackey

SQUARE
FISH

ROARING BROOK PRESS
NEW YORK

For Donna—who, in so many ways,
made this story possible.
And for Sophia—who dances our
whole family into life.

SQUARE FISH

An imprint of Macmillan Publishing Group, LLC
120 Broadway, New York, NY 10271 • mackids.com
Copyright © 2019 by Lindsay Lackey.
All rights reserved.

Square Fish and the Square Fish logo are trademarks of Macmillan and
are used by Roaring Brook Press under license from Macmillan.

Our books may be purchased in bulk for promotional, educational, or
business use. Please contact your local bookseller or the Macmillan
Corporate and Premium Sales Department at (800) 221-7945
ext. 5442 or by email at MacmillanSpecialMarkets@macmillan.com.

Library of Congress Control Number: 2019932582

Originally published in the United States by Roaring Brook Press

First Square Fish edition, 2022

Book designed by Elizabeth H. Clark

Cover photo girl by Mohamad Itani / Trevillion Images; Cover photo turtle by
Mirelle / Shutterstock; Back cover photo landscape by Chendongshan /
Shutterstock; Back cover photo tree by olegganko / Shutterstock

Square Fish logo designed by Filomena Tuosto

Printed in the United States of America by Lakeside Book Company,
Harrisonburg, Virginia

ISBN 978-1-250-61890-0 (paperback)
1   3   5   7   9   10   8   6   4   2

LEXILE: 630L

Bumblebees are impossible.

They break the rules of physics. Their tiny wings should not be able to carry their fat little bodies through the air.

The truth is, a bumblebee's wings work differently than people realize. For a long time, everyone thought their wings flapped up and down, like a bird's. But they don't. Their wings actually flap forward and back, really, really fast. So fast that a bumblebee creates its very own tornado. And that tornado picks up the bumblebee and carries it from one place to the next.

Which, if you think about it, doesn't seem impossible at all.

Chapter 1

The wind came from her mother.

Some moms pass along their freckles or their laugh or their flat feet. Red's mother shared air currents and chaos. Clouds that twisted between earth and sky like a wet rag being wrung out.

But Red kept the wind under her skin.

She had to.

The more she swallowed down her own storms, however, the angrier the sky above her became.

Though the day had started clear and crisp, the sky was now dark with rain clouds that churned above the quiet Denver neighborhood. One minute, leaves were crunching under the feet of schoolchildren. Jack-o'-lanterns smiled from porch steps, their faces so freshly carved that their skin was not yet spongy or speckled with mold. The next minute, the air hissed and whistled, and every leaf was sucked up up up, twirling and spinning. Carved pumpkins rolled and bounced and shattered, their pulpy flesh smearing like paint against the sidewalks.

In a small living room that smelled of air freshener and dirty socks, Red stood, her thoughts as deep and dark and full of holes as the pockets of her coat.

She did not look at the swollen-faced woman who constantly referred to herself as "The Mom."

The Mom said, "It's not easy being The Mom to three boys, you know."

To three boys. But not to Red.

The Mom looked at Red, then at her own hands. Her fingernails were a bright slash of yellow. Red's hair tickled her cheeks like tears, but her eyes were dry. Outside, the storm swelled as Red held her breath. *No no no.*

The Mom glanced out the window toward the thrashing trees. Her eyes darted back to Red, then to Ms. Anders, Red's social worker. "It just isn't a good time to bring a foster child into the family."

Red released her breath a little, then pressed her trembling lips together. The wind howled and The Mom flinched.

Ms. Anders put a hand on Red's shoulder. "Of course," she said. Her voice was as taut and charged as an electric wire. "All set, Red?"

Red nodded. All her belongings fit into an orange backpack that—thanks to The Mom's three boys— smelled like peanut butter and dog vomit. Still, a smelly backpack was better than the plastic bag she used to carry.

"We are so sorry about this, like I said before." The Mom's eyes were a little too close together, making her whole face look pinched. "It's The Mom's responsibility to protect her children. Sometimes things just aren't a good fit."

A familiar ache started between Red's ribs, but then anger, sharp and slick, snaked through her, burying the hurt. Across the room, the pages of an open magazine lifted, flapped, and fluttered. Red clenched her fists in her pockets.

No no no. She couldn't let her wind out, no matter how much it boiled beneath her skin.

A crash of thunder split the air and The Mom yelped.

Ms. Anders pursed her black-cherry lips, her fingers tightening on Red's shoulder ever so slightly. "Come on, Red."

Red hiked up her backpack and stepped from the house without looking back. Her caseworker let the screen door slam as she exited. She didn't acknowledge the gray-green clouds that had bruised the clear blue of the morning sky. Ms. Anders yanked open the rear door of her sedan. The fabric of her skirt was a snapping flag around her knees.

Red climbed into the familiar car. As always, there was a package of peach gummy candy on the seat for her. Affection for her caseworker flickered in her stomach.

The Mom opened the screen door, leaned out. "We really did try!"

Red hugged her knees to her chest, tucking the candy into her coat pocket. Fat, angry raindrops left dark spots on Ms. Anders's gray blazer as she ran around to the driver's side. She shook her short, tightly curled hair, and Red could smell powdery hair product under the sharp, cold scent of the wind.

Ms. Anders pulled out of the driveway and leaned forward to look up through the windshield. The wipers moved frantically against the glass. She clucked her tongue.

Red pushed away a clump of hair that was stuck to her damp forehead. Her storm still thrummed in her bones, whirled between her ribs and toes and ears, as familiar as her own breath. It wanted out, wanted to join the angry sky. She couldn't let it.

"This weather," Ms. Anders said. "Someone's gonna get hurt." She shook her head at the shame of it.

Red wanted to say, *Someone's already been hurt*.

Instead, she said nothing. She just leaned her head against the window and watched the sky have its say.

Chapter 2

"I have a new family for you." Ms. Anders spoke above the clatter of rain. "They're excited to meet you." She squinted at the sky. "Hopefully this storm peters out before we get farther east. Storms are usually worse east of the city."

Red drew slow, deep breaths and counted to ten, like her therapist, Dr. Teddy, had taught her to do. The wind buzzing in her veins slowly quieted as she watched the new-build neighborhoods unravel into business complexes and strip malls and parking garages. The longer they drove, the more the weather cleared. The angry clouds squeezed out their last tears and began to settle into fading swirls of violet and gold as the sun dipped toward the line of mountains along the western horizon behind them. Red ate her peach candies, which were so sweet they turned sour on her tongue.

"This will be good," Ms. Anders said.

Red met her eyes in the rearview mirror, which Ms. Anders always kept cockeyed so she could see the back seat. From the mirror, a small crystal angel dangled on a pink ribbon, bobbing and swaying with the rhythm of the car.

"The Grooves are very kind people," Ms. Anders said.

Red said nothing.

"You'll like them."

Red said nothing.

"They'll be a good fit. You'll see."

A good fit. Impossible. Nobody could be a good fit. Nobody except her mother. Red felt the pulse of the wind in her heart. *Three hundred ninety-seven days*, she reminded herself. Three hundred ninety-seven days until her mom got out. Three hundred ninety-seven days until Red would be *a good fit*.

She could feel her caseworker's stare, but ignored it. Once, when Red had to be removed from a family in the middle of the night, Ms. Anders had arrived so fast, it was as if she'd been waiting around the corner. Her hair was standing up in jagged peaks, and her shoes were mismatched. The buttons of her shirt weren't aligned with the holes, making her blouse bunch and gap in the front like crooked teeth. But she was there. She'd held

Red's hand and carried her plastic bag of clothes. That was the first time there had been a package of peach gummies on the back seat of the car.

That night, Ms. Anders had said quietly but firmly: "You've got edges and corners and curves to your soul, Red. We all do. But yours are special. Hear me? It might take some time, but someday, you're gonna find the folks who fit just right. You'll see."

That was almost three years ago. Red was only nine then, and didn't yet understand that kids were like shoes. They could be kicked off, left behind, returned when they didn't quite fit.

She'd be twelve in five months. She understood a lot more now.

Something flashed ahead. She blinked. A giant turtle stood by the side of the road. It was almost as tall as a stop sign, and had a grin packed with square white teeth. A black-and-white animal stood on top of its green shell. A . . . goat?

Ms. Anders slowed and turned onto a dirt road, giving Red a better view of the enormous reptile and its companion. At the top of the strange pyramid, above the goat's back, words were painted in big purple letters.

"Turn here for the Groovy Petting Zoo," Ms. Anders read aloud, then chuckled.

Red twisted around in her seat, eyes glued to the

sign as they passed, the sound of her caseworker's laughter stirring something in her she couldn't quite identify.

After a few miles, their sedan turned down another dirt road. This one was a driveway and was flanked by a row of skinny trees. Yellowing leaves skittered and danced along the thin, white branches. The end of the tree tunnel framed a two-story house with at least six different colors of paint. To one side, there was a rambling garden. Drooping sunflowers hung their huge, wilting heads against the top of a white fence. Near the gate sat an old bathtub bursting with the bright globes of marigolds. The sun was slinking behind the horizon now, and tongues of pink clouds licked the sky.

The startling joyfulness of the place made the feeling Red hadn't been able to identify fizz to life in her chest again. *Hope.*

"It's like something out of a storybook," Ms. Anders said. She put the car in park and turned around. Her smile made Red's stomach spin a pirouette. "Like I said, I think they might be a great fit."

Red swallowed her tiny bubbles of hope and looked away. A gust of wind peppered the side of the car with dirt.

The front door opened and a pack of dogs tumbled from the house, careening toward the car in an

11

avalanche. Their tails whipped back and forth, causing their butts to waggle in unison, like synchronized doggie dancers. A man followed the dogs, whistling for them, but they barely glanced at him before returning their attention to the car.

Ms. Anders climbed out. Red stayed put.

Over the yelping and snuffling, Red could hear Ms. Anders greet the stranger. He shook her hand with both of his, nearly lifting her off her feet in his enthusiasm. His smile was wide and bright, and he wore a dusty baseball cap that said, *I Like Big Mutts*.

Three of the four dogs gathered around the two adults, while one enormous pile of black fur remained at the car, staring eagerly at Red through the window. Its tail moved in a slow, easy wave, and its rosy tongue dangled out of its mouth. There was a black freckle right in the middle of its pink surface. The dog looked friendly. As friendly as a drooling black mass of fur could look, actually. But she wasn't quite ready to open the door and meet the beast face-to-face.

Just then, a woman emerged from the fairy-tale house, warm blossoms of pink on her otherwise pale cheeks. She was somehow both normal and remarkable all at once. Her curly hair billowed from her head like the gold and silver clouds of a sunrise. Her eyes paused on Ms. Anders and the man with his mutts, but they were seeking something else, and kept moving until they found it.

Red's heart tumbled around in her chest more wildly than the dogs had tumbled toward the car.

The woman's eyes were shining directly on her.

Chapter
3

Red held her breath. Only Gamma had ever looked at Red the way the lady with sunrise hair was looking at her. It was a look like, *You're here.* Like, *I see you there.* Like, *You aren't too old or quiet or broken at all.*

Ms. Anders opened Red's door, and cold evening air rushed up to kiss Red's cheeks. "Come on, Red. Come meet the Grooves."

Red looked away from the sunrise-hair lady and slid out of the car. The giant black dog pressed its nose against her thigh in greeting. The other dogs bounced and jostled and snuffled her. She gently pushed their heads aside. It was like swimming through a river of fur and tongue and drool.

Ms. Anders ushered Red over to the man. He was tall.

So tall that Red was sure he could reach up and pluck stars from the sky if he wanted to. Maybe he'd snatched some clouds at sunrise once and given them to his wife for hair. Red snuck a glance at the woman—Mrs. Groove—as she shook the enormous hand of Mr. Groove.

"This is Ruby Byrd," Ms. Anders said, her hands on Red's shoulders.

Mr. Groove was beaming. "I can't tell you how happy we are to have you, Ruby! When Ms. Anders called to see if we wanted to meet you—Down, Frodo! Stop that!—we were just—*Brontë!* Get down!"

He shooed two floppy-eared labs away, but the border collie took their place, sniffing Red's shoes.

"Honey, could you get these mongrels away?" he asked.

Mrs. Groove, who had come up alongside him, snapped her fingers once. The dogs, every single one of them, turned to face her and sat down.

"Porch," she directed. All of them obeyed, except for the black furbeast. It stayed by Mrs. Groove's side, tongue lolling as she scratched its dark ears.

"My," Ms. Anders said. "They're well trained!"

Mr. Groove shook his head and threw up his hands. "They only do that for Celine. I'm the vet, but she's the boss."

His wife was still smiling at Red. It brought a tickling wind to Red's skin. She shivered and wrapped her arms around herself.

15

"Ruby." Mrs. Groove's voice was deeper than Red expected.

"I go by Red." She clamped her bottom lip between her teeth, struggling against the swell of nervous wind in her chest.

"Red?" Mr. Groove asked. She could tell what he was thinking: *But her hair is brown.* "Red. Okay."

But Mrs. Groove's eyes hadn't left Red's face. "Welcome," she said. "It's so nice to meet you."

The sky was darkening as the sun disappeared behind the distant mountains, and a sudden gust of autumn air pushed against Red, driving her toward Mrs. Groove. She resisted, took a step back. Ms. Anders made a quiet *tik* with her tongue against her teeth and patted Red between the shoulders. The touch felt like, *It's okay.* Like, *Remember your manners.*

Red tried. "Nice to meet you," she said.

The giant black dog whined, its tail wagging and its tongue hanging long and pink from the side of its mouth. Stepping forward again, Red dropped to her knees and lifted her hands to the massive dog's head. Its hot breath smelled of maple syrup.

Mrs. Groove crouched so she was at Red's eye level. "This is Gandalf." She wiggled the dog's drooping lips with her fingertip. A line of drool swung back and forth from Gandalf's jowls like the little crystal angel in Ms. Anders's car.

"I wanted to name her Beauty," Mr. Groove said, kneeling beside them. "As in *Black Beauty*? But Celine was set on Gandalf, despite the fact she's not gray or white. And she's a girl, of course."

Mrs. Groove touched her nose to Gandalf's. "But she's magic."

"So is Hermione. That's a girl's name," Mr. Groove said.

Celine laughed. "I said she was magic. I never claimed she was brilliant."

At their words, the bubbles of hope sparkled again in Red's heart. "Hermione, like in *Harry Potter*?" she whispered.

Mrs. Groove nodded, just as Ms. Anders cleared her throat.

"Uh . . . should we go inside?" Ms. Anders asked. "Get Red settled?"

"Right!" Mr. Groove clapped his hands once and stood. Gandalf looked up at him, smiling her dog smile.

Mrs. Groove stood and dusted her knees. "Are you ready?"

Red stood, too, mimicking Mrs. Groove's knee-dusting.

Her caseworker and new foster father started toward the house. Mr. Groove took Red's backpack with him. Gandalf surprised Red with a slobbery tongue on her cheek before gamboling after them.

"She sneak-attacks with love," Mrs. Groove said.

Red wiped her face and they walked together.

"You go by Red?" Mrs. Groove asked.

Red frowned. "It's what my mom calls me."

Mrs. Groove paused on the top porch step. "I see. Red, it is. You can call me Celine."

A lot of foster parents wanted Red to call them *Mr.* or *Ms.* Whatever. Some even wanted a combination of *Mom* or *Dad* with their first name. *Mom Judy. Dad Frank.* Red hated it. None of them were her mom.

They never would be.

Still, she'd never been invited to call a foster parent by their first name alone. She bit her lip, sneaking a look at her newest foster mother.

Celine smiled and held the front door open. "Welcome home."

Chapter
4

The inside of the house was just as bright and mismatched as the outside. Mr. Groove—"Call me Jackson, kiddo," he said—led them into a crowded but comfortable living room. The walls had ornate wallpaper covered in gold birds hanging from tangled branches. A sagging denim couch was framed by a leather recliner and an antique rocking chair. Two differently patterned rugs splashed across the hardwood floor, each accented with clumps of dog hair. There were plants on shelves and tabletops, pillows embroidered with inspirational quotes, and stacks of magazines and books overflowing the bookcases. A pile of firewood next to the hearth filled the room with the sweetness of pine.

The whole place felt like an adventure.

"My," said Ms. Anders, eyeing a collection of cartoon-character cookie jars on built-in shelves outside the kitchen.

Jackson laughed. "*My* is right. The house was my mother's. We moved in to care for her the last year of her life. When she passed, we stayed. And despite all our best intentions, we haven't gotten around to redecorating."

"Oh, I didn't mean—I'm just impressed," she said. "That's quite a collection." Ms. Anders's lips puckered like she was embarrassed.

Jackson clapped her on the back, booming a bass-drum laugh. "You're welcome to them! You'd be doing us a favor. I keep telling Cee we should sell them on eBay."

"Nobody'll want those," Celine said, shaking her head. "Let's take Ru—Red up to her room before we sit. I'm sure she's eager to see it."

"Great idea," Ms. Anders said. She smiled encouragingly at Red. "I'll wait down here."

Celine led the way up the creaking staircase. The air upstairs was warmer and didn't have the same freshness as the piney living room. The faint scent of rose perfume conjured a sudden memory of Red's grandmother. Gamma had roses everywhere. On dishes and towels and bedspreads. On little glass bottles of perfume. Red used to love rearranging them on top of Gamma's dresser, sniffing each one.

"That's Mama and me," Jackson said, his voice jolting

Red back into the hallway. He pointed to a picture hanging among a constellation of smaller framed photos. A woman with thick glasses and Jackson's curved nose and miles-wide grin had her arms wrapped around a little boy with an afro that matched hers. The photo was yellowing around the edges, like it had been held and looked at and loved almost as much as the boy himself.

Red snuck a glance at Jackson as he smiled wistfully at the photo. She'd never had a Black foster parent before. She'd lived with a Latino couple once, and the house mother of one group home was Korean American, but most of the foster families had been white.

Jackson caught her looking at him. "Can't imagine me with that much hair now, can you?" He lifted off the baseball cap, revealing buzz-cut hair that was graying at the temples, and winked.

Red swallowed a smile and shrugged.

"This one is yours," Celine said, opening a door at the end of the hall. "I tried to keep the dogs out in case you're allergic."

"I'm not," Red said as Gandalf pushed past Celine into the room and began sniffing around.

Celine shook her head. "Good thing. Gandalf is no respecter of persons, as you can see."

Red stepped in after the dog. The room was surprisingly normal, considering the rest of the house. The walls were a soft gray, and the furniture buttery yellow.

The top of the dresser gleamed, and Red smelled the citrusy tang of furniture polish. There was a stack of books on top of it, and Celine's face lit up when Red touched their spines.

"Those are for you," Celine said. "Ms. Anders said you enjoy reading."

She did. In fact, The Mom would get mad at Red for reading too much, and used to take books away as punishment. Red turned from the stack, suddenly feeling prickly. Nobody had ever picked out books for her, like they *knew* her, knew what she'd like. Scowling, she faced the antique double bed situated under a large window that looked out over the backyard.

Red startled. Two large copper eyes were staring at her through the window.

"Oh," Celine said, spying the creature on the other side of the glass. "Billie wanted to say hello, too."

Billie. The thing staring at her had a name. And two floppy black ears framing its long white face.

A goat. There was a goat outside her window. Her *second-story* window. Red's brain hiccuped these facts together. "It's in a tree?"

"Billie's a Moroccan goat," Celine said, as if that explained everything.

The black-and-white goat was standing on a thin branch of the oak tree behind the house. It had ventured out so far, Red was amazed the wood hadn't snapped under its weight. A few browning leaves were disappearing into the goat's mouth as it stared at them, chewing chewing chewing.

"Is he gonna fall?" It seemed to Red like one wayward gust of wind could shake the goat right off.

Jackson said, "Nah. She's amazing. She hasn't fallen once."

"They really are incredible climbers," Celine said. "I'll show you pictures later. I have a book about the tree goats of Morocco downstairs. You might see twenty of them in one Argania tree."

Billie bleated, her pink tongue darting out from between her teeth, like, *Quit talking about me*. Red chewed her lip.

Celine was watching her. "Do you like your room okay?"

It wasn't *her* room. Just *another* room in a long line of rooms she'd had to sleep in. She shrugged. Nodded.

Celine said, "The furniture was Nicole's—Jackson's daughter—when she was young. But it's your room, so you can decorate it however you'd like." She pressed her fingers into the slope between her neck and shoulder on the right side. "What's your favorite color?"

"Green." A cold draft blustered from Red's skin. She could have said anything. Blue, yellow, pink. But green? Green was the truth, and she tried not to hand truth out too easily.

Celine's hair danced around her face for a moment. She caught some, tucked it behind her ear, and glanced at the closed window. She smiled at Red again. "Green! Well, there's not a lot of that here, is there?" She crossed her arms. "We'll have to do something about that."

No no no. Red didn't need a room with green. Not at this house.

"No, it's okay. I like it like this."

Celine waved a hand. "If my girl wants green, she gets green."

My girl.

For a moment, Red was swirly and feather-light. Then she shifted her weight between her feet and clenched her fists around the summery breeze of Celine's words. *I'm not yours,* she thought. *I'm not, I'm not.*

Outside, the branch beneath Billie's hooves shuddered and bowed, but the goat did not fall.

Dear Mom,

447 days.

I wish you could come back sooner. I hate it here.

I lost my closed-door privileges, so I have to change clothes in the bathroom again. The Mom got mad at me for screaming. She didn't get mad at her son for making me scream, though. The boys have a bet to see who can give me the biggest welt from pinching my arms. Winner gets all the Halloween candy next month.

Oldest Boy is going to win.

He keeps sneaking up on me or chasing me home from school to pinch me. Today he woke me up with a pinch. I wore short sleeves to breakfast, but The Mom just looked at me, then told me to put my dishes away like everything was normal. I know she saw the bruises.

I am not trying to worry you. I can take care of myself. I just wish you could get out sooner. I saw a TV show where a prisoner got out early because of good behavior. Is that true, or just a TV thing?

I wish it was true. I miss you.

Love,
Red

Chapter 5

"Come on, Fezzik! Don't be such a—*oof*—diva!"

Jackson recoiled as a small, shaggy donkey tried to head-butt him in the stomach again. He—Jackson—was attempting to get the donkey into a fenced arena behind the barn. The donkey—Fezzik—was the last of the animals from the barn to make his way to the arena, and he didn't seem happy about it.

Red was straddling a thick branch of the oak tree outside the bedroom window, watching the action below. It was the tree Billie had been in two nights ago, when Red first arrived. Now the goat was in the arena, munching her way through a pile of veggies, hay, and oats with the other goats. The Grooves were rearranging hay bales, setting up tables, and wrangling the animals into the arena, preparing for that day's Groovy Petting Zoo.

The Groovy Petting Zoo was what Red had seen a sign for on the highway with Ms. Anders. The black-and-white goat on the sign was Billie herself, it turned out. And the turtle was actually an enormous tortoise named Tuck Everlasting. Tuck for short. Celine and Jackson had introduced Red to Tuck the day before, along with the rest of the goats, a cranky llama named Lancelot and a less-cranky llama named Merlin, two horses, Alfonzo and Flicka, a bunch of chickens who looked more like feather balls than birds, three rabbits, and Fezzik the donkey.

Red had never been around horses or llamas or a giant tortoise before. In the last three years, she had been in a few foster homes with dogs or cats. One even had a guinea pig. But the closest she'd ever gotten to farm animals was reading *Charlotte's Web*.

She was nervous at first, especially because the bay horse nickered and stomped when Red came into the barn. But Celine had spoken softly to the horse and shown Red how to feed him apple slices from the flat of her palm. The animals responded to Celine like the dogs had that first day. They seemed eager to be near her, their heads turning as they watched her move around the barn. If she told them to do something, like step back from the gate so she could get into their stalls, they would.

It didn't take long for Celine's ease to calm Red's nerves, too. Red even laughed when Billie, Goat, and Gruff, the three goats, ate oats from her hand, their velvety lips tickling her palm.

Jackson beamed. "You're a natural. They love you!"

Except for Lancelot the llama. He spit at Red before she even got close. Merlin wasn't as wary as Lancelot, but he didn't seem too eager to be Red's friend, either. Jackson said they were guard llamas, and took their job of protecting the goats seriously.

"They'll warm up to you," Celine had promised. "You have to earn a llama's trust."

Now, watching from her tree, Red could see Celine patting Lancelot's long, shaggy neck. Like the other animals, Lancelot was relaxed with Celine and allowed her to lead him into the arena without complaint.

The Groovy Petting Zoo was open every other Saturday afternoon, June through November, weather permitting. Jackson said he and Celine had started rescuing animals a few years ago, after they got married. His daughter, Nicole, helped them out before she and her husband moved to Seattle. Aside from zoo days every other Saturday at the farm, the Grooves held zoo events to raise funds for all kinds of community things, Celine

28

told her, like children's programming at the library and their church.

That was how they decided to become foster parents. They'd taken the zoo to a foster care fund-raiser in Denver that summer. Red remembered that fund-raiser, though she hadn't visited the petting zoo. The Mom's boys hadn't wanted to go, and Oldest Boy faked a stomachache so they could leave and play video games at home.

Even though Celine had shown her how to feed the horses that morning, Red wasn't interested in helping with the petting zoo. It was a family thing. And they weren't Red's family. Since Jackson had said Red could help out with the zoo as much as she wanted, she opted not to help at all.

Gandalf stood beneath the oak, looking up at her. The dog's tongue bobbed as she panted, and she let out a quiet wuff every now and then.

"Go away," Red said, shooing the furbeast.

Gandalf just looked at her like, *Come down!* Like, *Play with me!* Red sighed and ignored her.

It was late October, but the weather was warm and bright. The grove of aspens in front of the house still had yellow leaves and the distant patches of scrub oak were turning red. Though the air was cool, the sun toasted everything. Red stared across the sweep of golden fields behind the house. The Grooves lived outside Bramble, which was far enough east of Denver that the mountains looked tiny. Just a thin strip of jagged teeth along the horizon.

Red ran her hands over the notebook in her lap. The cover was battered. Its corners were wrinkled and strips of the green patterned paper had been torn off to reveal the brown cardboard beneath. Several layers of tape hugged the spine, holding it together.

The notebook was fat with wavy, stained pages. More than once, Red had had to rescue it from the snow or mud, where foster siblings had tossed it. She used to hide it under her mattress, but when The Mom's three boys found it, she'd started carrying it with her all the time.

There weren't any foster siblings to worry about at the Grooves', but she couldn't break the habit of carrying it around. What if Ms. Anders came back and said there'd been some mistake, and Red had to leave? What if the Grooves decided they didn't want her?

No. It was better to hold on to it.

She lifted the cover. It always opened to the same page. The page covered in tape that held down the shreds of torn paper she'd collected from the bushes and grass and rocks that day at the park.

Gently, she tried to smooth out the collection of ragged papers. Their edges curled up, like they were trying to fly away from the page, but the tape held them fast.

The writing on each of the scraps was a little smeared and faded, but Red didn't need to see the words to know what they said. She'd read them so many times, she knew every one by heart. There were words missing, of course. A lot of them. Words written on scraps that she hadn't been able to snag before the wind blew them away.

The holes left by those missing words made the puzzle that much more difficult, but over the years, Red had grown used to their absence. She filled in the gaps a thousand different ways in her own mind, but she knew she couldn't make everything fit together perfectly. Not yet, anyway.

Not until her mom got out of prison.

A goat bleated, and she squinted toward the petting zoo arena. Billie was bouncing around, knocking into the other goats. Lancelot nipped at her, clearly irritated. Billie ignored him, bounded toward the chickens, scattering them. Then, with another happy bleat, she jumped onto Tuck's shell, just like the goat by the sign on the highway. Jackson and Celine laughed, and Celine looked up toward Red's tree, shielding her eyes from the sun and grinning.

Red pretended not to notice.

Chapter
6

"There's a Brownie troop coming at two." Celine was scanning the petting zoo reservations on her tablet. "But it'll be a quiet day." She looked at Red. "I'm sure the Kapules will stop by so you can meet Marvin. I can call our church youth group leaders, too, if you want. See if some of the kids would like to come out."

Red puffed a sigh through her lips and shook her head, pulling her ham sandwich into pieces.

Celine clicked off the tablet's screen. "I thought you'd like to meet some of the kids you'll be in school with. Maybe it will make Monday easier."

Red shrugged. All of her first days at new schools blurred together. There'd been a lot of them, and they'd never been very fun. But they were just something she had to deal with until her mom came back and they started their real life again.

Celine's eyes crinkled at the corners. "Red, sweetie, you're allowed to have an opinion. Our family talks about things."

A whoosh of air ruffled their hair as Jackson opened the back door and stepped into the kitchen. Red dropped a few chunks of sandwich on the floor for Gandalf and Frodo while Brontë and Limerick scurried to greet him.

"Fezzik is still in a mood," he said, dragging the baseball cap off his head.

Celine frowned. "What's gotten into him?"

Jackson shrugged. "The animals seem a little off this morning. Maybe a storm is coming or something."

"It's not mine," Red blurted. They both looked at her, confusion lifting their eyebrows.

"What's not yours?" Celine asked.

Red dropped the last of her sandwich onto the plate. "You said *our family*, but this isn't my family."

A stack of mail on the table fluttered. Celine and Jackson exchanged a quick look, and Celine laid her hand over the papers.

"We want it to be," Jackson said, taking a cautious step forward.

"No!" Red stood up. "I have a family! My *mom* is my family!"

"Of course she is," Celine said. She held up a hand,

palm out, like she did when soothing a startled horse. "We just—"

"Can I go upstairs?" Red interrupted. Her hair danced around her face and she pulled in a breath, trying to still her blustering emotions.

Celine pressed her lips together, exchanging another look with Jackson.

"Yes, Red. You may," she said.

Red hurried out of the kitchen and up the stairs. Gandalf followed her, pausing at the bottom of the staircase and looking at her questioningly.

Red rolled her eyes. "Come on, then."

The dog bounded up the stairs and followed Red to the bedroom.

Red watched from the window as a group of little girls in matching brown uniforms arrived a while later. They chattered and danced around until Jackson and the lady they came with finally got their attention. She could hear Jackson's deep voice as he gave them information about the animals.

She turned from the window, sinking down against the headboard. Gandalf was stretched out across half the bed. Her dark eyes followed Red's movements and she huffed a sigh that made her lips balloon a little.

"Quit looking at me like that. I'm not going out there."

The dog yawned and smacked her chops. Laughter filtered up from the arena. Red resisted the urge to turn around and spy on the activity. Instead, she picked up the green notebook again, opening it and carefully turning past the page of collected scraps.

At the top of another page, in handwriting that looked like it was dancing, was the word *IMPOSSIBLE*. She ran her fingertips over the inked letters, feeling the gentle dents they made in the paper. Under the word was a list.

Flying
Going to the moon
Climbing the world's tallest mountain
Bumblebees

It went on for more than a page. Red remembered the day Gamma had written the list. Red had woken to the sound of her mother and Gamma fighting again, but by the time she came into the kitchen, her mother was gone. Gamma was forcefully cheerful, like she always was after they fought. Beethoven's Fifth Symphony was playing on the ancient CD player, and Red knew instantly that Gamma was in a mood. She once said she only listened to Beethoven's Fifth Symphony when her emotions were so big, they started leaking out. Beethoven gave her feelings somewhere to go.

They listened to the whole symphony together while Red ate her cereal. It was a long symphony, but Red had always liked it. The rhythm of the violins, the hum of the cellos and bass, the climb and fall of the flutes. She liked how it sounded angry one moment, then happy or sad or calm the next. Gamma was right. Beethoven really did give feelings somewhere to go.

When it was over, a hush settled around them for a few moments, and Gamma closed her eyes. Then she told Red to hurry and get dressed, and they went to the dollar store. Gamma said she needed to buy something special, something new and fresh. She marched Red to the office supply aisle, and they picked out the notebook together. Red chose green because green seemed like the freshest color of all.

When they got home, Gamma sat Red down at the kitchen table. Her cheeks were flushed and her voice shook a little when she spoke.

"We're gonna start us a project, Ruby." She opened the notebook and wrote the word *IMPOSSIBLE* in big letters across the top of a page. "We're gonna start collecting impossible things."

"Why?"

Gamma bit her lip, shaking her head a little. "Because knowing the difference between *hard* and *impossible* is important, baby girl. Lots of things in life are hard. But *nothing* is impossible. Remember: It always *seems* impossible . . ." Her voice trailed off and she looked at Red expectantly.

Red knew her line. "Until it's done!"

Gamma smiled. It was her favorite quote. "Right. So we're gonna make ourselves a list of all the things the world thought were impossible, until someone came along and got it done. That way you won't ever forget when—"

Red frowned. "When what?"

"Just . . . never. So you'll never forget," Gamma said.

After Gamma made the list, she and Red started learning about some of the things on it. Gamma taught her about the Wright brothers, who were credited with flying the first airplane. She also taught her about a woman named Jeanne Genevieve Labrosse, who was the first woman to pilot a hot-air balloon, in 1798, and the first woman to parachute, in 1799. Gamma was especially eager to talk about her.

"There's *always* a woman hidden in history who did as much or more than any man," Gamma said. "All you gotta do is look for her."

Together, they'd filled several pages of the notebook with what they discovered, the ways impossible things weren't impossible at all. But they'd only made it partway through the list. There were still so many impossible things left.

They just hadn't had time to find them all before everything changed.

Still, Red kept the notebook, even after her mom was

arrested and Red was sent into foster care. Over the years, she'd lost things. Clothes, books, toys. Misplaced. Left behind during a sudden transition. Stolen, sometimes. Or thrown away by a new set of foster parents or the social workers.

But not the impossible notebook.

It was Red's most valued possession. Often, it was her *only* possession. The only thing that was really, truly hers.

Gandalf lifted her head, snuffled Red's knees. Red scratched the dog's ears.

Something clattered against the window behind her. Red turned around and nearly fell off the bed in surprise.

A boy was sitting in the tree, grinning at her.

Chapter
7

Red leaped off the bed. The boy was smiling and waving, like it wasn't weird at all that he was looking into a stranger's room. Gandalf sat up, her bulk making the bed sag, and wuffed.

"What are you doing?" Red asked.

The boy tipped his head to one side and cupped a hand behind his ear. She shoved the notebook into the nightstand drawer and unlatched the window, raising it just enough to talk through.

"What are you doing?" she said again.

Two fingertip-deep dimples punctuated the beginning and end of his grin. His glossy black hair was standing up in every direction.

"I'm saying hi." He adjusted his seat on the branch,

glancing down like he'd just realized how high up he was. "But now I'm also thinking about plummeting to my death." He made a face of exaggerated fear. "Holy bananas, this is high!"

Red crossed her arms, frowning at him.

"I'm Marvin," he said, as if his name explained everything.

She raised her eyebrows and said nothing.

He knuckled his nose, then wiped his hand on his pant leg. "I'm Marvin," he said again. "I live down the road. Didn't they tell you about me?"

He looked genuinely hurt at the possibility that Celine and Jackson hadn't mentioned him. Gandalf clumped up the length of the bed in two bouncing strides and stuck her nose out the open gap of the window. Her tail began to wag.

Marvin brightened. "See! Gandalf knows me!"

Red tried to push back the dog's enormous head. "Why are you in my tree?"

"Your tree?" Marvin laughed. "I've climbed this tree, like, a million times! Have *you*?"

"I've climbed it," Red said, bristling.

He met her scowl with a grin. "So are you coming out or what?"

Gandalf was crushing into Red now, trying to push her nose farther out the window. She whimpered, then sprayed a sneeze that splattered across the glass.

"Gross." Red grimaced.

The sound of Fezzik the donkey heehawing floated up from the petting zoo, followed by the squeals of delighted little girls.

"You should come outside! Jackson's gonna let Fezzik feed the chickens. Have you seen that yet?"

Red shook her head. A prickling heat stung her cheeks. Fezzik could feed the chickens? Why hadn't Jackson told her?

Marvin laughed, making the tree branch shake. He grabbed hold of it with both hands, his laughter screeching to a halt for a moment. His dimples reappeared as he steadied himself. "Well, *come outside*, then! You have to see it. It's hil-*ar*-ious."

Gandalf jumped off the bed, stumbling when she hit the floor, then shook her head, blowing little half sneezes of excitement.

Marvin started to climb down the tree. "Come outside!" he said again. "Hurry!"

Red watched him until he reached the ground and walked toward the arena. She didn't want to follow this weird, nosy boy to watch a donkey feed chickens.

Gandalf whined at the door.

Red sighed. "Fine."

She opened the door and the dog bounded out, booming a happy bark. Red paused, then followed Gandalf down the stairs and out to the backyard.

Marvin stood on the bottom rung of the arena's metal fence with his arms draped over the top. Red stepped up onto the fence next to him.

"See those beanbags?"

She looked to where he was pointing at the far side of the arena. "Those have chicken feed in them," he said. "Watch!"

Jackson took one of the small bags over to Fezzik, who was munching hay from a bale in the center of the circle. The Brownies were seated on surrounding hay bales, and the feather-explosion chickens were wandering aimlessly in the space around Fezzik's hooves. Off to one side, the two horses and three goats were happily chowing down, ignoring everything else. Celine held one of the rabbits in her lap and the other two were cuddled near her feet.

Jackson patted Fezzik's shaggy neck, then held the beanbag out to him like it was an apple. The donkey picked it up, his lips twitching.

"He got it! Watch this!" Marvin whisper-shouted.

Fezzik started nodding his head up and down, making the beanbag flop and shake. He dropped it on the ground, cuffed it with his hoof, then picked it up again. His ears were forward and he pranced a few paces, clearly having fun. He didn't look anything like the donkey who'd head-butted Jackson that morning. This was a game, and Fezzik loved it. A high, screeching donkey-laugh erupted out of him as he played with the bag, shaking it. Each shake sent chicken feed raining down. The chickens clucked and darted for the food, nimbly avoiding Fezzik's hooves.

Fezzik shook the bag until it was empty, then dropped it and returned to his own hay. The discarded cloth landed on the head of one of the birds. The chicken took off running, its head still covered, bumping into the hay bales and other chickens until Jackson caught hold of it and snatched the fabric off. The crowd of little girls laughed at the spectacle.

Marvin turned to Red, beaming. "Fezzik *always* drops the empty bag on a chicken! He makes it look like an accident, but I swear he does it on purpose."

"You came!" Celine appeared on the other side of the arena fence. "And you've met Marvin, I see."

Red wanted to say, *He climbed my tree.* But it wasn't *her* tree.

"Can I show Red how to feed Tuck?" Marvin asked.

Celine looked delighted. "Of course! If Red wants to."

Red frowned. She hadn't wanted to help Celine feed the tortoise that morning. His sharp, snapping beak made her nervous. But Marvin was already heading toward the barn. Gandalf and the other dogs yapped and chased one another, following him.

Red sighed. She was tempted to ignore Marvin and go back to her room.

No. Not *her* room. The room she was staying in until her mom got back.

Three hundred ninety-five days. Just over a year. One more year wasn't *too* too long. She'd already been in foster care for three years, so one year sounded easy. Kind of.

"Hey!" Marvin called, waving at her.

Red sighed again. Marvin acting like the Grooves' house belonged to him was making little clouds of dust billow around her ankles. She closed her eyes and took a deep breath. *It doesn't matter. It doesn't matter.*

The mini–dust storms lurched and settled.

"Come *on*, Red! I wanna show you something!" Marvin's voice was rimmed with irritation at her slowness.

She exhaled in a whoosh of renewed frustration.

"Whoa!" He gasped, stepping back as a cloud of dirt peppered him. He brushed himself off, unfazed. "Come on!" he said, and disappeared into the barn.

Chapter
8

When Red stepped into the barn it was sparkling. *Actually* sparkling. She stopped, gaping, as light twirled around her, dancing off every surface like a million giddy stars.

Marvin stood in the center of the space, arms held out, grinning triumphantly.

"Isn't it *cool?*" His arms thwapped against his sides and he stared up at the dancing light.

Red followed his gaze and saw a silver ball hanging from the ceiling. It was about the size of a basketball and was covered in hundreds of tiny mirrors, each reflecting light from a lamp attached to the beam across from it. How had she not noticed it when the Grooves had introduced her to the animals?

"It's a disco ball," Marvin said. "On cold days, they have the petting zoo in here. And it's *groovy*. Get it?" When she didn't laugh, he started pumping his arms in a weird dance move. "Groovy? The Groovy Petting Zoo?"

The twirling beams of light painted his face and body with bright strokes as he danced.

She shook her head. "It's kind of a dumb name."

He stopped dancing. "No, it's not."

She felt a little buzz of satisfaction at his tone. "They should call it something else. Like the Dancing Donkey Petting Zoo."

Marvin's dimples reappeared and the irritation evaporated from his voice. "Nah. Fezzik's cool, but he's not even the best part."

"What is?"

He motioned for her to follow him. "Tuck!" he said, stopping at the tortoise's pen.

Tuck's pen took up a large portion of the back corner of the barn. The barn itself was really nice, nothing like Red had first expected a barn to be. Everything was clean and organized. There were even framed photographs on one wall of Jackson's mother as a young woman riding horses in a rodeo. Tuck's corner was lined in plywood that was scuffed and gouged from being knocked into by his shell. There was a Tuck-size door in one wall that led to his outside habitat. Strips of thick, clear plastic hung over it, kind of like a dog door. Tuck was in the back corner under his large heat lamp. It turned his green-brown shell a molten orange. He didn't move when Marvin opened the gate and stepped into the pen.

"You probably shouldn't go in there," Red said. Jackson had told her Tuck was friendly and safe, but she didn't like Marvin marching around like he owned everything.

Marvin patted Tuck on his shiny head. The tortoise blinked and shifted slightly. "He's fine," Marvin said. "I hang out with him all the time."

The loose straw on the floor around Red's feet skittered away from her. Marvin shivered in the breeze.

"Look at this," he said, waving her into the pen.

She stepped in, keeping some distance between her feet and the tortoise's head.

"See that?" Marvin pointed to a deep dimple in the front of Tuck's shell, right between where Red imagined his shoulders would be. The center of the dimple was filled with something grayish and solid, almost like cement.

Yet another thing she hadn't noticed when Jackson and Celine showed her the animals. She frowned, the breeze from her skin calming as she concentrated on Tuck's shell. "What is that?"

"A scar." Marvin's eyes were wide, like he was getting ready to tell her a ghost story. He stroked Tuck's shell gently around the old wound. "You know how Jackson found him, right?"

47

Red shook her head, irritation prickling again.

"Well, you know Jackson is a veterinarian?"

"Yes," she said. Finally, something she did know.

"He worked with a lot of exotic animals. One day he got a call that some dumb frat boys in Boulder had a giant tortoise. Someone reported that the tortoise was hurt, so he went out there with the police to get it, and it was Tuck. There was a huge *screwdriver* sticking out of his shell, right here!"

Red stared, trying to imagine it. The air suddenly felt hot and thick in her lungs. "S-somebody did that to him?"

Marvin nodded gravely. "The frat boys swore it was there when they found him in Arizona. They said he was wandering around the desert and they were trying to help him, but who knows if it's true. Jackson said Aldabras aren't from Arizona, so he was probably a pet that somebody abandoned when he got so big. Maybe that person hurt him. I don't know. But Jackson had to do surgery on Tuck to get it out. And he thinks whoever stabbed him in the shell also hurt his head." Marvin pointed to a second, J-shaped scar that hooked around one of Tuck's eyes.

The tortoise's eye glinted up at Red as she knelt to get a closer look. Gently, she touched his cool skin, traced the scar. "Geez."

"I know." Marvin was kneeling, too, one arm draped

over the tortoise's back. "That's why Tuck lives here now. He needs special care from Jackson."

Red looked into Tuck's eye. She wanted to tell him she understood what it was like, not being able to go home. Living with strangers.

He stared at her like, *I know*.

When she moved her fingers over his head, Tuck stretched out his long neck, wanting her to rub it. She bit back a smile as he leaned in to her hand, almost like a dog.

The twirling disco lights blinked over and across their faces. Marvin showed Red the refrigerator in the barn's food storage room where fresh vegetables were kept. Tuck stood on his stumpy legs and came over to Red when she held out a cucumber for him.

"Hold it up kind of high," Marvin instructed. "It's good exercise for him to reach for it."

Red obeyed, marveling at the strength in Tuck's jaws as he crunched into it. He was a messy eater. Before long, his face was covered in chunks of soggy vegetables.

Suddenly, Tuck's whole body jolted. For a second, Red didn't know what had happened. Then a stream of snot came flooding out of Tuck's nostrils in long, sticky strands. Red stepped back to avoid the river of mucus.

"He sneezed! Sick!" Marvin said, clearly delighted.

"Bless you," Red whispered to Tuck. He stretched his neck toward the last bit of cucumber in her hands.

"Billie loves Tuck," Marvin said, trying to feed the tortoise a carrot. Tuck ignored it. "They're totally BFFs."

"I saw her on his back this morning."

"Yeah, she does that all the time." He tapped the carrot against Tuck's lips, but the tortoise turned away. "Billie is a rescue, too. All the animals are."

Red ran her fingers down into the soft, leathery folds of Tuck's neck skin. "How do you know so much about them?" she asked.

Marvin tried again to feed Tuck the carrot. Red wanted to swat his hand away.

"I hung out here a *lot* when our parents were getting certified."

The air stilled, cooled. Red narrowed her eyes. "*Our* parents?"

Marvin stroked Tuck's shell. "Yeah. My parents are Support Friends to yours. So they can take care of you, too. In case yours need help or something."

"Jackson and Celine *aren't* my parents."

He looked up, startled by the ice in her voice. "Oh, yeah, I know. Sorry. I meant foster parents. I know your real parents—I mean, I know they aren't around."

"You don't know anything about me!" Red's hair whipped around her face, and the gate to Tuck's pen rattled.

Marvin glanced at the gate, then back at Red, eyes wide. "Sorry, I—"

"I don't even know who your parents are! Why would they take care of me? I'm not staying here forever."

Marvin was stone-still now. Dry grass and shriveled leaves of lettuce from Tuck's food bowl were spinning across the floor, swept up by the flurries of Red's outburst and catching in his shoelaces. His cheeks turned scarlet. "I didn't—"

"You keep acting like you know everything, but you *don't*!" She stood, fists clenched. "I didn't ask you to come here and be my friend. I don't NEED any friends!"

He shrank back, bumping into the tortoise. "I just—"

The barn door slammed open with a clatter. The dogs, who had been hanging around outside it, yelped and scattered. Sunlight poured into the semidarkness, gobbling up the tiny fragments of twirling light. Marvin jumped up, looking at Red like she'd hit him. His eyes filled with tears and his chin began to tremble. She stepped aside as he rushed past her and out into the sunlight.

Welcome!

Ms. Anders told me you like to read. I do, too! These are books I loved when I was your age. I thought you might enjoy them—they're yours to keep. I hope you'll especially like A Wrinkle in Time. It is one of my very favorites. Feel free to explore my library downstairs, too. You're welcome to any book you'd like.

If there's anything at all you need, just ask. Our home is yours.

Happy reading!

Love,
Celine

Chapter
9

Someone knocked lightly on the door. Red sat on the bed and hugged her knees to her chest as Celine stepped into the room.

"I brought you some cocoa," Celine said, holding out a steaming mug. One corner of her mouth tipped upward in a small smile. "Cocoa is the best medicine, in my opinion."

Red took the mug. It was hot, but not too hot to wrap her hands around. She breathed in the smell of chocolate and cinnamon.

Celine sat on the foot of the bed. Gandalf followed her in, and put her head on Celine's lap.

"Marvin sure rushed out of here fast," Celine said.

Red took a sip of the cocoa. Shame heated her cheeks.

"Earlier today, you said something that I want to address," Celine continued after a moment. Red stared into her mug, watching the chocolate swirl slowly around a single large marshmallow. Celine's hand slid toward Red on the bed, but stopped short of her feet. Red curled her toes.

"You said that you aren't our family." Celine's voice was low and calm. She didn't sound angry or upset. "Red, I want you to know that we aren't trying to replace your mom."

"Good." The word rushed out of Red's mouth, hard and flat. "Because I don't need you to be my family."

Celine sat back a little, hurt shadowing her face before she spoke again. "It's okay if you don't want to get involved in things like the petting zoo right now. That's your choice."

Celine's hand slid a little closer to Red's foot, and Red tucked her feet under her body.

"But we do expect you to help out with some chores around the house. This is a busy place. Everyone has to pitch in."

Red scowled.

Celine let out a little laugh. "You don't have to look so worried! I'd actually like you to pick the chore you want to do. Something you'd enjoy."

"Like what?"

"Did you like feeding the animals this morning?"

Red thought about this. "I liked feeding Tuck today."

Celine smiled. "Perfect! Let's start with that, then."

"He sneezed when Marvin and I were giving him a cucumber."

"Ugh." Celine made a face. "That's gross, isn't it? I think he must get veggie juice up his nose or something."

Red smiled, nodding. "Yeah. It was like a snot fountain."

Celine shuddered, laughing, then ruffled the top of Gandalf's head and stood. "Okay, tomorrow I'll show you Tuck's routine. Sound good?"

Red nodded.

"I'm about to go for my nightly walk. Would you like to join me?"

Red shook her head. "No. Thanks."

Celine pressed her knuckles into the curve between her neck and shoulder. "Maybe next time," she said. She snapped her fingers, and Gandalf trotted after her.

"Celine?"

Celine paused at the door as Red opened the drawer of her nightstand and took out three envelopes.

"Can I mail these? They're for my mom." She held the envelopes against her stomach, suddenly unsure of herself. The Mom hadn't liked how often Red wrote to her mother in prison. She'd said it was a waste of postage, especially since Red's mom rarely wrote back. She told Red to send emails instead. But Red hadn't been allowed to use the computer, and as far as she knew, her mom couldn't use email anyway. But Red preferred writing letters by hand. She liked the idea that her mom's fingers would touch the same paper her hands had touched. It made her mom feel closer somehow.

Celine smiled. "Of course. I'll put them in the mailbox for you. Remind me tomorrow, and I'll show you where the stamps are, too. You can send as many letters as you want."

Red released a breath and nodded. "Okay." She handed the envelopes to Celine. "Thanks."

Celine gave Red another small smile at the door. "I'm glad you're here, Red."

Then she was gone.

Red heard the back door open and close a minute later. From her window, she saw Celine walk out into the yard, Gandalf behind her. At the edge of the circle of light cast by the back-porch lamp, Celine stopped and looked up into the sky, a thin veil of breath hovering around her face. Red glanced up, too. Above Celine, the clouds had unraveled into a near-perfect circle. Stars glimmered in the patch of revealed sky, bright and bold and warm. For a moment, Red thought she heard a faint whisper, like distant music.

An ache blossomed in her chest as she watched Celine fade into the night, Gandalf at her heels and starlight in her hair.

Chapter 10

"There are a couple of things you need to know about tortoises."

Celine unlatched the gate to Tuck's pen and stepped inside. Red followed her. Tuck was munching on a pile of long dried grass, his head bobbing with each bite.

"Number one," Celine said, "they need to stay warm. See how we have several types of lights set up for him? That one is a ceramic heater." She pointed toward one of the lamps hanging a few feet from the floor in the back corner. "And the others give off heat as well as UVB rays. He needs them to stay healthy.

"Number two: tortoises love to eat." Celine held up a bucket filled with vegetables and greens she'd brought along. "Tuck mostly eats greens and grass, like the stuff in his bowl. When he's outside, he grazes on grasses, dandelions, and leaves. But I'll tell you a secret." Celine dug into the bucket and pulled out a banana. "These are his absolute favorite treat."

As if on cue, Tuck lifted his head from the bowl of dried grass and immediately started shuffling toward them, eyes on the banana.

"He's fast!" Red said, amazed at how quickly the giant tortoise could move. The claws on the toes of his elephant-like feet scratched against the wood floor as he approached.

"Oh yeah. Especially when there's a banana on the line. Here, hold it by the stem. He'll gobble it right up, peel and all."

Red held the banana as instructed. Remembering Marvin's advice the day before, she held it up a little. Tuck stretched out his long, leathery neck and chomped into the fruit. Red grinned as banana goop smeared across his face with each bite.

"Great job!" Celine said, looking impressed.

Although Tuck's jaws were powerful, Red wasn't nervous about feeding him anymore. She was careful to keep her fingers clear of his sharp beak, however.

"Told you," Celine said when Tuck finished the banana in three bites. "Loves 'em." She handed Red a cucumber. It crunched as Tuck bit into it. "You're holding it perfectly. Well done! When we let kids feed him in the zoo, we usually spear chunks of veggies on the end of long sticks for them to hold. That way their fingers stay safe."

Red nodded and rubbed Tuck's neck when he finished the cucumber. "I don't think he'd bite me."

Celine watched the way Tuck turned his head into Red's palm and smiled. "I think you're right."

Celine explained how to vary Tuck's diet by giving him different greens, grasses, and even some special pellets.

"In the summer, most of his food comes from outside. We grow several kinds of grass for him and he loves dandelions, which is great because we have those in abundance," she said. "This time of year, we supplement his diet with a few more vegetables. I like to give him cucumber and other watery things to keep him better hydrated. Everything is grown here in my garden and greenhouse, whenever possible. What we do get from the store is always organic." She grinned. "He's a very spoiled tortoise, isn't he?"

By the time Tuck finished eating, his face was covered in globs of vegetables and bananas. He didn't seem to mind, though, and Red thought he looked cute. Gross, but cute. He followed Red around the pen as Celine showed her how the timer for the lights worked, how to clean up his poop, and where to put fresh straw.

"We keep a pig blanket under this pile," Celine said, pushing back some of the straw to show Red a thick plastic heated mat on the floor. "It keeps him nice and warm at night and on really cold days. We just have to keep an eye on the cords. Jackson secured them inside this PVC pipe, but tortoises have a tendency to plow into things and get tangled up."

Red laughed when Tuck knocked into her from behind as he made his way into the straw.

"See?" Celine said, patting the tortoise's shell. "He's proving my point."

They toured the outside habitat, too. Jackson was planning to remodel it over the winter since Tuck would spend most of that time indoors. It was a big area with lots of grass, dirt, rocks, and logs. Celine said Jackson was building a sort of obstacle course for Tuck.

"It's good for his legs if he has to work a little to get over things. He weighs four hundred pounds, so it's important that his legs are healthy," Celine said. "He also loves to push boxes around. They're his favorite toy. He may be old in years, but he's young at heart."

Her words made Red think of Gamma, who used to describe herself the same way. Whenever a grocery store clerk offered to carry her groceries or someone thought she couldn't do something because she was too old, she'd laugh and wag her finger at them. "Don't go treating me like an old lady, now! I'm young at heart!" And then, just to prove her point, she'd wiggle her hips in a funny dance.

Red patted Tuck's shell and he stretched his neck toward her. Celine laughed.

"He's really taken to you."

Red chewed on the corner of her smile and shrugged. "He likes neck rubs."

When Celine went back into the house, Red sat against a bale of hay in Tuck's stall. He stayed close to her, nosing her shoelaces and letting her pet his scaly knees.

He's really taken to you. Celine's words made hope fizz up inside her again, as it had when she'd first arrived at the Grooves'. Tuck's head bobbed into the pile of grass near her feet, his jaws clacking as he ate. When he looked up at her, long strands stuck out of his mouth, like whiskers. She grinned and tickled his chin, avoiding the still-slimy parts.

"I've never had a friend before," she whispered.

He looked at her like, *Me neither.* Like, *I see you.* Like, *We both need a friend.*

Red hadn't wanted a friend here. She wasn't staying. Not forever. And friends just made it harder to say goodbye.

Tuck bumped his nose into her knee, then went back to eating. A string of slime from his gooey face dripped from her jeans, reminding her of his sneeze. She smiled, thinking of Marvin's reaction.

After Marvin ran out of the barn the day before, Red had stormed around, looking for the switch to turn off the disco ball. She'd wanted the wind to blow it all away—the dancing light, the way Marvin said *our parents*, like family was the easiest thing in the world, the hurt look on his face when she'd yelled. She hadn't even tried to control the gusts rolling off her, kicking up dust and straw and making the air inside the barn hazy.

But then she saw Tuck, with his rippling scar and glinting black eyes. Maybe it was crazy, but something in his eyes made her feel more at home than she'd felt in years.

So, sitting on her knees next to Tuck, she'd leaned forward onto his shell, her arms folded over it, cheek pressed against it. Tuck's dimpled shell scar looked softer from this angle. Like a wave in a murky, unmoving sea.

She understood that scar. And being alone. Being different.

Tuck had let out a long sigh that shifted his whole body beneath Red's. She'd closed her eyes, felt her storm's energy evaporating. Slowly, everything settled into silence. Her breath steadied, deepened, as Tuck's solidity and stillness gave weight to her bones. For the first time in a long time, she wanted to stay right where she was.

And so she did.

She was still draped over Tuck's shell when Jackson started bringing the animals into the barn. Red had woken from her half trance, half nap with creases in her cheek that were the mirror image of Tuck's shell pattern.

And even though part of Red still wanted to be angry, still wanted to rage and bellow and blow, there was a deeper kind of quiet in her now. And with it, her anger at Marvin had blown out like a candle. Instead, all she felt was the sharp pinch of regret.

Now, watching Tuck, one hand on his shell and his gooey slime smeared on her knee, she wondered if she might have the courage to make room in her heart for two friends.

Chapter 11

"Nervous?" Celine asked. Gravel pinged against the underside of the car as they drove down the dirt road.

Red shrugged. This was her fifth new school in three years. Being the new kid, the new *foster* kid, was generally the same every time.

"Your teacher is Ms. Bell. I hear she's everyone's favorite." Celine massaged her right shoulder—a frequent habit. "What school did you go to before?"

"You mean this year?"

Celine's eyes widened. "Have you switched a lot?"

Red stared at the blur of golden fields. "Kinda."

"Well, I think you'll like Bramble. It's a small town, so everyone goes to the same school, kindergarten through high school. No more switching for a long time."

Red frowned. She'd be switching again, as soon as her mom got out. *In 393 days . . .*

Celine glanced at her again. "Do you feel okay?"

"Fine," Red said. She slumped in the passenger seat. The ghost of her face was reflected in the window next to her. Her dark eyes and hair skimmed over the fields and fences, like frightened birds.

"Marvin is in your class," Celine said. "So you'll already have a friend, at least."

Red chewed her lip and said nothing.

They turned off the highway onto the town's main street. Celine was right—Bramble was tiny. There were a few blocky buildings, no taller than two stories, as part of "downtown." A doughnut shop, a diner, and the Mercantile, whatever that was. Farther down the road, a rusty water tower stood like a giant mushroom overlooking all of Bramble. A faded, rust-orange *B* was painted on its face.

A long line of cars and buses ran down the length of the main road and curled into the school parking lot. The school was a low brick building with windows wrapped around its sides. A sign on a strip of dead grass near the parking lot entrance read, BRAMBLE K–12 SCHOOL: HOME OF THE BRAMBLE BOBCATS!

A third of the school was designed for younger kids. Paper shapes were hung in some of the windows, and there was a playground to one side of the building. The

65

far side of the building had a courtyard with metal picnic tables and a few basketball hoops. Teenagers stood in tightly grouped clusters on that side.

But the part of the building with kids Red's age was in chaos.

A zombie was chasing Iron Man around and around the merry-go-round. Three princesses in wispy purple dresses covered by puffy coats were twirling and playing with their hair by the swings. A lopsided pumpkin, a pirate, something with enormous green hands, and a container of french fries were on the monkey bars. The french fries was having a hard time reaching the bars, and the giant-green-hands thing was crouched, punching the ground over and over and shouting at the others.

"Oh no," Celine breathed. She put the car into park and leaned forward, staring. "Oh no," she repeated.

A ninja streaked by the car, wailing as a giant octopus followed him.

"Oh, no no no . . ." She gave Red a helpless look. "It's Spirit Week! Today is the class costume party. I completely forgot!"

She pressed a fist into her forehead, looking so thoroughly upset that Red was alarmed.

"It's okay," Red said quickly. "I don't care."

"Look at everyone! Ms. Bell even reminded me. Oh, Red, I'm sorry!" Celine dragged both of her hands down her face, squishing her cheeks and lips together.

Red felt a shivery, nervous breeze in her bones. She knew Celine hadn't meant to forget, but now Red would be the new girl *and* the only kid without a costume. A fresh wave of regret for yelling at Marvin hit her.

"I'll go get you a costume," Celine said.

The last thing she wanted was her foster mother showing up halfway into class with some kind of princess skirt or kitty cat outfit. "It's okay. I don't need a costume." Her voice sounded harsh, urgent.

Celine looked at her for a long moment, then let out a breath. "Okay. I'm really sorry I forgot about the party."

Red shrugged. "I better go."

Celine nodded, unclipped her seat belt. "Come on. I'll walk you in."

Chapter
12

Red wished she were invisible. A thousand eyes needled her as she walked into the front office and then down the busy halls to Ms. Bell's classroom. After being forced to stand at the front of the room on full, un-costumed display, and share *three things we should know about Red* with everyone, Red's skin hummed with humiliation. Clenching her teeth, she struggled to keep her wind's anxious spinning inside.

She took her seat at a cluster of four desks near the window, not looking at anyone. Blood whooshed in her ears, like she had giant seashells attached to her head. Pages of a notebook on the desk across from her fluttered and flapped, and a line of colored pencils wiggled, then rolled onto the floor.

Not now, not now.

The girl next to her stood and closed the nearest window, which had been open a crack. Her brow furrowed when the papers on the desk continued to rustle and she glanced at Red.

Red closed her eyes. *Take time to reset!* The voice of Dr. Teddy, Red's state-appointed therapist, bubbled up in her brain. Dr. Teddy said that the best way to calm down was by controlling her breath. He called it *resetting*, and had taught Red how to do breathing exercises.

Of course, Dr. Teddy didn't know about her wind. He didn't know she'd knocked over The Mom's youngest boy by breathing a little too hard once, or that sometimes the only way to keep a storm inside was to hold her breath for as long as she could. Red had to be careful. Breathing did help sometimes, but not every time. Not if she was too upset.

The last thing she needed was to lose control on her first day of school. *Focus on your breath, not your stress.* That's what Dr. Teddy would say. She pressed her palms into the tops of her thighs, and counted backward from ten in her mind, slowly. Each number got a full breath.

In . . . and out. *Ten.*

It wasn't a big deal that she didn't have a costume.

In . . . and out. *Nine.*

She just had to get through the day. That was all. She could do that.

69

In . . . and out. *Eight.*

When she finally opened her eyes, the whoosh in her ears was quieter and the notebook across from her had stopped rustling. Ms. Bell was talking and everyone was turned toward the front, oblivious to Red. She relaxed a little.

"What are you doing?"

Red looked at the girl in the desk next to hers. She had a wide, square face and blond hair cut in a blunt line around her shoulders. Her cheeks had black cat whiskers drawn onto them. The right side was already smudged.

The girl raised her eyebrows. "What were you doing just now?" she whispered.

Red swallowed hard. "Nothing."

"You were talking to yourself."

Had she been? Red's face burned. She saw Ms. Bell writing something on the whiteboard.

"Sorry," she mumbled.

The cat-girl with the smudged whiskers rolled her eyes, her mouth twisting into a little curl of disgust. Finally, she turned her attention back to Ms. Bell.

Red glanced at the other students in her desk cluster. The two boys who sat across from her and cat-girl were turned around in their seats, backs to Red, listening to Ms. Bell. One of them had on a pirate's tricorn with fake dreadlocked hair tumbling out around his ears. The other wore a muscled Captain America suit. His glossy black hair stood up messily on his head. Red knew that hair.

Marvin.

She sank deeper into her seat.

"Journaling time!" Ms. Bell announced brightly. "Make sure you copy out today's topic in cursive, please. Yes, I'm aware cursive is unpopular and archaic. My students will still learn to use it, thank you very much."

A murmur of conversation floated up like freed balloons as the class started pulling spiral notebooks out of their desks. Red opened her backpack and unpacked the school supplies Celine had purchased for her. But even the novelty of shiny notebooks and sharpened pencils— notebooks and pencils that were all hers *and* brand-new—wasn't enough to ease the tension in her chest.

She felt Marvin's eyes on her, but his gaze darted away the second she looked at him. He focused on his journal, copying the topic in slow, curling handwriting. No matter how hard she stared at him, he wouldn't meet her eye.

Like maybe she was invisible after all.

Chapter
13

The class costume party was the last thirty minutes of the day. After lunch, it was practically impossible for Red's classmates to keep quiet and pay attention to the math lesson. Finally, Ms. Bell announced it was time for the party.

"Would the Weekly Star please collect the math work-sheets? And while Amber does that—Marvin? Would you like to tell us about the treat you brought to share with the class?"

Marvin, who had been picking at the star on the front of his costume, lit up.

"Sure!" he said, standing.

His Captain America shield—which he'd fastened to his back by tying shoestrings around his shoulders—got caught on his chair. He grunted, struggling to unhook himself. A few people snickered. Finally, Marvin broke free and hurried to the snack table, where Ms. Bell and a mom helper were setting out paper cups filled with carrot sticks and crackers. He took a large glass bowl from Ms. Bell's mini-fridge and set it on the table. There was some sort of purplish-gray pudding in it.

Marvin pulled the clear plastic wrap from the top of the bowl and crumpled it in his fist. He beamed at the class, totally oblivious to the worried looks a few kids were exchanging.

"This is poi. My mom helped me make it last night. It's a traditional Hawaiian food. If you want to see how to make it, you should check out my YouTube channel, *Kitchen Kahuna*. I posted a video of us working on it."

"What is it?" asked the boy in the french fries costume.

"It's basically mushed-up taro root. That's a plant. It's still kind of sweet since we just made it last night. It gets a little tangier when it's older, which I like, too. It's good with vegetables or on rice, or even by itself." Marvin gestured toward the cups of carrot sticks on the table.

Nobody looked convinced. But Marvin grinned at them, like he was waiting for them to leap from their seats and dive into his bowl of purple-gray pudding.

"Thanks, Marvin," Ms. Bell said. "We appreciate that you like to share your Hawaiian culture with us! Don't we, class?"

There was an unenthusiastic murmur of agreement.

"Marvin, would you please help me by serving the poi to people as they come through the line?" she asked, and he nodded happily.

Red joined the wave of her classmates as everyone hurried to the snack table. She hung back a little, letting people slip in front of her. They all eagerly took orange and black cupcakes, as well as fruit and cheese sticks. But when they got to Marvin and his purple poi, they made faces and declined.

After nearly half the class had refused to try the dish, Ms. Bell made everyone come back and accept a spoonful.

"Unless I have received notice of a poi allergy from your parents," she said sternly, "then I'm making it mandatory that you each take at least one bite of Marvin's treat. He worked very hard to share this with you."

The cat-girl asked in a whining voice, "Did my parents tell you about my poo allergy?"

Giggles scattered through the classroom.

"Poi. It rhymes with *boy*, Amber," Ms. Bell corrected. "And no. In fact, their email said they had some on their trip to Hawai'i last summer, and they were excited for you to try it."

Amber sighed, held up her plate, and rolled her eyes. Marvin's smile faltered.

When Red finally made it up to the table, there were only two cupcakes left—one for her and one for Marvin—

and all the other snacks were nearly gone. But Marvin's bowl was still almost full of poi. The look on his face sent a hot, dry wind through Red's bones. She bypassed the cupcakes and fruit and held her empty plate out to him.

"Can I have two scoops, please?"

For the first time that day, he made eye contact with her. She could see the ghost of their last conversation in his eyes and wished she could blow it away like dust.

"Please?" she said.

He tapped a blob of purplish paste onto her plate. She held it still, waiting for another spoonful. When he didn't give her one, she jiggled her plate, her eyebrows raised. One of those ridiculous dimples of his appeared in his cheek. He scooped another serving out and gave it to her, a smile creeping across his lips.

"Thanks," she said.

She looked around for a cup of carrot sticks, but they'd all been taken. Ms. Bell and the mom helper had moved on from the snack table and didn't notice their counting error. Red could feel Marvin watching her. She dipped a fingertip into the cold, goopy poi and slurped it into her mouth. Marvin's laughter made wind dance warmly through Red's hair.

"Technically, this is three-finger poi," he said. He scooped some onto a plate and then demonstrated. Using three fingers, he shoveled poi into his mouth and grinned. "See? Easiest to eat with three fingers, not one."

She mimicked him, taking another bite. The poi was cool and watery on her tongue. It tasted lightly sweet, with a note of sourness that she liked much more than she'd expected.

"It's not bad," she said.

"I know."

Then, quietly, she said, "I'm sorry I yelled at you."

Marvin nodded, licking poi off his fingers. "I'm sorry, too. Mom says I have a tendency to come on a little strong."

Red smiled and scooped another three-fingered load into her mouth. "Mmm. Better than cupcakes," she said around the poi on her tongue.

Marvin shook his head. "No way. Nothing's better than cupcakes!"

"That's true," she agreed.

They each grabbed one of the remaining cupcakes and returned to their desk cluster, grinning at the puddles of poi slowly soaking into the plates of everyone they passed.

Dear Mom,

Have you ever met a tortoise? Maybe when you get back, I can introduce you to Tuck. He's an Aldabra tortoise, and he weighs 400 pounds. He likes bananas and cucumbers and even cactus, which is weird to me, but he loves them!

This might sound crazy, but Tuck likes to read. I mean, he likes for me to read to him. Since there aren't any other tortoises here, I hang out with him in the barn a lot so he won't get lonely. The other day I brought a book and he kept trying to eat it. I told him it's not for eating, it's for reading, and then I showed him how. He sat there and listened to a whole chapter!

When I told my friend Marvin about it, he wanted to film Tuck for his YouTube channel. He came over to film, and his parents and grandparents were here, too. I didn't want to read in front of everyone, so Marvin tried instead. Tuck wouldn't listen! He kept digging around in the straw and ignoring everyone. Marvin's dad and his grandma both tried, but he only listens when I read to him.

I hope you can meet Tuck. I think you'll like him.

Did you get my last letter? Please write back soon. I miss you.

Love you,
Red

I've been trying

*two different things. And it's impossible
to be two different things at once, isn't it?*

It rained today. But the funny thing was,
there weren't any clouds in the sky. It was
bright and sunny... AND it was raining. The
weather was definitely two things at once.
   Did you know that Australia is the world's
BIGGEST island and it is the world's SMALLEST
continent? Did you know that a snail is MALE
and FEMALE at the same time?
   Sometimes I laugh when I'm sad, and cry
when I'm happy.
   Sometimes strangers feel like family.
   And sometimes my family feels like a
stranger.

Chapter
14

"If you keep the stitches loose, like this"—Celine leaned over to show Red the fabric of the small pouch she was sewing—"then the chicken feed can get out while Fezzik is playing with the beanbag." She snipped off the thread and held the bag out on the flat of her palm for Red to examine.

"We tried this trick with Billie once." Celine dropped the completed bag into a basket on the floor between them. "But she ate the whole thing."

"The whole thing?" Red asked.

Celine nodded. "Bag and all."

She showed Red how to fill each of the newly stitched bags with a quarter cup of chicken feed. Fezzik would shake the feed out during his next dancing-donkey trick at the last Groovy Petting Zoo of the year.

Red still hadn't wanted to help with the zoo that morning, but she had stuck around to watch everything going on. Afterward, when Celine said she needed to make more bags for chicken feed, Red asked to learn how, and the two of them set up camp in Tuck's pen. Empty fabric pouches were strewn around them like confetti. Red leaned against the tortoise as he munched on the veggies she'd put in his dish. The barn was golden with early-afternoon sunlight that poured in through the narrow windows along the ceiling.

Celine scooped another measuring cup of feed from a bucket. "I haven't found a fence yet that will keep Billie out of my garden. She loves to get in there and bite the heads off my marigolds. She doesn't eat them. Just decapitates them."

Outside, Billie bleated indignantly, like she knew they were talking about her. Red bit back a smile as Celine laughed. Tiny bits of chicken feed floated in the air between them, glinting like stars.

"We better hurry," Celine said, glancing at her watch. "The Kapules are expecting us in an hour."

She threaded another needle and started to stitch up the last two pouches. Pausing, she pressed her fingers into the slope between her neck and shoulder again, her expression tightening with pain.

"Are you okay?" Red asked.

The pain cleared from Celine's face. "I'm fine. I've just had a stiff neck lately. That's what happens to old ladies."

Red rolled her eyes. She knew Celine and Jackson were older than any of the foster parents she'd had before. Jackson was retired, even though he was still busy most days caring for animals at nearby farms. Celine worked three days a week at the library in Bramble, but technically she was retired, too. Still, Red didn't really think of them as old.

"But you're young at heart," she said, thinking of Gamma.

Celine's laugh was delighted.

"Marvin wants me to help him with a video for his YouTube channel tonight," Red said, packing up the chicken feed and measuring cups.

Celine raised her eyebrows. "It'll be a busy night! *Kitchen Kahuna* and a lūʻau. Sounds fun!"

Red planted a quick kiss on the top of Tuck's hard, cool head. "Marvin always has time for YouTube."

She'd already been to the Kapules' house twice for dinner, and they came to the Grooves' once a week. But Marvin had said that tonight, to celebrate Red's *three-week-iversary*, his family was hosting a lūʻau, which he described as a party, "Hawaiian style." Red wasn't sure what the difference between the other dinners and tonight's would be, considering Marvin had already cooked them one Hawaiian meal last week.

Tonight would be Red's first time on his YouTube channel. She was worried she'd mess it up, but Marvin was confident she'd be great. Even though she was nervous, she was happy he'd asked her.

Marvin loved *Kitchen Kahuna*. She and the Grooves had watched a few episodes together. Red had to admit she was impressed. In each episode, he would make some kind of Hawaiian meal or food. He usually worked alone, chattering away about everything he was doing, just like on cooking shows on TV. Sometimes his mom or his grandma would come in to help him with more complicated things. Once, his dad grilled up chicken kebabs for him. During that one, Marvin managed to work in a complaint, at least once per minute, about the fact that he wasn't allowed to use the grill unsupervised.

Red carried the bucket of chicken feed out of Tuck's pen and put it away. She took the basket of beanbags from Celine, who was rubbing her sore neck again.

"Thanks," Celine said. "Will you do me a favor and get the mail, please? I need to get the petting zoo smell out of my hair before we go to dinner."

As Celine headed inside, Red said goodbye to Tuck, then ran around the house and down the long driveway. Gandalf and the other dogs appeared out of nowhere, following her, their tongues dangling and their ears flopping as they ran.

It was mid-November, but the afternoon sun was warm against Red's back and hair. Frodo, Limerick, and Brontë started chasing a bunch of leaves that were spinning in the gentle wind. A sudden memory of *before* slowed Red's steps and made her smile.

When Red was little, before her mother started taking pills, they used to go to a big park by the museum to fly kites. It was one of Red's favorite things, but a lot of the time, the wind was way too gusty or not gusty enough for kite flying. Nobody could keep their kites up.

Except for Red's mother.

While all the other kids' kites would crash or get tangled in trees, Red's always floated perfectly and peacefully above them. She'd squeal and stomp her feet in excitement, clutching the string spool in her chubby hands. Her mother stood back, one hand shielding her eyes from the sun, and the other by her side, fingers dancing gracefully, creating little currents of perfect, kite-flying air.

It was one of Red's best memories with her mom.

She stopped walking. Could she do that, too? Could she make the air playful and gentle, like her mother used to? Her fingers began to tingle as she concentrated. For a minute, nothing happened. And then the breeze stuttered and stopped all together. Red frowned, pulling in a slow breath, and tried again.

A current, so soft she barely felt it at first, slipped

from her fingers. Red smiled, squinting in concentration. A tickling sensation spread from her fingers up into her wrist as the breeze grew stronger. The dogs barked and hopped excitedly when Red's wind lightly flipped some of the leaves over.

Red laughed, walking down the driveway again. The air came more easily now, and the leaves hovered just above the dogs' heads. They yapped and jumped, trying to snatch the brown and orange patches from the sky. Red kept the leaves floating just out of reach for as long as she could, then sent them skittering along the ground. The dogs went crazy, chasing after them like they were rabbits.

Red grinned, tired from the effort, but her blood buzzing with a warmth she hadn't felt before. Gandalf trotted back to her and snuffled her hand. Fingers still in Gandalf's fur, Red opened the mailbox and took out a fat bundle of envelopes.

The air stilled so suddenly that Gandalf whined and pressed her nose into Red's hip. Red pushed the dog away, her chest tight and hot.

There, rubber banded together on top of the bundled mail, were the last five letters Red had written to her mom, all marked *Return to Sender*.

Not one of them had been opened.

Chapter
15

Celine rang the Kapules' doorbell an hour later, glancing at the gray and black clouds that were stacking up above them, like crouching, watchful monsters.

"The weather sure changed moods fast," she said.

Red said nothing.

Marvin opened the door, holding a pineapple.

"Aloha!" he practically shouted.

"Aloha, Marvin," Jackson said.

Red forced down the roiling emotions snaking between her ribs. She wanted to focus on Marvin, on the lū'au.

Not on the letters.

The *unopened* letters.

A gust of wind nearly blew the pineapple out of her hand when Marvin gave it to her. All of them lurched and scrabbled for it. Red caught it before it hit the porch. She frowned, handing the pineapple back to him.

He motioned them inside. "Mom told me that pineapples used to be a sign of great wealth," he said grandly. "Rich people gave them to guests, probably to show off how rich they were." Then his dimples appeared and he laughed. "But we aren't rich. We just need it for *Kitchen Kahuna*. Come on." He led them into the house. "Have I told you what *aloha* means yet?"

"Doesn't it mean hello?" Red asked.

"Well, yeah," he said. "And goodbye. But it doesn't *just* mean hello or goodbye." He bounced on his toes, his eyes glittering with glee at being able to share so much information in the first ten seconds of her arrival. "It has a *spiritual* meaning, too. It's an expression of love and compassion. So you have to use it carefully. Keep the spirit of aloha pure."

"You amaze me, Marvin," Celine said. She took off her coat and ran a hand through her windblown hair.

"Thanks, Mrs. G. You amaze me, too!"

Celine laughed.

He led them into the living room. Mrs. Kapule greeted them there.

"Thanks for having us, Leilani." Celine hugged her.

"Of course! We're happy to celebrate this special girl," Mrs. Kapule said, smiling at Red.

Mrs. Kapule was only a few inches taller than Red

and had long, thick black hair that she wore in a braid down her back. Her face was round and, just like Marvin, when she smiled, a dimple appeared in the center of each cheek. She wore a dress with large pink flowers on it. A necklace made of delicate white blossoms was around her neck, and she had a pink flower in her hair above one ear.

Usually, Marvin's mom made Red feel at ease just by being there. There was a peacefulness about her that Red liked, and her dark eyes always sparkled. But even Mrs. Kapule's gentle smile wasn't enough to distract Red tonight.

Mrs. Kapule picked up a necklace made out of fresh flowers from the coffee table and held it out for Celine. It was a string of red roses, with some kind of smaller, white flower between them. "*Aloha nui loa,*" she said, looping the necklace over Celine's head.

"This is gorgeous," Celine said. "Thank you!"

Mrs. Kapule gave a similar flower necklace to Jackson, except his was made of red carnations.

Marvin grabbed Red's arm and pulled her closer to the coffee table. "Here's yours," he said, lifting a loop of fuchsia flowers. They glistened like spun sugar, and had a rich, sweet fragrance.

"It's a lei," Marvin said as he draped it around Red's neck.

She was afraid to touch the blossoms, worried they'd fall apart in her fingers. He watched her, his head tilted to one side.

"This is for me?" she asked.

"Mom and Tūtū made them. I picked out the flowers, though." His cheeks flushed and he grinned. "They're plumerias."

"You found plumerias in Colorado this time of year?" Jackson asked. "I'm impressed!"

Mrs. Kapule smiled mysteriously and shrugged. "Marvin is very determined. He left no stone unturned."

Red heard a door open in another part of the house. A moment later, Marvin's dad appeared, wearing a brightly patterned shirt and wiping his hands on a striped dish towel.

"You're here!" he boomed. "Aloha!"

Marvin looked a lot like his mother, but Red had learned that his personality came mostly from his dad. The first time Red met Mr. Kapule, he'd been wearing his Air Force uniform, and she'd expected him to be serious or scary. But he joked all the time, and his laugh was loud and a little high-pitched. She'd liked him immediately.

He hugged Celine and Jackson, and held up his palm to give Red a high five, which she gave half-heartedly. "You all look lovely tonight."

"Thank you," Celine said, looking at Red when she didn't respond.

Red was too distracted to notice.

"Marvin, where are your *kūpuna*?" Mr. Kapule asked.

"Behind you," came the voice of Marvin's grandfather.

Marvin's grandparents, Mr. and Mrs. Makani, were both short and slight, like Mrs. Kapule. They had brown eyes and wide smiles. Marvin's tūtū wore an orange dress similar to Mrs. Kapule's pink one. Her hair was almost completely gray, and the flower she had tucked into her bun was as yellow as a banana. Her husband, Marvin's papa, had thick white hair that stood up messily, just like Marvin's. He wore round glasses and had a gap between his front teeth that made his smile look impish.

"I got the kitchen set up for your video, Marvin," Mr. Kapule said.

Marvin did a little dance. "We're making pineapple kebabs," he said to Red.

Red was staring out the window, where two little pine trees in the Kapules' front yard were rocking, their branches whipping back and forth. The pressure in Red's chest was building. *Why were the letters unopened?* She clenched her fists against her stormy thoughts.

"Helloooo?" Marvin jabbed a finger into her shoulder.

She blinked and tore her gaze away from the trees.

"Sorry," she mumbled, starting toward the kitchen.

Celine's fingers brushed her arm as she passed, but Red ignored her worried expression, concentrating instead on keeping the rage of her wind under her skin.

Chapter 16

She barely said three words while they filmed the episode of *Kitchen Kahuna*. As Marvin narrated their actions for the camera, she dipped sliced pineapple into various spices, then slid them onto long sticks, like giant toothpicks.

She tried not to think about the swirl of storm clouds building just under her skin. But the more she ignored her own storm, the more the wind howled outside.

Focus on your breathing.

Not on the letters, now stuffed under the mattress in her bedroom.

Focus on your breathing. On pineapple. On Marvin.

Marvin didn't seem too concerned by her silence, at

least. He talked throughout filming, and before Red knew it, they were done.

Celine, on the other hand, kept glancing at Red during dinner.

"You okay?" she whispered as she handed Red a basket of golden-topped rolls. A crease between her eyebrows deepened when Red only shrugged.

"Try the potato mac salad," Marvin said, offering a bowl of creamy noodle and potato salad to Red from the opposite side. "Tūtū makes *such* good potato mac salad. Oh, and the kālua pig is ah-MAAAA-zing." He sang out the word, eyes squinched shut for emphasis.

Mrs. Kapule smiled. "Marvin helped plan the menu for tonight."

Marvin was glowing. "All my lūʻau favorites!"

Red tried to return his smile, but her face felt stiff and hot. She ignored the flow of conversation, focusing on breathing slowly and carefully. Her storm was drilling into her skull, roaring between her ears. But she couldn't let it out. It would ruin everything nice the Kapules had done for her.

She closed her eyes, saw the bundle of envelopes, wrinkled and smudged by the mail service, but otherwise unopened, unread, unwanted. *Why didn't Mom read my letters? What did I do wrong?*

She gripped her fork, brought food up to her mouth

that she didn't taste, her fingers shaking. *Don't think about it anymore.*

In . . . and out. *Ten.*

"In June we had a lūʻau for the entire church to celebrate Papa and Tūtū's fiftieth anniversary. Fifty years is a. Long. Time."

In . . . and out. *Nine.*

"Mom and Tūtū danced for everyone and I filmed it for my class. Did I tell you I'm taking an online filmmaking class?"

In . . . and out. *Eight.*

The pressure in Red's skull began to ease. She swallowed the food in her mouth. Her stomach cramped.

"We should have another church lūʻau next year, Mom. Then Red can come!"

In . . . and out. *Seven.*

"You'd love it, Red. We even gave a hula lesson to everyone. It was hilarious. All these old white ladies trying to move their hips."

In . . . and out. *Six.*

"Marvin, please speak respectfully of your elders."

"What? They *are* old white ladies! Saying the truth isn't disrespectful."

In . . . and out. *Five.*

"Marvin . . ."

"Do you like to dance, Red?"

Her throat was still tight and hot, and she didn't trust her voice, so she nodded.

Marvin's eyes widened. "You do? Awesome. I *love* dancing."

Red nodded again, the movement feeling less jerky and stiff this time, the rush in her ears fading. Her voice barely cracked when she spoke. "I used to dance. With my gamma."

"I dance with Tūtū! She's a *kumu hula*."

Tūtū's smile was proud. "Marvin is an excellent student."

Mrs. Kapule squeezed Tūtū's hand. "Mama and I taught together for many years. We are a good team."

In . . . and out. *Four.*

"Mom's gonna dance for you guys later, right, Mom?" Marvin reached for the plate of pineapple kebabs they'd made for *Kitchen Kahuna*. "Mom competed at the Merrie Monarch Festival once. I wasn't born yet."

In . . . and out. *Three.*

"Red?" Celine leaned in close to Red so nobody else could hear. "Are you okay?"

Red chewed her lip. The buzzing wind between her ribs was quieting some, but her stomach still ached. She whispered, "I'm not very hungry."

Celine nodded. "Okay. That's fine. Just eat what you want."

Red pushed the food around on her plate, struggling to focus on Marvin's chatter, on Celine's steady presence next to her, the musical laughter of the Kapules and Marvin's grandparents. She finished her breathing exercise, though it didn't make much difference.

Celine kept a close eye on Red, and Red even caught Marvin's tūtū looking at her with concern a few times. She tried to smile, tried to act normal.

"I believe we were promised some dancing," Jackson said once everyone else had finished eating.

Mrs. Kapule stood. "Yes! We're here to celebrate Red, after all."

Red's stomach cramped again. Gamma always danced when she was celebrating. Big things, little things. It didn't matter. She danced when the Broncos ran a touchdown. She even danced when they were losing, saying, "Someone's gotta dance the life back into their defense, baby girl!"

"What do you say, Red?" Mr. Kapule asked. "Would you like to see some hula?"

Marvin jumped up. "I'll get the 'ukulele!" He hurried from the room.

Red's throat was sandpaper. She followed the adults into the living room in silence. Celine's arm brushed hers as they moved toward the couch.

"Are you sure you're okay? Do you want to go home? We can," Celine whispered.

Tears sprang into Red's eyes and she turned her face away from Celine's. Her whole body ached with wanting to go home. Home to her mom. Home to before the pills. Home to Gamma.

But that was impossible.

Marvin bounded in with what looked like a tiny guitar and handed it to his grandfather. The Kapules moved a small table and a cushioned chair aside to make space for the dance. Tūtū sat next to Red on the couch. She patted Red's knee. Red wanted to pull away, but Celine was on her other side. Her skin felt as tight and thin as a balloon's.

Just breathe.

She clenched her fists. Behind them, the windows rattled as the wind outside grew louder. Jackson looked over his shoulder. Celine glanced at Red, the crease in her brow deepening.

Mrs. Kapule stood tall and strong before them, preparing to dance. She looked right at Red as she spoke. "We've had the privilege of walking beside Celine and Jackson as they became foster parents. We've seen them face each challenge with courage and love, and we know they were very, very eager to welcome you into their home."

Sweat prickled the back of Red's neck. The house creaked.

"The three weeks or so that you've been with Celine and Jackson have been our joy, too. We're so honored

95

that they asked us to be their Support Friends, and we're honored to get to know you better each day," Mrs. Kapule continued.

Celine had already explained that Marvin's parents were respite caregivers. That meant they could take care of foster kids without actually being foster parents. Except the Kapules were respite caregivers just for the Grooves. Or, really, just for *her*. They called it being a Support Friend. She'd never heard of anyone getting certified just to help out one specific foster family before, but that's what the Kapules had done. Celine had said it was a program sponsored by their church.

Mrs. Kapule continued, "We don't take that lightly. You're very special, Red. We consider you *ʻohana*. It means we are family. This dance is *mele ʻohana*."

Her words broke something open inside of Red. She wanted to tear a hole in the wall and fly out into the night. *Family* wasn't supposed to be strangers. *Family* was supposed to open letters, to write back. Family was supposed to *be there*.

Mr. Makani strummed the ʻukulele. The tone was soft and lilting—a sound so opposite the roar of the wind that Red gasped. She wrapped her arms around her stomach.

Celine leaned in to her as Mrs. Kapule started to dance.

"Red?" Her voice was low, urgent. "What's going on?"

Red watched Mrs. Kapule. Her movements were graceful, one flowing into the next like water. It was nothing like Gamma's dancing. Gamma's dances were all bounce and kick and silly wiggling.

Gamma.

Gamma would never have returned Red's letters. She would have read them. Every single one.

But Gamma was gone, too, and the ache of missing her was so big, Red couldn't contain it.

A rasping moan overtook the music. Red realized the sound was coming from her. She rocked forward, the part sob, part groan streaming out of her.

And with it, the wind.

Thunder cracked, so loud and close that Tūtū yelped, and darkness swallowed them as the power blinked out. Red's wind ripped through the room, rattling the pictures on the wall.

She felt a sudden weight on her back. Hands—Celine's hands, clutching her, drawing her in, holding her close.

She pulled away.

Glass shattered, and the storm outside came galloping in.

Chapter 17

This is my fault.

Red stood on the Grooves' back porch under a sky scrubbed clean and flecked with chipped-ice stars. Her cheeks were raw with salt and shame.

"Easy! Easy, Flicka! That's it." Jackson's voice was low, pleading. He held his hands out as he approached the spooked horse.

Flicka, the palomino mare, nickered and stamped, her ears flat against her head. A slice of dusty white moonlight illuminated the field, making the sweat on the horse's golden coat gleam. Red could see the whites of her eyes, even from a distance.

Finally, Flicka let Jackson slip a halter over her head. He stroked her neck, speaking too quietly for Red to hear.

Not that she could hear much above the guilt thundering in her veins.

She looked around the Grooves' field, her flashlight beam scrabbling over debris and splintered tree branches. The fence to the arena was a knot of twisted poles and hooked metal claws. A gaping black hole yawned across the front of the barn. The door had been ripped off and dragged into the night.

Flicka whinnied and chuffed, but followed Jackson without further resistance. Red watched him lead her into the dark mouth of the barn. Celine stepped out the back-porch door.

"The house seems okay. The library window is cracked, but that's it. Jackson will have to look at the roof tomorrow, though." She swiped her hand over her face. "Did he get Flicka?"

Red's mouth was sour and her throat burned. She nodded.

Celine let out a breath. "Good. Who's left?"

Red couldn't answer.

Jackson stepped out of the barn's black hole. He was at the porch in a few long strides.

"Everything okay?"

"Seems to be," Celine said.

"We'll have to cancel the last zoo." Air whistled between his front teeth. "I can't believe this. The storm took the door clean off the barn. Chewed up the arena pretty good. And of course—" He motioned to the oak tree behind Red's bedroom window. It had splintered straight down the middle of the trunk, top to bottom. Half of it lay on the ground while the other half stood above it like a tombstone.

"How are the animals?" Celine asked.

"Spooked. And Tuck's gone."

Red choked and coughed.

Celine frowned. "Gone—how?"

Jackson shook his head. "Vanished. None of the others were too far out. Flicka and Alfonzo were just out there." He pointed beyond the arena. "Lancelot and Merlin had the goats and Fezzik rounded up right next to the barn. I've accounted for all the chickens, and the rabbits were sleeping in their cage like nothing happened. But Tuck." He threw his hands up, let them fall against his sides. "I can't find him. The gate to his outdoor habitat was hanging off its hinges."

A crease deepened between Celine's eyes and she pressed her fingers into the curve of her neck. "Any sign which way he went?"

"Not that I saw," Jackson said. Exhaustion had etched holes in his voice. "But he has to have left a trail. He's basically a four-hundred-pound bulldozer."

Celine looked at Red, a little frown tugging on her lips. "Red?"

Red flinched, even though Celine's voice was quiet.

"Do you want to help us look for him tonight? Or would you rather go inside and rest?"

It's my fault. Tuck's gone, and it's my fault.

She swallowed the lump in her throat. "I want to look for him."

Celine nodded, pulled the hood of her jacket up. "Okay. Let's spread out a bit. Red and I will look that way"—she pointed north, past the arena—"and you go south. He couldn't have gone far."

"He's pretty fast when he wants to be," Jackson said.

"We'll find him." Celine squeezed Red's shoulder.

Jackson nodded. "Okay. You take Gandalf. The storm may have chased coyotes out of their dens."

Red shivered and tucked her nose into the collar of her coat, trapping hot breath against her neck. The thought of Tuck lost somewhere in the dim light of the half-moon, facing off with a snarling coyote, made her heart ache.

They set out, their boots crunching over dirt and dry grass. Red copied Celine and swept her flashlight back and forth in long arcs. Gandalf raced ahead of them, then circled back, sniffing and wuffing.

Just that afternoon, Red had sent leaves scattering for the dogs in a playful breeze. She hadn't felt wind like that—happy, gentle, warm—in a long time. And she'd never *made* her wind like that before. But this—splintered branches and twisted metal scattered across the ground. Things broken and battered and lost.

This was familiar.

When Red was little, her mom's wind could tousle Red's hair from across the room, turn the pages of a book she was reading, or send a stuffed toy scooting along the carpet in a tumbling dance. Red had loved her mom's wind back then.

Before.

But Red's wind had always been more like her mom's wind *after*.

After the pills. After the fights with Gamma. After the nights she didn't come home, even though Red cried for her.

Those winds of her mother's hurt. They didn't tousle Red's hair anymore; they bit at her cheeks with cold teeth. They blew relentlessly, making Red's skin raw and chapped. And when her mom got angry, the winds got bigger. Scarier.

Those were the winds Red had inherited.

Until she'd come to the Grooves', her wind had never felt light or playful. It wasn't always *bad*, necessarily. Sometimes it even helped her, like the last time The Mom's boys cornered her in the yard to pinch her arms. She'd let her wind swell, let it blow them off their feet in an angry burst. She didn't hurt them. Just scared them so they'd leave her alone.

Red was only protecting herself. She'd been sent away after that, though. The Mom was convinced she was dangerous, even though she didn't know what had happened.

Would Celine and Jackson think she was dangerous now, too? Would they send her away?

The thought brought a fresh wave of anxious flurries to her skin.

Maybe she *was* dangerous. As much as she wanted her wind to be good or playful like her mother's used to be, maybe it couldn't be. Maybe her wind was broken. Or maybe she was.

It was better for everyone if she kept it inside as much as possible. But whenever she did, the air *outside* churned and bellowed. Like tonight. It had splintered trees and ripped gates off their hinges.

How could she stop *that*?

And now, Tuck was gone. Because of her.

"We'll find him, Red." Celine's voice was solid in the darkness, her words sure-footed.

But Celine was wrong.

They didn't find him. Not even a trace of him. Not that night, and not the next morning.

The Kapules came over to help them search. They

walked through the fields and looked in Celine's garden. Jackson even drove the dirt road around their property with Red and Marvin in the back of the truck, each looking over one side, scanning for a glimpse of green-brown tortoise shell among golden grasses.

But Tuck had vanished.

Chapter
18

The next three days passed in a fog of silence for Red. When Ms. Bell called on her at school, Red didn't respond. Marvin tried talking to her, tried assuring her that Tuck would be found, but she ignored him, too. Celine and Jackson made her mug after mug of cocoa, leaving them on Red's nightstand, then taking them away again—untouched—a few hours later. Celine scheduled an emergency appointment with Dr. Teddy, but even he could only get a few shrugs out of her.

It wasn't that Red didn't *want* to talk.

It was that she couldn't.

Every time she tried, the words got stuck in the back of her throat. They piled up behind her tongue, heavy and sharp as stones.

My mom doesn't want to talk to me.

Tuck is lost.

It's my fault. Everything is my fault.

Celine and Jackson started having whispered conversations that would stop the moment she came into a room. Red knew her silence frustrated them. They weren't the first foster parents to be frustrated by her. Or maybe it scared them. Maybe they sensed the storms building inside her with each passing day and were afraid of what she could do, like The Mom had been.

Either way, she knew what the whispered conversations meant. It always meant the same thing.

They were sending her away.

The knowledge still couldn't free Red's tongue. Any day now, she knew Ms. Anders would come with her peach gummies to take her. To another house. Another room. Another starting over. So she packed a few things in her old backpack and kept it under the bed.

Waiting.

Ready.

After school on Wednesday, Red watched Jackson from her bedroom window as he cut the fallen half of the oak tree into logs and hauled them to the woodpile by the barn. Her throat burned with unspoken words, and her stomach ached with shame.

She turned away from the window and sat on the bed. Tomorrow would mark five days without Tuck. Five days. Days Tuck didn't have food or friends or his heat lamp. It was getting colder, and a steady, wintry wind had been blowing since Saturday night. It wasn't good for a tortoise to be out in the cold. Tuck was built for deserts, not frozen fields. Red shivered.

Tomorrow was also Thanksgiving. Would Ms. Anders come get her tonight, so Celine and Jackson could enjoy the holiday? Would anyone else want to take her in—a girl of storms and silence?

The questions chased her back onto her feet. She pulled the envelopes out from under her mattress and stared down at them. She'd examined them a hundred times, but there wasn't the slightest clue as to why they'd been returned. Tears pricked her eyes and she shoved them back under the mattress. She paced the room a few times. Swirling emotions skimmed off her skin in a restless breeze that rustled book pages.

Why had they been returned? What had she done wrong?

She tried to think back, struggling to recall if she'd written something that might have made her mom mad. But Red wrote so many letters, and she couldn't even be sure they were all sent. The Mom said she'd sent them, but Red once found a letter crumpled up in the bottom of The Mom's purse, grease-stained and forgotten after a tube of hand lotion had exploded.

But obviously some of her letters had been sent.

Because now they'd been returned to her. Unopened. Unwanted.

A gust of frustration made the blankets on Red's bed ripple. She stomped over and pulled one of the envelopes out from under the mattress again. It felt heavy, like disappointment and broken promises.

Heat rose up inside her, making hot, dry air circle the room in a blazing gust. She crumpled the envelope in her fist.

Her mother was supposed to be released from prison in 370 days. Red scowled.

No.

Mothers weren't supposed to be in prison at all. They weren't supposed to be addicts. Mothers were supposed to fly kites and share secrets and take care of their daughters. Her mom was supposed to be here, with Red. They were supposed to be together.

But they weren't.

And now, her mom didn't even want to read her letters.

Red tore the envelope in half.

She pulled the pieces of her letter out, and tore them, too. She tore and tore, ripping apart her sentences, shredding her words until they fell from her fingers in a flurry of papery snow. If her mom didn't want to read them, then *fine*. She didn't want her to read them now anyway.

Something hot and thick rose from Red's belly. She

108

clawed at her mattress, pulling out more envelopes, but refusing to let herself cry. Her wind whisked the tattered paper from her fingers and sent it scattering and skipping over the bed, across the floor, around her feet. The shards caught in the folds of her blankets and snagged in the curtains. They blew under the dresser, tangled with dust bunnies, and piled up against her pillow.

She stood, face burning, as the fragments of her letters flurried and drifted. Her breath came in ragged gasps, but the heat in her chest was cooling. She wiped her nose on her sleeve and went to the window. Outside, Jackson had finished chopping up the fallen oak. He wasn't in the yard anymore.

Red opened the window all the way. The cold November air smelled like freshly cut wood and coming snow.

Just before her mother was arrested, the two of them went to a park outside Denver. It was one of Red's favorite parks, with giant red rocks and a bunch of walking trails. Earlier that day, her mother had written a letter. She wouldn't let Red read it, but Red knew it was for Gamma. She'd seen Gamma's name at the top of it.

"What does it say?" she'd asked her mother as they walked.

"Nothing."

"But . . . it has to say *something*."

Her mother dragged a hand through her long hair. "Leave it alone, Red."

They stopped at the base of a trail that wound up into a thick grove of trees.

"Stay here," her mom said. "I need to be alone."

Red lagged behind, but still followed her silently, pausing behind trees when she thought her mom might have heard her coming. But her mother never glanced back. Finally, she stopped at a spot overlooking a field. The valley below was bright and bursting with wild-flower color. Her mother stood in the shadows of the trees and leaned her elbows on a fence along the edge of the trail. Her dark hair shifted around her face, even though there wasn't any wind. Red watched as she took the letter she'd written to Gamma from her pocket and stared at it. She didn't read it. Just held it in both hands, fingers gripping the edges so tightly, the paper wrinkled.

"You were wrong, Mom," Red heard her say. "Some things really are just impossible."

Then, to Red's horror, she ripped the letter to shreds.

A wind, cold and angry, scooped the pieces of the letter from her mother's hands and carried them up up up.

"Are you happy now?" her mother shouted into the sky.

The sky didn't respond.

Red's eyes followed the pieces of that letter swirling in the air, but her mother turned away and started back down the path, never seeing her daughter hiding in the nearby bushes.

Pushing aside the memory, Red began collecting the scraps of her own letters from her bedroom floor, grabbing at them in frantic, hurried swipes. She held out the bottom of her shirt like a basket and scooped the pieces into it. Then she returned to the window.

In the distance, the sun was sinking toward the mountains, casting ocher light that sent long shadows slanting across the landscape. Red held a handful of paper out and concentrated with all her might. Her wind, still frothy with hurt, whipped the bits of her letters from her fingers and carried them up up up, vanishing into the sky. She emptied handful after handful into the air, until the basket of her shirt was empty.

After her mother had disappeared down the path that day, Red had chased the fragments of the letter. She'd collected as many pieces as she could, later taping them into her impossible notebook. She taped them there because, at the time, she still believed impossible things could happen.

Now, though, she wasn't so sure.

As the last bits of her own letters disappeared, Red pulled the impossible notebook out of the nightstand drawer and opened to her mother's page. There were too many missing pieces for her to make out the whole letter, but it didn't really matter. All that mattered was the largest scrap on the page. The scrap where her mom had written her own list of impossible things.

it's all impossible. Being a good daughter. Staying sober.

Being a mom.

More than anything in the entire notebook, Red had wanted to prove these three things wrong. Wasn't that why Gamma had given Red the notebook in the first place? She wanted Red to remind her mom about the difference between *hard* and *impossible*, too.

But Red never got the chance. Her mom was arrested a week later, and Red was put in foster care.

And now, her mom didn't even want to read Red's letters.

Red slammed the notebook closed and threw it across the room. It hit the wall with a *thud* and fell to the floor, pages bent and spine twisted. Like a bird, broken after flying into glass.

Dear Mom,

I'm moving in with a new family tomorrow. Ms. Anders said I'll have my own room since the family has three boys and no girls. It'll be nice to have my own space, I guess. This group home has eight girls in it, and most of the time they're fighting. There's this girl, Alicia, who is always stealing stuff from people.

It's not so bad here, though. The other day they took us to a movie. I was thinking about how you taught me to stand by the screen during the end credits with my arms in the air and look up so it feels like falling. I was going to show some of the girls, but the house mother made us leave right away. I'm glad, though. I don't really want to do that trick with anyone else. That's our thing.

It's lights-out, so I better go. I'll send you my new address in my next letter so you can write me back.

I miss you.
Red

Chapter 19

Thanksgiving morning, Red didn't come downstairs. What was the point? Words were still lodged behind her tongue. Tuck was still missing. Shivering currents were still skimming across her skin. Celine and Jackson wouldn't want her sitting silently at their table, ruining their holiday.

It was better to stay away.

Her orange backpack was under the bed, stuffed with clean underwear, a pair of jeans, two sweaters, and the books Celine had given her. Even though it wasn't touching the bed, she could feel it under the mattress, heavy and cold. Across the room, the impossible notebook stayed where it had fallen. She'd already decided:

if Ms. Anders came for her, she would leave the notebook behind.

She was curled up on the bed, knees hugged under her chin, staring at the bent pages and broken spine of the notebook, when someone knocked on the door.

Red said nothing.

"I'm coming in," Celine said. She opened the door and Gandalf came bounding in. The dog immediately jumped on the bed, making Red's whole body bounce, and lay down at Red's feet, licking her socks.

Celine was holding a newspaper. She sat at the foot of the bed and stroked Gandalf's ears, newspaper folded in her lap. Red waited for her to say something. But Celine just sat there, letting the silence circle and settle between them like a dog on a pillow. Outside the window, the fractured trunk of the old oak creaked softly.

After a long time, Celine reached over and squeezed Red's foot gently. "We'd love for you to join us today, Red. Marvin and his family are coming for lunch. We thought we could go out and search some more after we eat."

Red said nothing.

"I know what it's like to miss someone," Celine said. Her voice was quiet in a way that made Red think it was true.

But Red said nothing.

"We all love Tuck very much. And I promise you, we

are not going to abandon him. We'll find him, Red. We'll do everything we can."

A tear slipped over the bridge of Red's nose and soaked into her pillow.

"We won't give up. That's not who we are. We're Tuck's family," Celine said.

Red said nothing.

Celine unfolded the newspaper and set it next to Red's arms.

Red looked at it, then uncurled her body and reached for it, hands shaking.

There, on the front page of the *Bramble Bee*, was a picture of Red sleeping with her arms slung over Tuck's shell. His face was turned toward her, and it looked to Red like he was smiling.

BELOVED TORTOISE GOES MISSING, the headline read. **FAMILY ASKS COMMUNITY FOR HELP**.

Celine stood. "We'd love for you to join us today. For lunch, and for searching. For whatever you want to be a part of."

Red said nothing.

But her heart ached from wanting to.

Chapter

20

The ache in Red's heart swelled when the doorbell rang in the middle of lunch. Celine went to answer.

"Oh my goodness!" Her voice was filled with genuine surprise.

From the dining room, where Red, Jackson, and Marvin's family were eating lunch, they could hear the sound of feet shuffling and people murmuring. They all got up and joined Celine at the front door.

A crowd of people were on the porch. Neighbors, people from church, kids from school. Even people Red had never seen before. Dozens of folks, all wearing heavy coats and looks of determination.

A man with sandy hair and a thick mustache shook Jackson's hand.

"Bill," Jackson said. "What's going on?"

"I hope we didn't interrupt your Thanksgiving meal," Bill said. "We're here to help find a tortoise."

"We saw the article," a woman in a knit cap said. "So we organized a little search party."

Hope surged through Red, hot and bright. She looked at Marvin, who was grinning at her.

"We'll *definitely* find him now!" he said.

Marvin's grandparents offered to clean up lunch while Jackson and the man, Bill, organized three groups out on the front drive. Red, Marvin, and Celine headed out in the third group. Afternoon sunlight illuminated everything in deep gold, and the sky was clear and blue and wide. The cold winds that had been spinning around Red for the last few days had warmed, but only a little.

"Still not talking?" Marvin asked her as they walked.

She sank her fingers into Gandalf's fur and bit her lip.

Marvin nodded, as if he understood. "That's okay."

Ahead of them, someone was shouting, "Tuck! Where are you? Tuck!"

Marvin shook his head. "Can you believe all these people came because of that article? It's so cool."

She'd read the newspaper article three times that morning. It told Tuck's entire story. How he'd been found in the desert of Arizona by some college students at CU

118

Boulder. That they'd kept him in their frat house for several months, and Jackson had been called in because Tuck was so badly wounded.

"This tortoise is a fighter," says Jackson Groove, the tortoise's rescuer and now caretaker. "He's a survivor. But he's family, and we miss him. My little girl especially misses him. I want to bring him home as soon as possible."

The Grooves' foster daughter, Ruby, is pictured above with the hundred-year-old tortoise. Groove says the two share a special bond, and that Ruby has been looking for the tortoise since he disappeared on Saturday night, when an unexpected windstorm saw gusts of seventy miles per hour in parts of Bramble.

Red stared at the picture for a long time. Jackson must have taken it on his phone the day she met Marvin and later fell asleep with her cheek pressed against Tuck's shell. She hadn't known the picture existed.

The article proved that Celine meant what she'd said. They weren't giving up on Tuck. And now, dozens of people were fanned out across the fields behind the Grooves' farm, searching for him.

"We'll find him," Celine murmured to Red, as if she'd read her mind.

"Let's take a spin-eo!" Marvin said, grabbing Red's hand.

119

They were in a small grove of trees near the back of the Grooves' property. Rays of light angled through the bare tree branches and birds sang above them.

"A what?" Celine asked.

"A spin-eo! It's when you take a video selfie and spin in a circle to show people where you are. I made it up."

Celine laughed. "Is this for your YouTube?"

Marvin nodded. He was bouncing on his toes. "Can we use your phone, Mrs. G.?"

Celine pulled her cell out of her back pocket. "It's kind of old. I don't think the camera's very good."

"That's okay. Everybody! Stand together for a sec. Let's show the world Tuck's search party! Maybe we'll make the news," he said to Red.

Everyone gathered together, smiling and shaking their heads at Marvin. Marvin fiddled with Celine's phone and made a face.

"It doesn't have a forward-facing camera." He sounded appalled.

Mr. Kapule laughed and stepped away from the crowd. He traded his phone for Celine's and handed hers back to her. "Sorry my kid is such a tech snob."

Celine winked at Red as Marvin held up his dad's phone. He held it high, spinning in a slow circle. "Here we are! The fearless tortoise search party!" he said. "Everyone wave!"

The crowd obeyed, laughing and cheering as the camera panned by them.

"We're gonna find him, Red!" Marvin shouted.

"Yeah!" they all agreed.

Red's heart surged with hope.

They were going to find him.

They had to find him.

After Marvin's spin-eo, the crowd got down to the business of serious searching. More than thirty people looked for Tuck in knee-high grasses, behind rocks, under bushes, and around all the buildings on the property. Some people went past the fence line, others walked miles down the dirt road, scouring the ditch on either side. Marvin talked the entire time, filling the space around Red's silence. Her footsteps fell to the rhythm of his voice, and she felt the logjam of words in her throat start to loosen.

We're coming, Tuck. We'll find you.

But one hour turned into two, and no sign of him.

Sunlight blinded them as the day slipped away. People held their hands to their eyes and checked behind rocks they'd checked twice before. Nobody shouted Tuck's name anymore. Slowly, the mood of the search party shifted, quieted. The knots in Red's chest tightened as the sky began to darken. Holes opened in Marvin's chatter. A few people shook Jackson's hand and went back to their cars. Then a few more.

Three and a half hours after it had begun, the search slowed and finally stalled. Darkness was closing in around them. Darkness was closing in around Red, too.

The Kapules stayed another hour, helping them search with flashlights in hand. But eventually, even they had had enough.

"We'll look again tomorrow," Marvin said. He gave Red a stiff hug before climbing into their car.

"I'm sorry, kiddo," Mr. Kapule said, a hand on her shoulder.

"Don't lose heart, Red." Mrs. Kapule brushed her fingers against Red's cheek.

Red stood on the porch, watching a pale cloud of steam rise around the Kapules' car when Mr. Kapule started the engine. A frosty wind shivered from her fingers and stirred through her hair.

Marvin rolled down the back window and waved. "We'll find him, Red!" he shouted. "I know we will!"

Red watched them go, and said nothing.

Chapter
21

Long after the Kapules' taillights faded into the night, Celine joined Red on the porch and set a hand on her shoulder.

"Let's go for a walk," she said.

For the last few weeks, Red had seen Celine head out for her nightly walk, with Gandalf and the other dogs at her heels. Red didn't understand why, but every time she watched Celine leave, she felt a sense of loss. Celine hadn't invited Red to join her since that night during Red's first weekend, though.

Celine touched Red's hair lightly. "Come on. I want to show you something."

Even bundled in their coats, the night air stung. White, misty clouds slithered around their faces with each breath. The cold made worry for Tuck gnaw at Red's heart.

Celine carried a solar camping lantern that cast a pale yellow glow on the ground in an arc before their feet. Spindly shadows stretched out behind the dried stalks of grass as they passed.

"Here we are." Celine paused, waiting for Red to catch up, and held the lantern higher.

A large flat slab of stone jutted out of the ground at an angle. Red had seen this rock during their search. From a distance, she thought it looked like a misshapen Frisbee caught in a gutter. Now she could see it was as big as a table.

Three of the dogs kept wandering around, sniffing the grass and playing together, but Gandalf hopped onto the rock like she'd been there a hundred times. Celine put the lantern down and spread out one of the fleece blankets she'd been carrying. The dog lay across the top portion of it.

Celine lowered herself onto the blanket, propping her head against Gandalf's ribs, and patted the space next to her. Red stretched out beside her foster mother, and Celine covered them both in the second fleece blanket. Red squirmed, opening a gap of cool air between her arm and Celine's. She closed her eyes, trying to push back the emotions still twisting inside her. Gandalf, however, sighed, as if this rocky cuddle puddle was all she'd ever wanted in life.

Red let out her breath and opened her eyes.

Above them, the galaxy shimmered. The Milky Way curved through space with such clarity, Red could see the blue and purple and green and yellow of it, like flecks of crystal in candlelight. The moonless sky was inky, and stars burst through the velvety blackness with a kind of recklessness. A wildness so bold, Red could hear it.

She could hear the stars.

The night was alive, humming with the deep thrum of orchestral strings and the soaring trill of sopranos. It sounded like one of Gamma's symphonies, but bigger and even more full of emotion than Beethoven. A shooting star dripped from the top of the sky toward the horizon, its song spinning out of it as it fell.

"Can you hear them?" Celine asked.

This wasn't possible. The stars didn't sing. *Did they?* Red shook her head in disbelief.

Celine tilted her head toward Red's. "I asked them to sing for you."

Red felt a familiar tickle on her skin. It was the same tickle she felt when she made the wind play tricks with leaves for the dogs. The same tickle that came whenever she and Gamma had written in the notebook.

It was the tickle of impossible things.

She sat up, scooting away from Celine. How was she doing this? How did someone *ask* the sky to sing?

She didn't. She can't, Red thought. *It's impossible.*

It always seems *impossible* . . .

Gamma's words whispered in her mind. Red closed her eyes and shook her head. *No.* She didn't want to believe in impossible things anymore! A sharp wind sliced through her ribs, making the fleece blanket flap. Celine caught it easily and held it down.

"I love coming out here. I've wanted to bring you with me, but I knew you needed time," Celine said.

Red frowned, watching Celine's easy movements. She glanced back up at the sky, goose bumps rising on her arms as the music crescendoed.

Celine pointed to a small shimmering patch of stars. "That's my favorite. Pleiades. Also called the Seven Sisters. In Greek mythology, they were seven beautiful sisters that Zeus turned into stars."

Red glanced at her foster mother, uneasiness still coiling its breath between her fingers. *She asked the stars to sing.*

"The sisters' father, Atlas, was punished for rebelling against the gods. He was sentenced to hold the heavens on his back for all eternity, and could never return to his children. The sisters' grief was so terrible, it destroyed them."

Red looked at Pleiades winking above her. The stars

126

were small compared to other constellations, clustered together like a tiny version of the Big Dipper. One of the Sisters was dimmer than the others, barely a whisper of starlight.

Celine continued, "Their death was mourned by all the gods. But Zeus wanted the sisters' beauty—not their grief—to define them, and so he turned them into stars."

The music pulsing in the night air seemed sad now. Lonely. As her eyes grew more accustomed to the darkness, Red thought she could see the loneliness. There, twining between the stars. A blackness, deeper than the night sky, like a scar across the heavens. It looked as if someone had carved out a ribbon of starlight, leaving a gaping emptiness behind.

The ache between Red's ribs throbbed with each heartbeat.

Celine said, "I like Pleiades because I understand them. I understand loss. How the hurt of losing someone can feel like it's swallowing you up."

Red shivered and hugged her knees to her chest.

After a brief silence, Celine said, "I lost my son." Her voice was quiet but steady. Surprise snaked through Red.

The celestial symphony softened as Celine spoke. "Roan. He—he passed away when he was six. He got sick. One day he was fine, and the next . . ." Her lips pressed together and she swallowed hard. "Meningitis."

She cleared her throat. "It was a long time ago, but it still hurts. I miss him. Every day."

Silent tears sparkled on Celine's cheeks.

The sadness on her face reminded Red of the way Gamma had looked sometimes, after Red's mom left. It was a raw, wide-open kind of sadness. A sadness too big to look at. Red turned back to the stars and listened to their music. Something loosened inside of her.

"I miss Gamma."

Celine closed her eyes at the sound of Red's voice. Red was a little surprised by it herself.

"Your grandmother?"

Suddenly, tears were in Red's eyes, too, and she couldn't blink them away. "Yeah."

Celine turned her face toward Red. "What happened?"

Red closed her eyes against the memories. *Gamma's skin turning gray like ash. Her arms so thin that her bones were sharp. The bruises that bloomed like flowers at even the lightest touch.* There were other memories, too. Of her mother. Of the pills Gamma tried to hide, but her mother always found, always took for herself. Of the way her mother disappeared when Gamma needed her most.

"She got sick, too."

Celine shifted, rolling onto her side. Her voice was soft, warm. "Remembering can hurt sometimes."

Red kept her eyes on the stars. The music was faint now, barely audible above the gathering wind.

"It still hurts me, too. But not like it used to. It used to feel like I was caught in a hurricane. Like I couldn't move or breathe without being bowled over by the hurt." Celine let out a slow breath, and the star-music faded even more.

"Grief changes us. It can turn us into something we don't recognize. But this—" She gestured toward the sky. "The music reminds me I'm loved. It brings me into life."

Red's throat tightened. Gamma used to say something similar about dancing. If the toaster was burning everything, she would shake her rear end and jump with her arms held high. When the car died, Gamma would waltz around it, touching the hood with each pass.

"I'm dancing it into life!" she'd say, twirling, her hands in the air.

And it worked.

The toaster quit burning things. The car started. The broken things came back to life, and Gamma would smile like she had a secret, and hug Red close.

Red shivered.

Gamma could dance things into life. Celine could make the stars sing. All of Red's impossible hopes pulsed within her. Finding Tuck, reuniting with her mom, being a perfect fit.

Ever since Gamma died, Red had stopped looking for the impossible. She'd kept the notebook because it was all she had left of Gamma, but the impossible things she'd collected in its pages felt cold and empty. As hollow as broken promises.

Before, Red had hoped for all kinds of impossible things. She'd hoped her mom would come back. She'd hoped Gamma would get better. She'd hoped and she'd hoped.

But Gamma didn't get better.

And her mom didn't stop taking pills.

After Gamma died and her mother was arrested, Red lost everything. Her family, her home. Her belief.

But tonight, the sky was singing to her. All because Celine had asked it to. If the impossible—like singing stars—could happen, then maybe the things she hoped for could happen, too. If she believed.

But did she?

Her heart ached with wanting to.

She turned to her foster mother. "I want to show you something," she said.

Chapter
22

"What's this?" Celine righted the pages of the battered notebook gently.

Red pulled off her coat and sat on her bed. "My grandma gave it to me." She reached out and smoothed another page, hating that they were bent and creased, and that it was her fault. "We made it together."

Her foster mother looked awestruck. Seeing the impossible notebook in Celine's hands made Red feel as if, for the first time in years, the world was standing right-side up. Gamma would have loved hearing the stars sing, and she would have loved Celine. Red knew it, as suddenly and as deeply as she'd ever known anything.

Celine turned to one of the creased pages labeled *IMPOSSIBLE*.

"Gamma really liked impossible things, so we started collecting them," Red said.

Celine's eyes were wide as she examined the page. "Collecting them?"

"Yeah. Gamma wrote down things that people used to think were impossible, and then we proved how they weren't really. See?"

She pointed to the words *Climbing the world's tallest mountain*, written in Gamma's handwriting.

"Gamma taught me about Mount Everest. It's in Nepal. People thought it was impossible to climb because it's so tall and cold, and there isn't very much air at the top of it. Lots of people died trying."

Celine was looking at Red now. Her eyes were shiny, like she was going to cry again, but she was smiling.

"But then there was this guy—"

"Sir Edmund Hillary," Celine said, nodding.

"Yeah. He climbed it in 1953 with a guy named Ten . . . Ten—" Red frowned, squinting at the name she'd written so long ago.

"Tenzing Norgay," Celine said.

"Yeah, him." Red shrugged. "Gamma and I looked up all kinds of stuff like that. But we didn't have time to finish it."

Celine turned a couple of pages, reading the entries Red had written about going to the moon and climbing Mount Everest. As she read, she massaged the right side of her neck and shook her head a little, a small smile on her lips.

"This is pretty amazing," she said. She leaned in to Red's shoulder. "*You're* pretty amazing."

Red blushed.

Celine turned another page. "Bumblebees?"

"They say it should be impossible for bumblebees to fly because their bodies are too fat for their wings," Red explained.

Celine nodded. "They say bumblebees defy the laws of physics."

"Yeah. Who's *they*, anyway?"

Celine laughed. "I don't know. But *they* don't sound like my kind of people at all."

Red smiled. "Mine, either."

Celine read the short entry and pointed to Red's words. "*A bumblebee creates its very own tornado.*" She smiled. "I was actually reading an article about bumblebees the other day. It said that a bumblebee's wings create *two separate* vortices, one on each side of its body. But they never join up. If they did, then bumblebees would be more aerodynamic. They could fly more easily. Instead, bumblebees have adapted to the chaos."

Red stroked Gandalf's head and thought about bumblebees, about two separate tornadoes spinning beneath their wings, carrying them through life. She wished her wind could be like that—controllable. Maybe bumblebees weren't aerodynamic, but at least they could control when their tornadoes happened.

Celine read a few more entries. She especially liked the parts about women who'd done amazing things that weren't recognized in history books.

"I think I would have liked your grandma very much," Celine said. She put an arm around Red's shoulders. Red didn't pull away.

"Thank you for sharing this with me, Red. It's really special. You're—" She shook her head, like she couldn't find the right words. "I'm really proud of you."

Red didn't know what to say. She took the notebook from Celine and focused on petting Gandalf. Celine stood and stretched.

"It's been a long day," she said.

"Celine?" Red thought she could still hear the distant sound of Celine's singing stars. She smiled. "I think Gamma would have liked you, too."

Chapter
23

The next day—after video-calling Jackson's daughter, Nicole, and her family; after spending a few more hours searching for Tuck; after playing a game of Scrabble against Jackson, with Celine on her team; after helping Jackson fetch big plastic bins of Christmas decorations out of the attic—after all of that, Red went into her bedroom and unpacked her smelly orange backpack.

She no longer believed the Grooves would send her away.

And she was right. Ms. Anders never came.

Marvin and his family visited on Friday evening, too. They brought food, and Marvin even talked Red into filming another episode of *Kitchen Kahuna*. He told her the episode she'd been in with him had gotten more views than any of his other ones.

They spent Saturday morning looking for Tuck. Red and Marvin made flyers Friday night that they printed and handed out around the neighborhood Saturday. People promised to keep an eye out for him. Jackson even reported Tuck's disappearance to the police, just in case.

"I seriously doubt anyone took him," he said. "But I want to explore every option."

The longer Tuck was gone, the more impossible finding him felt. But Red couldn't stop thinking about impossible things. She explored Celine's library, looking for books about big things that had been lost. She found a book about a city called Pompeii and another about the *Titanic*.

Celine took her to the library in Bramble that afternoon, too, and Red discovered all kinds of amazing books. Books that brought a familiar tickle to her skin. She learned about frogs that froze to death in winter, only to come back to life in summer. Jellyfish that never died. Doctors that were learning how to grow human body parts—like hearts and even brains—in laboratories so that someday they could use them to save peoples' lives.

The idea of so many impossible things in the world made Red light-headed with wonder.

And so, Sunday evening she pulled out the impossible notebook. She hadn't added anything to it in years, except for the picture of Tuck from the newspaper, which she'd cut out and carefully taped into its pages. But now she couldn't help herself. She'd learned so many amazing things in the last few days, she *had* to write some of them down.

Red sat in Tuck's empty stall, books open in front of her and the notebook in her lap. But she couldn't concentrate. She kept staring at the Tuck-shaped holes all around her. A few days ago, Celine had scrubbed the stall clean, scouring tortoise pee out of the wooden floorboards and tossing out the old straw and food. She said she was getting it ready for him, so he'd have somewhere nice to come home to.

Red wished he'd hurry.

"Red?"

She jumped. Celine stood by the gate. Red hadn't heard her come into the barn.

"How's it going in here?"

"Fine." Red snapped the notebook shut. She'd been too distracted to write anything anyway.

Celine stepped into the stall and looked around, her fingers massaging the slope of her shoulder. Her eyes were full of missing Tuck, too. After a moment, she sat down on the hay bale with Red. Red pulled her knees up under her chin.

"We need to talk."

Something in Celine's tone sent a nervous shiver through Red. The fresh straw on the floor beneath them skittered back, away from Red, away from whatever Celine wanted to say. Red clenched her fists, pressed them into the tops of her shoes.

Celine watched the straw for a moment. "I spoke with Ms. Anders."

Icy tingles started in the tips of Red's fingers, zinging up her arms, straight toward her heart. Had she been wrong to unpack her backpack? Were they sending her away after all?

She closed her eyes. *Three hundred sixty-six days*, she reminded herself. Even if Celine and Jackson didn't want her, she only had 366 days left in the system. Her mom would be out then, and things would go back to normal.

Next to her, Celine brushed a piece of hay off her pant leg. "I told her about your mom's letter. The one that was returned," she said. "I found it when I was changing your sheets yesterday." Celine looked at her sadly.

Surprise jolted through Red's body. Hadn't she torn them all up?

"Was there more than one?" Celine asked, watching Red's expression.

Red bit her lip, tears stinging her eyes.

"Oh, Red. Why didn't you tell me? We could have faced it together."

Red blinked. Shrugged. She'd wanted to tell Celine, but was afraid that would be betraying her mom. The letters were private. They were *their* thing. She shifted on the hay, adding to the space between them.

Celine ran a hand over her face. "Ms. Anders talked to your mom's lawyer. I guess he was able to petition for early release. She completed her rehab, and the judge decided to grant the petition." Celine stopped and shook her head in a small, tight movement.

The tingles in Red's arms became bolts of lightning, white-hot. Red looked at Celine, at the way her lips pulled into a frown. Celine's fingers were balled into fists in her lap. She looked . . . *angry*.

"So . . ." Red tried to make the words fit together. "Does that mean my mom is getting out of jail early?" Her skin suddenly felt too tight, like it was holding her down when everything in her wanted to fly.

Celine's green eyes glistened with tears that Red didn't understand.

"Red." Celine paused, barely shook her head again. "Your mom is already out. She was released three months ago."

Chapter
24

After Gamma died, Red and her mother started over.

"No more pills," her mother promised. Red watched her mother pour two bottles of little white pills into the toilet. *Splook splook splook.*

"I don't need them anymore," she said, and squeezed Red against her. "I've got what I need."

They spent the day at the Denver Zoo, holding their noses in the monkey house and hanging out at the polar bear exhibit, hoping the sleepy bear would wake up and do something exciting.

The sun illuminated the copper and blond highlights in her mother's dark hair as she said, "What would Gamma do?"

Red scrunched up her nose in thought. Her mother started shaking her hips slowly, her arms crooked at the elbows.

Red laughed. "Dance him into life!"

"Right!"

So they did. They twirled and jumped, spun and clapped, bobbed and twisted. When they leaped like gazelles, the wind lifted them higher. When they fluttered together in their own fairy circle, the breeze brushed through their matching dark hair, swirled it around their faces, and tangled it up with their laughter. People stopped to watch them, even filmed them on their phones.

"It's working!" cried Red.

The crowd gasped and cheered. The polar bear was on his feet, bobbing his big head to their rhythm. He chuffed and turned his whole body around as Red and her mother did the same.

"We did it!" Red laughed. "We danced him into life!"

They grasped hands and spun so fast that all Red could see was her mother's laughing face, her flowing hair and bright brown eyes, clear and sharp against the blur of the world.

36 MONTHS AGO

Red heated a frozen dinner of macaroni and cheese in the microwave. It was the last meal in the freezer.

It was the last meal in the whole house.

As she pulled the plastic wrapper off the top, carefully avoiding the steam, she thought of a story Gamma used to tell her about Jesus. How one time he only had a little bit of food, but he did an impossible thing, and the food became enough to feed five thousand people.

Red wished for her own miracle. She didn't need enough for five thousand people. But she did need her mother to remember to get groceries. Soon.

When someone pounded on the door around midnight, Red hoped it was her mother coming home at last. Her stomach was rumbling again.

But it wasn't her mother.

Red screamed when the door burst open. She ran to the bedroom and scrambled under the bed she and her mom shared. From the front room, several loud male voices boomed, and then the husky voice of a woman quieted them. A few minutes later, Red saw a pair of scuffed black shoes in the doorway.

"Ruby?"

It was the husky female voice she'd just heard. Red curled tighter, tried to hold all of herself in.

But the wind gave her away.

A terrified current rippled from her skin, sent dust bunnies and balled-up receipts and cigarette butts fluttering out from under the bed. Red flattened her hand against papers by her head to keep them from rustling.

Too late.

The shoes stepped closer. Ankles bent. Knees appeared, pressed into the carpet. Hands. Then a face—oval, with brown skin and high cheekbones and full, black-cherry lips. Thick natural hair, cut short.

"There you are," she said. "Ruby, honey. My name is Ms. Anders. I'm afraid I have some bad news about your mom."

11 MONTHS AGO

"What's this?"

Oldest Boy appeared out of nowhere and snatched the letter out of Red's hands. His eyes scanned it, grew wide with glee.

"Did your *mommy* finally write to you?" His sharp, flat laughter drew Middle Boy and Youngest Boy to him like moths to a light. They laughed as Oldest Boy held the paper above his head to keep it away from Red.

"Give it back!" Red jumped, swiped for it, missed.

"What's it say?" Oldest Boy asked. "Did she finally remember who you are?"

Red jumped again, missed. She clenched her fists and glared at him. "Give it *back*."

"I'm surprised your mom even knows *how* to write!"

Dried leaves skipped over the grass and wrapped themselves around the ankles of the three boys. Wind chimes on The Mom's back porch started dinging, then clanging.

"It's not yours," Red said. Her voice shook.

The younger boys didn't notice the shiver in the air, but Oldest Boy did. He sneered, stepped closer. His zip-up hoodie ballooned open.

"I don't think you should read this," he said. "Every time you get one of these, you just cry yourself to sleep for the next week, like a *baby*."

He held the letter out, let the paper crinkle in the wind. Red snatched at it.

"Give it back!"

He dodged her hands and laughed again.

"What's going on out here?" The Mom appeared at the back door. She narrowed her eyes. "Adrian, what is that?"

Oldest Boy dropped his arm and his face transformed into innocence. "I was just helping Red out. Wasn't I, Red?"

She glared at him, but he spoke again before she could.

"She dropped her letter and it almost blew away." He shoved it into her hands. "Here. *You're welcome.*"

The Mom sighed and told them to come inside, wash up for dinner. Red folded her mother's letter carefully and tucked it into her pocket. Oldest Boy was right— she did cry at night. But not because of what the letters said.

She cried because she'd gotten a letter at all.

Mom,

I hope you got my last letter. I miss you a lot.

I miss Gamma a lot, too. I've been thinking about her lately. About when she died. There was a bad storm that night. Do you remember? You never talked about it, and you weren't even there, but I always thought maybe it was your storm.

I remember the nurse in the hospital room with me and Gamma. I liked her. She chewed cinnamon candy and always snuck Spanish words into her sentences.

I held Gamma's hand. It was thin like paper and cold like snow. The nurse said, "You hang on now, Rose. She'll be here any minute." She kept saying it, even though Gamma wasn't awake anymore, and her breathing was wet and thick sounding. Then the machine that beeped with her heart cried one long note, until the nurse turned it off.

When you finally got there, the weather was all rain and bright flashes of lightning, and I remember being so cold in the hospital room. You ran in, and you were soaking wet from the rain. You didn't even look at me at first. You just stared at Gamma lying there, small and still. Then you sat in the chair by the bed and held Gamma's hand and cried. Do you remember?

The wind howled and the lights flickered. You finally called me over, and hugged me so tight I thought my bones might crack. And you said, "I'm sorry. I'm sorry I wasn't here. I'm sorry I'm sorry I'm sorry," just like that, over and over. "I promise I'll do better," you said.

And I hugged you back and told you, "It's okay, Mommy." Because it was. Because even though you hadn't been there for Gamma, I knew you would be there for me.

I can't wait for you to come back, Mom. I miss you.

3 MONTHS AGO

Red's mother walked out of prison, and never even told her.

Chapter
25

"She's already out?"

The whole world was spinning. Red dug her fingers into the hay bale beneath her.

Celine laid her hand over the back of Red's. Red tried to jerk away, but Celine held on. "Red, look at me, please."

Red realized she was gasping. There was not enough air or light or space.

Her mother was already out. But she hadn't come for her. Hadn't even told her. For three months.

"She could have . . . I could have gone with her." She looked up at Celine. "I didn't have to come here! I could have gone home with her instead!" Her voice was getting louder, higher with each word. "Ms. Anders brought me here! Why would she do that?"

Celine's hands moved to Red's shoulders, like she was trying to keep her from flying away. "Ms. Anders didn't know, Red. She thought your mom was still in jail. She's upset, too. There was some error in paperwork—I don't know. It doesn't matter."

Red rocketed to her feet. "You lied to me. You all lied to me!"

"No." Celine's voice was so firm, it stopped Red's accusations. "We did *not* lie to you, Red. Jackson and I do *not* want to keep you from your mom. We care about you." She tilted her head, chasing eye contact when Red looked away. "Do you hear me? We want whatever is best for you. And if—if that's your mom"—her voice hitched a little—"then we'll work toward that. Do you understand me?"

Red crumpled to the floor of Tuck's pen. Celine followed her down, sat next to her with an arm around Red's shoulders. Red didn't try to shrug her off.

"I don't know why your mom didn't tell you she was out," Celine said. "But she wants to see you now. Her lawyer asked Ms. Anders to set up a visit." Her eyes searched Red's face. "Do you want to see her? Or would you like some more time?"

Just like that, Red's anger evaporated and hope took

its place. *Of course* she wanted to see her mom! And of course her mom wanted to see her. Maybe it had all been a mistake. Maybe her mom wanted to take her back right away.

A memory uncoiled in Red's mind like a sleepy snake. She and her mother curled up in bed, their foreheads almost touching. Her mother's breath hot on Red's face when she spoke.

"Do you love me?"

Red spread her hands out wide. "I love you times this much!"

Her mom poked her belly button. "I love you times infinity!"

"Infinity!" Red giggled. She took her mother's cheeks in her palms, squeezed so that her lips pooched out. "I love *you* times infinity, plus *one!*"

Her mom tickled her, and Red squirmed, still shrieking, "*Plus one! Plus one!*"

Another memory-snake uncoiled, hissing at the heels of the first one.

Ms. Anders saying her mother wasn't coming back. That Red had to live with someone else.

"Gamma?" she'd asked, even though she knew Gamma was dead.

"No, baby girl. Somebody else."

Red wanted to say, *But they're strangers*. She wanted

to say, *I can wait. I just need some more freezer dinners, that's all.* She wanted to say, *She'll be back. I know she will.*

Round and round the memories went, each followed by twisting clouds of hope and fear in her heart. Ribbons of cold air rippled from her hands and arms, stirring the straw into a small cyclone. She watched it spin until Celine wrapped her fingers around Red's hands and the wind stilled.

Red leaned in to Celine's side, suddenly tired. Celine smelled like lavender and starlight, and was soft and warm and steady.

"Why didn't she come for me?" Red asked.

"I don't know." Celine's voice was as small as Red's now. She smoothed Red's hair, tucked it behind her ears.

Red laid her head in Celine's lap and let her tears fall. Her foster mother held her tight.

For once, the wind was silent.

Once, a scientist caught a jellyfish and kept it in a jar in his kitchen.

Then he forgot about it.

When he came back later, the jellyfish was gone. Instead, there was a tiny little blob at the bottom of the jar.

But it wasn't just a blob. It was a baby jellyfish.

How did it get there? What happened to the grown-up jellyfish that he had in the jar before?

Turns out, that baby jellyfish WAS the grown-up jellyfish. When the scientist forgot about the grown-up jellyfish, it should have died. But instead, it decided to start over. It transformed back into a baby until it was safe. Then it became a grown-up all over again.

This species is called the immortal jellyfish. Whenever an adult feels scared or gets hurt, it can turn back into a baby until things settle down. Then it grows up and keeps going.

When life gets hard, it starts over and tries again. As many times as it takes.

Chapter
26

Ms. Anders guided Red toward a small room at the back of the agency offices. If it hadn't been for the pressure of her caseworker's hand between her shoulders, Red might have turned around and hightailed it out of the building. Then again, she might have hightailed it straight into her mother's arms. She wasn't sure. She wanted both things at the same time.

For the last five days, confusion had made Red blustery. One minute she was thrilled, almost giddy with excitement to see her mom again. The next, she stormed around the house, as quarrelsome as Lancelot the llama. She would open the front door, ready to run out and keep running. But then, staring at the long slice of dirt road in front of her, her arms would suddenly ache with wanting to hug Celine, and she'd stay put.

But now, as she got closer to the visitation room, anxiety made her fingers and toes tingle. Just twenty more steps until she saw her mother . . . Just ten more steps . . . Five . . .

The room was squat and square. Fluorescent lights flickered above, and daylight poured in through the back windows. The room looked over the parking lot on one side, and was looked over by an office full of shabby cubicles on the other.

A woman sat in one of the fabric-covered chairs by the window. At first, Red didn't recognize her. There was a softness about her that was unfamiliar. She was less bone and angle and sharp corners than the last time they'd been together.

"Hello, Wanda," Ms. Anders said.

"Ruby." The woman slipped off the chair and onto her knees, arms out. Like an angel.

The sound of her voice squeezed every ounce of breath from Red's lungs. Her vision blurred and she clenched her teeth to keep the tears from escaping. She didn't even feel her feet moving as she crossed the room. Arms lifted. And then she was wrapped around her mother, tight and snug.

"Hello, you," her mother whispered into Red's hair.

Red said nothing. She just held on.

Wanda's sable hair was long and thick and wild, like Red's, and always seemed to be moving. It tickled Red's cheeks as they hugged and hugged. Red breathed her in. She was wearing a cool, fresh perfume, like the lingering scent after rain. Under that was the familiar, cloying fragrance of cigarettes and salt. The perfume was unfamiliar, but the tang of smoke smelled like home.

"Well," Ms. Anders said briskly, her voice sliding between them like a scalpel. A single flash of anger sizzled through Red at the intrusion. "This is a supervised visit, so I'll be just over here." She motioned to a chair in the far corner.

Wanda pulled back from Red's embrace. Her brown eyes skimmed over the caseworker. "Thanks so much, Mrs. Anderson. I'm excited to see my little girl again."

Ms. Anders pursed her lips as if physically holding back words.

Wanda put her hands on her hips, examined Red. "I can't believe how grown-up you are!"

Red flushed.

"Go on, spin for me. You're practically a young lady."

Red obeyed, turning in a slow circle. The look of approval on her mother's face was sunlight.

"My, my. You really do look like me," Wanda said.

"You're beautiful." Red felt shy and awkward next to her mother.

"Thank you. I've put on some weight, I'll be honest."
Wanda ran her hands over her hips. "But I'll get things
under control now that I'm home. Come on. Let's sit."

Red admired Wanda's glittery golden high heels.

"So," Wanda said, folding her hands into her lap.

"So," Red repeated. Her heart was pounding so loudly,
she could barely hear her own thoughts.

Wanda lifted a perfectly shaped eyebrow. "Tell me
about yourself, Ruby."

She tucked a strand of hair behind her ear. "Um,
people still call me Red."

Wanda frowned. "Why?"

Why? Red blinked. "Because . . . that's what you
call me."

"Oh, right." Wanda looked Red over, top to bottom, a
smile snaking up her lips. "I remember. Ruby was way
too fancy for a kid like you." She combed her fingers
through the length of her hair, laughing.

Red's mouth felt like sandpaper. She stared at Wanda's shoes, watched her long legs bouncing up and
down.

"So, how's school?"

"Okay."

"Do you have a special boy?"

A *special* boy? "Well, there's Marvin," Red said.

"Ooh!" Wanda pressed her lips together and lifted
her shoulders, gleefully conspiratorial. "Marvin! Is he

eighty? Because that sounds like an eighty-year-old's name."

"No. He's ten."

"I was kidding." After another awkward pause, Wanda said, "I'm getting my degree soon." She leaned back in her chair and crossed her arms. "I started business classes at Community College of Denver. I still have two semesters left, but I'll have an associate's degree soon. Doesn't that sound important? Associate's degree. I'm going to frame it, like doctors frame theirs in their offices."

"Will you be a doctor?"

Wanda's smile flipped over on her face. "No, silly. Doctors go to school for, like, twenty years or something."

"Oh."

Her mother dragged air through her nose and smiled tightly. "So, tell me about your fosters. What's their name?"

"Celine and Jackson. Groove."

"Groove?" Wanda giggled. "Are they *groovy*?"

She laughed. Red mimicked her.

"They're pretty nice, I guess."

"They better be." Wanda squeezed Red's knee.

Red's fingers knotted and unknotted around one another in her lap. There were too many questions in her head. They kept knocking into one another, clattering against her ears, piling up on the way to her lips. *Where have you been? Why did you leave? Why didn't you tell me you were back? What happens next? When can I come home?*

But the questions didn't matter. All that mattered was that they were together. That they could *always* be together now. Red sniffed and wiped her nose with her sleeve. "I brought something to show you."

She got up and went to her backpack, which she'd dropped by the door on her way in. Keeping her back to her mother, she pulled out the green notebook, staring at the cover for a moment, a nervous breeze whispering down her spine. The binding had a new layer of tape holding it together since she'd thrown it against the wall. Celine had gotten her sparkly green duct tape. She glanced at Ms. Anders, who was watching her curiously. Her caseworker gave her a little smile.

"Here." Red opened the notebook to one of Gamma's *IMPOSSIBLE* pages and held it out.

Wanda stared at it blankly as she took it. "What's this?"

"It's—just something I've been working on. I thought you'd like it."

Her mom read a few words, then turned to the next page. She looked up, eyebrows raised in question. "So . . . it's for school?"

Red forced her voice to stay cheerful. "No. Gamma gave it to me. See?"

She took the notebook and flipped to the very first page.

It always seems impossible until it's done.
—Nelson Mandela

A little smile appeared on Wanda's face. "She said that all the time," she said, her voice wistful. Then she laughed, but the sound was brittle. "She never stopped believing in the impossible." She sniffed, snapped the notebook shut, and handed it back to Red.

Red hugged it against a pang of disappointment in her chest. She had thought her mom would want to know more about it, that she'd be impressed by everything Red had written. But instead of looking happy, her mom looked upset.

"Are you okay?" she asked.

Surprise flashed across her mother's face. "Yeah, baby. I'm okay. Are you?"

Red nodded and shrugged at the same time. She could feel Ms. Anders's eyes on her.

"Hey." Her mother's voice was softer, more familiar than before. "Look—I'm sorry I didn't get in touch right away. I've had some things I needed to work out."

A chilly breeze stirred against Red's face and hair. She tried to hold it in. Outside, clouds darkened the sky. "You could have told me," she whispered.

Wanda leaned forward in her chair. "I know." Her dark hair brushed against her cheeks and she swept it back. "But I'm here now."

Ms. Anders cleared her throat. "It's three thirty."

Wanda stood and opened her arms again. "Give me a hug."

Red obeyed. The fabric of Wanda's blue shirt was cool and liquid against her face.

"I miss you, Red. I'm so glad we get to see each other again."

"Me too." She meant it.

Wanda stepped back and lifted Red's chin with two fingertips. She smiled her dazzling smile. "Do you still love me?" Her voice was soft, fragile.

The wings of Red's heart opened, stretched wide. "Infinity plus one."

Her mother's smile sweetened. "Plus one." She ran her fingers lightly over Red's jaw, then turned and picked up her purse. "We'll do this again?" she asked Ms. Anders.

The caseworker nodded. "I'll be in touch."

"Great." Wanda blew her daughter a kiss and swished out of the conference room. Red watched her golden shoes glitter until she disappeared around a bend of cubicles.

Chapter
27

There was a tornado building in Red's rib cage. She tried to push it down, but emotions whirled and knotted around her heart, and questions whirred and tangled in her mind. Her mother was back! *Why hadn't she told her sooner?* She was getting better; she was going to school. *Did she want her back?* She loved her, infinity plus one. *Didn't she? Didn't she? Didn't she?*

Celine and Jackson made careful conversation from the front seat of the car, but Red didn't hear them. The noise in her head was too loud. She sat with her feet tucked up under her and stared out the window, but her eyes didn't see the thrashing trees or swinging power lines or whipping flags. She didn't notice the way Jackson's hands gripped the steering wheel, or the sudden lurch of the car as it was buffeted by wind on the highway. And it wasn't until Celine breathed, "Look at those clouds," that Red even noticed there *were* clouds.

A solid blanket of steel gray covered the sky, bulging like hundreds of enormous pieces of popcorn. The setting sun illuminated the crests silver against the darker pockets, making the whole world eerie and cold.

Another gust of wind shook the car. Jackson clicked off the radio, as he always did when he needed to concentrate on the road.

"It's supposed to snow," he said.

The vortex in Red sizzled and slithered between her ribs. She squeezed her arms around her middle. *Did her mother want her back? How could her mom forget her name? What would happen now?*

Celine gave Jackson a worried look. "Has there been any news about Tuck?"

The words lassoed Red, yanking her back into the car, into the small, warm space they all shared.

Tuck. Her whole body tensed in an effort to rein in the brewing storm. She couldn't do that to Tuck. Not again.

Since the news that her mom was out of prison, Red had been distracted. She hadn't even looked for him. She'd broken her promise to him.

"We have to keep looking," Red said.

Jackson seemed surprised that she'd spoken. "We've searched everywhere. There's no sign of him," he said.

"We have to look again! Maybe he's trying to find his way back," Red argued.

Jackson sighed, but Celine turned to look at her. After a moment, she nodded.

"Maybe he is," Celine said. "Tuck knows we love him. And love can do impossible things."

Red hoped that was true. She took long, slow breaths and focused her thoughts on Tuck. Gradually her tornado began to unspool. Finding Tuck before the snowstorm rolled in became all that mattered. It pushed out the roiling hurt and disappointment and confusion, and filled her with determination.

When they got home, the three of them searched until it was too cold and dark and snowy to see. A bitter wind was blowing—a wind that wasn't coming from Red. Still, Red tried to make it stop. She did her breathing exercises, and clenched her fists and even tried holding her breath. But she couldn't blow the storm away.

Long after they'd all gone to bed, Red stared out her bedroom window, her face a pale reflection against the darkness. Where had Tuck gone? *When could she live with her mom again?* How far could a storm carry a giant tortoise? *Didn't her mom want her back?*

The questions twisted and knotted within her as she watched the snow pile up in the yard.

It wasn't fair. Tuck was out there somewhere, lost. He was alone—just like Red had been. After Gamma died. In foster care. It wasn't his fault he was lost, just like it wasn't Red's fault her mom got arrested and left her behind. Her mom was supposed to come back for her. She was supposed to get out of prison and fly straight to Red and take her home. She was supposed to *be there*.

But she hadn't been. She'd left Red alone in foster care.

"I won't leave him," Red whispered to her reflection.

She got out of bed and started pulling on layers of clothing, as many as she could fit. Three pairs of socks. Fleece-lined tights, flannel pajama pants, and a pair of jeans. Two T-shirts, a sweater, a hoodie, and her coat. Carrying her snow boots, she tiptoed downstairs, avoiding the squeaky step at the bottom. Gandalf followed her, whining softly when she ordered her to stay in the dog beds with Frodo, Brontë, and Limerick.

Red pushed her feet, fat with wool socks, into her boots, and pulled a pair of Celine's mittens over her own. Then she wrapped two scarves around her neck and reached for the big flashlight Jackson kept by the back door. Celine's too-big mittens brushed against it and it clattered to the floor.

She froze, listening. All four dogs were looking at her,

ears perked. When the ceiling above her didn't creak with the sound of Jackson or Celine getting out of bed, Red let out a little breath.

Steeling herself, she opened the door and stepped into the storm.

Chapter
28

The cold stole her breath. She hunched forward, clicking on the flashlight, and tucked her nose deeper into the scarves around her neck. Snowflakes prickled against her forehead, and she pulled her hood up.

The snow was as deep as her ankles in some places as she trudged across the dark yard. Instinctively, she headed toward Celine's stargazing rock. Her legs began to burn with exhaustion. All she could see in every direction was whirling gray snow against the black. The wind shrieked and drove the flakes straight into Red's eyes. She swept the flashlight beam back and forth, but all she could see was the writhing white.

"Tuck!" she called. "TUCK!"

Snow crunched under her boots. Her foot hit a rock

buried in the snow, and she stumbled. She dragged herself upright again.

"Tuck! I'm here, Tuck!"

Her nose was running and her breath made the scarf wet against her lips and chin. She kept walking, unable to even look up at times.

"I won't leave you alone!" Her voice cracked. "Come home, Tuck! Come back!"

The only answer was the howling wind.

She stumbled again, and her knee cracked against another rock. The flashlight flipped out of her hand and disappeared into a snowdrift. Pain and despair made her want to curl up and cry. But she couldn't. Tuck needed her. She was his family, and family didn't give up. Eyes stinging, she crawled forward and dug out the flashlight, then sat back on her heels and looked around.

Nothing looked familiar. She thought she had been going toward the stargazing rock, but she should have reached it by now. There was no sign of it, though. She twisted around, squinting into the darkness. The flashlight wasn't much help.

"TUCK!"

Climbing to her feet, she managed to walk a little farther. Something emerged from the darkness. A gnarled shape she didn't recognize. Coming closer, she realized it was a clump of scrub oak, twisting branches sticking out of the snow like broken bones.

Fear clawed at her. She tried to shake it off. Where was she? How far had she walked? Her body shivered and her lungs burned.

Her next footstep sank more deeply than she expected and she fell, her leg twisting painfully behind her as she slid down some kind of embankment. Branches grabbed at her clothes and gouged her face. She lay in the snow for a moment, heart hammering in her ears. Wind—her wind—blustered from her skin, shaking snow from the bushes onto her face.

She groaned and sat up, cradling her leg. Snow and sorrow swirled around her and through her, hollowing her out, crystallizing under her skin. She was too tired, too cold, too empty to move.

Maybe it was stupid to believe it was possible for her to find him by herself. Celine had said love could do impossible things, and Red loved Tuck. She loved him so much it made her heart hurt just thinking about him being lost. But what if her love wasn't enough to bring him back?

Something knocked into her from behind, and she fell forward into the snow again. She scrambled away, twisting to see what had bumped her. A shadow emerged from the gnarled arms of the scrub oak. She almost screamed, but the sound caught in her throat.

Clack.

She gasped, squinting.

Clack.

"Tuck?"

Clack.

"TUCK!"

The enormous tortoise clacked his jaw again and took a step back into the tangled scrub oak. His black eyes glinted in the beam of her flashlight.

"Tuck!" She crawled toward him in disbelief and pressed a mitten against his shell. It was firm and solid and *real* beneath her hand. Joy surged through her and she wrapped her arms around him. His head pulled into his shell, then slowly peeked out. Laughing, Red planted a kiss on the top of it before he ducked back in.

"You're alive! I found you!" She hung on to him.

Looking around, she tried to see through the blizzard, unsure of what came next. How could she get him back to the farm? It wasn't like she could carry him.

"I'm sorry. I'm really sorry, Tuck. I'm sorry about the storm. I'm sorry you were lost." The dark and snow crowded in on them, and panic gripped her. "Now we're both lost."

The tortoise blinked, his head still mostly inside his shell. She didn't know how to get Tuck home, but she could try to keep him warm. She tugged off her mittens with her teeth and stuffed them into the space around Tuck's head, then unwound the two scarves and wrapped them around the base of his body, covering his scaly feet.

Turning toward where she hoped the house might be, she screamed as loud as she could. "HELP! I FOUND TUCK!"

She screamed until her voice disappeared and she could taste the tang of iron on her tongue. Then she unzipped her coat and swung one leg over Tuck's shell and sat on his back. Opening her coat, she draped herself over the tortoise, her stomach and chest pressed against his shell, and her arms and coat dangling like a blanket.

"Hold on, Tuck."

She squeezed her eyes shut and tried to push back the storm again, but it wasn't hers to control. The snow was so thick now, it stuck to them in wet sheets. The tortoise was still and cold beneath her.

"Please," Red whispered. "Please hold on, Tuck."

The roar of the blizzard was deafening. Wind shrieked and screamed in Red's ears. A dry sob burned in her throat. She wished Celine was there. Celine would know what to do.

A whistle trilled in the darkness, clear and bright against the wind. Red lifted her head. Her whole body was stiff with cold.

She heard the whistle again. Like the song of a flute.

Hope sparked hot in Red's heart. She twisted around, looking up at the sky.

"There! Look, Tuck! Look!"

Behind them, a small patch of clouds unraveled into a near-perfect circle. Pleiades peeked through, shimmering boldly amidst the storm. Red could hear the song of the Seven Sisters clearly now, warm and beckoning.

"WE'RE OVER HERE!" she shouted, but the storm buried her voice.

Red closed her eyes, listening to the star-music. She pulled in a deep breath and felt a familiar tickle. Warmth spread down her arms and into her hands. Music swirled around her, strengthened her. She concentrated on the joy still buzzing through her. She thought of Tuck, of Celine. And of the music she knew was meant for her.

"We're over here," she whispered. "Please hurry."

And a breath of wind, as warm as a summer breeze, carried her words right where she needed them to go.

back? When something that big
is lost, it's gone forever.

The RMS Titanic was a really big, really nice
boat that could carry more than 3,500 people
on board. For its very first journey, the Titanic
was sailing to New York from Southampton,
England. On April 15, 1912, it hit an iceberg and
sank in the Atlantic ocean. More than 1,500
people died that night.

Everyone thought the boat was lost forever.
Lots of people looked for it. But for a long time,
the Titanic stayed lost.

Then, seventy-three years later, on September
1, 1985, it was found more than thirteen nautical
miles from where everyone thought it would be. It
was 12,000 feet under the water, and had become
a part of the ocean floor.

Thirteen miles away and 12,000 feet deep. Lots
of ocean-floor camouflage. That's why it was
impossible to find for so long.

They were looking in all the wrong places.

Chapter
29

"We're gonna visit my uncle on the Big Island. He used to live close to Kīlauea, before the last really big eruption." Marvin jumped off a hay bale, which startled the goats. "The lava destroyed his house. But he says all that matters is that his family is okay."

They were in the barn, feeding the animals and hanging out with Tuck. Today was the last day of school before winter break, and all Marvin could talk about was his family's upcoming trip to Hawai'i.

"I wish I was going somewhere warm for Christmas," Red said. The weather had been cold since the night she found Tuck, almost three weeks ago. The snow was gone. It was just freezing and dry all the time. Her lips were constantly chapped because of it.

"Yeah, it's nice. But I've never had a white Christmas. Maybe you will."

Red laughed. "I've lived in Colorado my whole life, and never had a white Christmas. It's always brown!"

Marvin made a face. "Colorado weather is so weird."

"You can say that again." She held another apple slice on her palm for Billie, who was standing on Tuck's back. Every morning since Tuck's return, Red had come into the barn to find Billie in Tuck's pen, snuggled up next to him or standing on his shell.

"I kind of wish we were staying in Colorado, though," Marvin said, tossing his apple slice at Lancelot's feet.

"Why?"

He drop-kicked a carrot and it skittered through the straw into the goats' stall. "Tūtū and Papa are talking about going back to Hawai'i."

"So?"

"I mean, they want to *go back*. For good."

"Oh." Red glanced at him. There were tears in his eyes. "That sucks."

He wiped his nose. "I'm not allowed to say that word. But yeah. It does."

"Why do they want to go back?"

"That huge windstorm really scared Tūtū. She hasn't stopped talking about moving back since. She's afraid of tornadoes."

173

Spikes of guilt jabbed at Red. "Haven't they always lived with you, though?"

Marvin kicked another hay bale. "Yeah. Ever since I was a baby. When Dad got transferred here, Tūtū said she couldn't go a day without seeing her *honu* and so they came, too."

"Honu?"

His cheeks flushed. "That's what they call me. It means turtle."

She bit back a smile. "Oh. Right."

The blush of embarrassment faded from his face. "Dad said they're just homesick. He doesn't think they'll want to move back if we go visit. But I don't know. What if they decide to stay there?"

He looked so dejected that Red reached out and took his fingers in her own.

After a moment, he dropped her hand. "But I have a backup plan."

"You do?"

He nodded. "Yup. I'm making a video. I have to make one for that online film class anyway. So I'm gonna make one that will convince Papa and Tūtū to stay here."

"How?" Red fed Billie another piece of alfalfa.

"I'll just show them everything they love about Colorado. And me. *Lots* of stuff about me. Just to remind them how much they'll miss me if they go." He grinned mischievously.

Billie bleated from Tuck's back, wanting more food.

"Has Tuck been okay?" Marvin asked.

Red nodded. "Yeah. Jackson says it's a miracle." She scratched Billie's soft ear. "Billie won't leave him alone. She missed him. I think she's worried he'll blow away again."

"Blow away?"

Red flinched. "Run away. Whatever."

Marvin wandered over to Fezzik's stall and rubbed the donkey's velvety nose. Fezzik turned so that Marvin would scratch his ears, too.

"Are you seeing your mom for Christmas?" he asked.

It was Red's turn to kick a hay bale. "No. Not on Christmas. She has to work. She got a job at a restaurant."

"That's good, right?"

Red nodded.

Things with her mom were going pretty well. They even got to see each other once a week now. Last week, Ms. Anders had told Red what the judge said Wanda had to do to get custody of Red. Basically, she needed to prove she could take good care of Red. It wasn't complicated. Just keep a job, get an apartment. The most important part—and what made Red the most nervous—was that her mom couldn't start taking pills again. She had to stay sober.

"Not a problem," Wanda said. She'd squeezed Red's

hand, and her face was serious. "I've got what I need right here."

Red squeezed her hand back, hard, like a promise. Like, *I'll be what you need.*

Red offered Fezzik some alfalfa. "Hopefully she likes her job okay. She worked in a restaurant when I was little, but hated it. She used to tell my gamma it was eating her soul."

Fezzik snuffled the alfalfa, then turned away. Marvin took it from her and started twisting it with another piece. "What are you doing for Christmas?"

Red watched as he braided the alfalfa into a skinny crown. "Jackson's daughter and her family are coming."

"Cool!" He sounded genuinely happy at the news. "I met Nicole when they visited last summer. I liked her. She's a really good cook."

Red didn't say anything. Of course Marvin liked Nicole. Marvin liked everybody. And everybody liked Marvin right back. It wasn't so easy for Red, though. Nicole was all Jackson talked about lately, and it made Red whirly with nervousness. And maybe a little jealous, too. Jackson cared for Red, she knew that. But Nicole was his *daughter* daughter. How could Red compete with that?

Red hadn't ever known her dad. Her mom refused to talk about him whenever Red asked, and Gamma had only ever said that Red's dad "wasn't up for a kid." Red didn't even know his name. Once she'd seen her birth certificate in her state file. The box where her father's name was supposed to be was empty.

Gamma used to tell her not to worry about it. "Don't let anybody take up brain and heart space he don't deserve, baby girl," she'd say. So Red hadn't. But lately, listening to Jackson talk about Nicole, seeing the way his eyes softened around the edges when he said her name, made Red wish that she could have a dad who loved her like that, too. Did Nicole know how lucky she was to have Jackson? If she did know, then why had she moved so far away? Red didn't think she'd ever move away from Jackson if he was her dad.

Red and Nicole had talked on video-chat a few times, and she seemed nice. But what if Nicole didn't like her when they met in person? Would Celine and Jackson still want Red around if Nicole didn't like her? She thought of The Mom's three boys, how much they'd hated her. Bio kids had a way of making parents change their minds about being fosters.

"HOLY BANANAS!"

Marvin's voice made her jump. He pointed toward the stack of hay bales in the back of the barn. "I swear I just saw something," he said.

"What?"

He shook his head. "I dunno. I think it was a rat or something. If it was, it was the biggest, hugest, most enormous rat *ever*!"

They went over to investigate, peering behind the stack and even jostling a few hay bales to see if something ran out. But nothing was there.

Marvin held his hands about two feet apart. "I swear I saw it! It was, like, this big!"

There was still no sign of it a few minutes later when Celine called them in for dinner. But as they left the barn, Red thought she heard a quiet rustling from the back corner. She shivered and pulled the door closed behind her.

Chapter
30

"Merry Christmas Eve!" Jackson said. He filled a pot with water and set it on the stove to boil for oatmeal.

Red was still rubbing sleep from her eyes. It was the first day of winter break, but she was up early for barn chores. The animals had to be fed, even on Christmas Eve. "Morning." She yawned.

"Gonna catch flies with that thing," Jackson teased.

She covered her mouth belatedly. The dogs were sniffing for crumbs under the table. Gandalf's huge backside kept bumping into Red's chair.

"Are you excited?" Jackson asked.

He was, obviously. All week long he hadn't been able to get through five minutes without mentioning Nicole. *Nicole's a reader, too, Red, I bet you've read the same books! You should taste Nicole's chili, Red, she makes a mean one. You'll love Nicole's boys, Red, they're torna-does with curls.*

That last one made Red squirm. She didn't want any tornadoes—toddler-size or otherwise.

Red grabbed Gandalf's tail to keep it from whacking her in the arm again. Jackson hummed as he made breakfast, his music rustling up excitement in the dogs, too. Celine came into the kitchen a while later and ruffled Red's hair.

"Happy Christmas, my family!" Celine was pale, but her smile was bright. Her damp hair smelled of lavender and mint.

"I'm making oatmeal," Jackson said, kissing her as she opened a cupboard and fished out a mug.

Celine smiled. "Nothing beats old-lady oatmeal!"

"Old-*fashioned*, not old-lady, thank you." Jackson peered into his pot and sniffed. Celine winked at Red and poured herself a cup of coffee.

"What time does their plane get in?" Celine asked after Jackson set bowls of oatmeal—lumpy, sweet, old-fashioned oatmeal—in front of them.

"Around ten. They should be here by noon, I expect. I told them we'd pick them up, but Nicole said it'd be easier to have a rental car. She also said the twins will need to go down for a nap when they arrive."

Celine laughed. "Good luck with that! Those boys will want to see every animal, and they'll want to play with Red." Celine reached across the table and squeezed her arm.

Red ate a few bites of oatmeal and snuck the dogs several sticky lumps. Celine didn't seem to have much appetite, either. She picked up her mostly full bowl and dusted her hand over Red's hair on her way to the sink.

"If anyone is going to be your favorite in this family, my girl, it'll be Nicole. Just you wait," Jackson said.

Red was sitting on the floor of the living room helping Jackson assemble a set of toy train tracks under the Christmas tree a few hours later. They'd almost laid the last piece in the figure-eight design when they heard the sound of gravel crunching under tires in the drive-way. Brontë and Frodo came barreling through the room, sending tracks and train cars flying in every direction.

Jackson leaped to his feet and clapped his hands, a grin as wide as the sky on his face. "Cee! They're here!"

"I hear that." She came from the kitchen, massaging the curve of her neck and shoulder.

Red lagged behind as Celine and Jackson hurried outside. From the window, she watched the dogs run happy circles around the car, pressing their noses into every new leg they saw.

Nicole was tall and thin with a mass of brown and red and blond ringlets. Her hair was cut so that it was longer on one side of her head than the other. Her husband, Anthony, was a shorter, somewhat pudgy man with a brown, close-cropped beard. Their boys, Noah and Jack, tried to run after the dogs, little arms outstretched and faces split open with joy.

"The airport was a nightmare. It took us an hour to get our bags. And then the rental place only had this thing. We asked for a midsize and the guy kept saying, *I have something just a* little bit *bigger*. Ha!" Nicole laughed. Her laugh was as musical as her father's.

"Let me help, Nic." Jackson hurried toward her and wrapped her in a hug. "Hey, Bear," he said.

She kissed his cheek. "Hi, Daddy."

They rocked back and forth for a moment. Finally, Nicole pulled back and reached for Celine. Red tucked herself back into the curtains when Nicole's eyes searched the porch.

"Isn't Red here?" she asked.

Red's heart fluttered and flapped, and she didn't catch Celine's reply.

The group tromped noisily into the house. Jackson hung up Nicole's coat and bent to lift one of the boys. He tossed him into the air, and the boy laughed and shrieked with glee.

"Hello, there, my little prince!" They rubbed noses.

The boy grabbed Jackson's cheeks with his fingers, pinching them together so that Jackson's lips puckered.

"Pappaw!" He forced Jackson's mouth to move as if he were speaking. "Pappaw!"

The second toddler bumped against Celine's legs, hands outstretched. She unloaded bags from her arms and lifted him. He nestled against her chest, head tucked under her chin, and yawned.

"They're so tired," Nicole said. "They didn't sleep at all last night."

"Too excited about Pappaw and Nooni's house." Anthony grinned and patted the back of the boy in Celine's arms.

"They're so big!" Celine murmured into her toddler's curly head. "Push pause, for heaven's sake."

The six of them were still and quiet and shining for a moment that stretched out like gum wrapped around a fingertip. Red stood back, watching like the outsider she knew she was. She didn't belong, but her heart ached with wanting to.

"Oh my gosh." The moment pulled softly apart as Nicole's eyes landed on Red. "Red? Dad, what are you even doing." She grabbed his arm. "Introduce me to my sister in person!"

Jackson grinned as he looked between the two of them. "Come here, Red," he said, waving her forward. "This is my girl."

He put his hand on Red's shoulder and squeezed lightly, and Red realized he was still talking about her. *This is my girl. Red. Red is my girl.*

"Hi." She waved awkwardly.

"Look at you!" Nicole stepped around the dogs and held out her hand. "It is good to see you in *real* life, instead of on a screen!"

Red shook her hand. She was surprised by the strength in Nicole's fingers. "Hi," she said again, more confidently.

Nicole's smile was magnetic. "Can I hug you? I'm a hugger. And you're my *sister*! I have always wanted a sister!"

She smelled like applesauce and stale airplane air, and her hair tickled Red's cheek and ear. Red wanted to say, *I'm not your sister*. But Nicole's hug made her feel like maybe she could be.

Anthony had a lopsided grin. He took his glasses from his nose and polished them with the hem of his shirt. "Good to see you, Red."

The twins squealed and squirmed, ready to be released to the level of wagging tails and tongues. Bags were shifted and wheels went *pluuuhh* against the hardwood as Jackson dragged suitcases toward the guest room.

The twins were definitely not interested in taking a nap. Everyone gathered in the living room for a while. Nicole and Anthony stationed themselves on the floor, acting as roadblocks between the twins and the pile of Christmas presents. Red rebuilt the train track and switched on the electric train, effectively distracting the boys. Nicole gave her a grateful smile. Red kept her attention on the boys as the adults talked, occasionally sneaking glances at Nicole.

She was nice. Maybe having a foster sibling would be different this time. Maybe Nicole wouldn't turn Jackson and Celine against Red. Maybe she really would treat Red like a sister.

Later, Red and Nicole helped Celine finish up dinner preparations. They were having an early dinner before that night's Christmas Eve church service. Celine and Nicole chatted, moving around each other in a familiar dance. When Nicole was called out of the kitchen for a diaper changing, Red stepped in to take her place. She and Celine worked in comfortable silence, each knowing their part of the kitchen choreography.

"If they don't sleep tonight, I am going to lock myself in the barn and sleep with the horses," Nicole moaned when she came back, dropping onto a stool at the counter.

Celine smiled. "They just need food in their bellies."

Nicole rested her head on her hands. "I hope they'll be okay for the Christmas Eve service tonight."

"They'll be angels. Put this on the table?" Celine lifted a giant bowl of sweet potatoes and Nicole took it and disappeared into the dining room.

"Red, will you take this, please?" Celine asked. She reached across the counter with a basket of rolls. Suddenly, she cried out, dropping the basket, and gripping her side.

Red jumped off the barstool where she'd been sitting to stir sugar into the pitcher of tea, and tried to catch the flying rolls before they flipped off the counter. "Are you okay?"

Celine's face was gray and she sucked a breath in through her teeth. After a moment, she straightened again. "Yeah, yes. Sorry." She closed her eyes a second. "I'm okay. Thanks for catching the rolls."

Nicole came back into the kitchen. "You should see the fort they're building out of Christmas presents! I—" She stopped in her tracks. "Cee? What's wrong?"

"Nothing, I'm fine." Celine waved the question away. Some color was returning to her cheeks.

Nicole and Red exchanged a look and Red shrugged, unsure if she should betray Celine by admitting what had happened. She picked up the basket of rolls and hurried into the dining room. Before long, the two women followed her with the rest of the food, calling the men and boys to the table. Red took her seat next to Celine's.

"I'm okay," Celine whispered, noticing Red's concern.

Red nodded, wanting to believe her. But when she took her hand for the prayer, Celine's fingers were as cold as ice.

Chapter 31

Celine was quiet at dinner and barely ate anything, but otherwise seemed fine. Or at least better than she'd been in the kitchen. When Celine caught Red looking at her nervously for the third time, she leaned toward her.

"I'm okay," she reassured. "Just not very hungry."

Red tried to believe her.

"So, Red, what should I know about you?" Anthony asked during dessert. "Do you like any sports or play an instrument?"

She swallowed her bite of pumpkin pie. "I like the animals."

Jackson laughed. "You should see her with Tuck! That tortoise is nuts about this girl!"

"That's what I hear!" Nicole took a bite off Noah's

plate. "Dad told me he got lost and you found him in the middle of a blizzard." She gave Red an impressed look. "Sounds like an amazing story."

Red blushed. "I found him, but Celine found me."

When Celine had emerged from the snow and darkness that night, Red wept with relief. Celine stared at the two of them—girl and tortoise—for a moment, like she couldn't believe her eyes, then bundled Red into her arms. "I'm here," she'd whispered, over and over in Red's ear. "I'm right here."

Later, when Jackson asked how on earth Celine had run straight to Red through the storm, she'd just given Red a small smile and shrugged.

"I don't know. I heard Red's voice on the wind, I guess," she'd said.

Pushing away his empty dessert plate, Jackson clapped his hands together once, a childlike look of happiness on his face. "Okay! You know what time it is!"

Nicole laughed, wiping smears of pumpkin pie off Noah's cheeks. "We have time before church?"

Jackson stood, lifting Jack out of his booster seat. "There's *always* time for presents!"

"Peh-zents!" chirped Noah, pushing his mother's hand away.

"Okay, little man." Nicole snuck in one last wipe of Noah's face, then lifted him out of his seat. He squirmed from her grip before she could get his rubber bib off and dashed toward the living room. She shook her head. "Prepare yourself for chaos, Red."

They all followed the twins into the living room. It was getting dark outside, even though it was just after four o'clock, and the room glowed with the warm white lights of the Christmas tree. Jackson, still holding Jack, snagged Noah before he could rip into a large present near the edge of the pile.

"Whoa, buddy. That one is for Red. Come here and let me take that bib off you."

Anthony stepped forward and took Jack out of Jackson's arm. "Boys, remember what we talked about. We're only opening *one* present each tonight."

Nicole draped her arm around Red's shoulder affectionately. "Christmas Eve tradition," she said. "Everybody opens one present before church. Just *one*." She lifted her voice at the last part, eyebrows raised toward the twins. Then, shaking her head, she smiled at Red and whispered, "Good luck with that."

Red grinned and glanced at Celine, who was leaning against the doorway. She had one arm wrapped around her stomach and the other massaging her shoulder. Her expression was a little vague and her eyes glassy.

"Come on, Red! Pick out the one you want to open." Jackson finally wrestled the bib off Noah. Nicole took it from him and knelt between her boys in front of the tree.

Celine blinked, then caught Red's eye and smiled encouragingly. "Go on," she said. "Any present you want."

Anthony and Jackson were helping the boys pick out a gift each.

"Small ones, please," Nicole said, shaking her head at a large, oblong package Noah was reaching toward. "And hopefully something quiet they can take to church?"

Red bit her lip, looking over the stack of gifts. There were so many. Anthony and Nicole had added some before dinner, and she had a feeling Jackson must have snuck a few more in, as well. She'd never seen so many gifts under a Christmas tree before, especially so many that had her name on them. She felt like crying and laughing at the same time.

"Cee, I don't have my phone," Jackson said. "Are you filming this?"

He looked over his shoulder as Red reached around him, bypassing the biggest box with her name on it and going for a smaller, book-shaped gift. Jackson wrenched around suddenly, nearly knocking Red over as he thrust Noah into her arms.

"Celine!"

Red stumbled, and the startled Noah—angry at having been ripped away so unexpectedly from his gift—began instantly to cry. His shriek was hot in Red's ears. She twisted to see Jackson grabbing for Celine, who had crumpled forward. He caught her, and her head lolled against his chest.

"I'm gonna be sick." Her voice was thin and hoarse.

Nicole was standing now, too. She followed as Jackson rushed Celine out of the room toward the bathroom down the hall. Red was a bag of sand, heavy and useless. A moment later, the sound of retching bounced off the wooden floors and plaster walls. It was a violent, tearing sound that turned Red's insides to ice.

Anthony took the shrieking Noah from Red's arms. He thrashed until his father put him on the floor near the gifts again.

Down the hall, the noises continued. Horrible, wrenching sounds that made Red's whole body shake.

Nicole was back in the doorway a few minutes later, her eyes wild and her voice tight. "Anthony, call 911."

She was gone again.

Anthony pulled his phone out of his pocket and dialed. There was a clatter of Christmas ornaments knocking together, and Anthony reached for Jack, who'd just tumbled over boxes and fallen face-first into the tree. He lifted the now-crying Jack by one arm.

"Yes, I need an ambulance . . . My mother-in-law is sick. I'm not sure, actually. They just—" He patted Jack's back, trying to quiet him. Noah, meanwhile, had started tearing into several packages at once. "Red? Can you help?" Anthony pleaded.

Red sucked in a breath, focusing on the twins. "Here," she said, reaching for Jack.

Anthony gave her a grateful look and hurried from the room, speaking urgently into the phone.

Jack wasn't happy in Red's arms and cried for his father. When Red held him tighter, he began to scream. She pulled her head back, trying to get him to look at her. His little face was contorted and shone with fury, and he pushed his fists against her shoulders, trying to get away.

"Let's go outside!" Her voice sounded cartoonish. With her free hand, she pulled on Noah's sleeve. He lifted a small truck he'd managed to unwrap, his face bright with glee.

"Twuck!"

Down the hall, the sound of retching was now punctuated with sobs. Red blinked back her own tears.

"Yes, a truck. Come on! Let's show it to the chickens!"

Noah was thrilled. He bolted toward the back door, and Red ran after him, Jack still struggling in her arms. She had to get away from the sounds coming from the bathroom. She had to get out. *Now.*

Red balanced on one foot to keep the dogs from getting inside and held the door open for Noah. He slipped under her raised knee and took off toward the barn. His quicksilver body drew the dogs' attention away from the door long enough for Red and Jack to get outside.

She pulled the door closed, and immediately the world stilled. Jack's screams silenced as abruptly as they'd started, and he laid his head on her shoulder. His breath came in hot little waves against her neck. The air smelled like snow. Out here, she could no longer hear the agonized sounds coming from down the hall. Out here, she could close her eyes and pretend everything was okay.

Chapter
32

Noah banged his truck against the new barn door. The dogs yapped and bounced around him. Both boys were shivering already, and Red knew she should have grabbed their coats, but there hadn't been time. At least the barn would be warm.

The air inside smelled like sweet hay. Noah beelined for the chicken coop. His curls flopped around his ears, and, smiling, he pointed a fat, dimpled finger. Jack was still nestled against Red. He curled into her, tucking his hands between his chest and hers when she tried to show him the chickens. His breathing was ragged and wet sounding.

"Come on," she said, hiking him up. Gandalf was at her side, peering at her with worried brown eyes.

Noah pressed his face against the rings of chicken wire, sticking his nose and lips through one of the holes. When he lost interest in the birds, he turned to the goats, who were inside because of the cold. He drove his truck over hay bales and along the rough floorboards. Red showed Jack how to hold long strands of hay out for Billie and Goat to nibble. Gruff was uninterested and stayed in the back corner with Lancelot and Merlin, watching them with a grumpy expression. Jack stayed cuddled against Red as she fed the goats. His skin was tacky with the sweat of crying and his ringlets stuck to her neck.

What was happening in the house? How long would it take an ambulance to arrive?

She pushed the questions from her mind. Tried to focus on keeping a two-year-old boy's fingers far away from sharp goat teeth. Tried to keep the anxious spinning in her chest from leaking out into the air.

Noah grew bored with the truck after a while, abandoning it to Billie, who nibbled at it curiously. His feet thumped over the wooden planks of the barn floor toward the mountain of hay bales stacked against the back wall. Jack finally squirmed down and followed his brother.

Red trailed them, only half watching as they started to scramble onto the bales. The sound of Celine sick and in pain echoed in Red's mind.

I should have told Jackson. She sat on one of the bales, offering Jack a finger to steady himself with as he climbed. Guilt and fear roiled in her. She should have told Jackson that Celine had dropped the rolls, that something was wrong. But maybe it wouldn't have made a difference.

The barn creaked softly in the gathering wind. Red focused on her breathing. *She'll be okay. She'll be okay.*

"Mousy!" Noah squealed.

A new panic cut through Red. She looked up to where Noah was pointing. There, atop the stack of hay, stood the most enormous rat Red had ever seen.

She leaped to her feet, stumbled back. The twins started climbing with renewed excitement, heading straight for the silvery rodent. If this was the thing Marvin had seen, then he was right—it was huge. It eyed the boys warily, its whiskers twitching. When she tried to shoo it, it hissed at her. What kind of a rat *hissed*? Fear twisted in her like a screw.

"Don't touch it!" she barked.

But they were climbing straight for it. She grabbed the first tool her hands found—a heavy metal rake. Lifting it above her head, she whirled around, aiming for the rat and his glinting black eyes.

"GO AWAY!"

Her scream let loose a whoosh of air, and the entire mountain of hay trembled. The curls on the twins' heads flattened under the force of the gust, and Noah's fingers lost their grip. Red watched in horror as he fell. She couldn't move, couldn't react. Noah slammed into Jack, who was below him. There was a sickening crack of bone against wood when the boys hit the floor. The rat gave a single trilling squeak and disappeared into the shadows as the rake fell from Red's hands.

Nicole was suddenly there. Red hadn't heard her come in, but the barn door was open, and Nicole was running toward her children, her feet *thunk thunking* across the floorboards. The boys, both of them this time, fractured the air with their screams.

"No! No no no," Nicole breathed, trying to scoop them up. Jack fought her, more scared than hurt, but Noah was screaming in his mom's arms. "What were you doing?" Nicole snapped, looking up at Red.

Red stood, helpless, numb with horror.

"Noah? Sweetie, shh, let me see your head." Nicole brushed back his curls, looking for signs of damage.

"Shh, buddy, you're okay. Jack, did you get a bonk, too?" Nicole pulled Jack closer. Amazingly, he was calming down. His eyes were glued to his brother, who was still screaming.

Anthony appeared. "What happened?"

Nicole stood, Noah in one arm, and Jack's hand grasped tightly in her free hand. Her eyes were rimmed with red. "The boys fell. Noah hit his head. Hard." She looked toward Red but not exactly at her.

Anthony hurried over and lifted Jack, and they

started toward the house. Anthony said over his shoulder to Red, "The ambulance is here."

She watched them go, her hands and feet still tingling with shame. Was she supposed to follow them? Would Nicole want her anywhere near her family now? Even if she didn't, Red wanted to see Celine, to make sure she was okay.

Running from the barn, she circled around the house, following the sound of barking dogs. An ambulance was parked in the driveway, its lights flashing painfully bright in the dim light. Three paramedics lifted a gurney with Celine on it down the porch steps. Red slid to a halt in the gravel. Celine was alarmingly white and the sunrise was gone from her hair. Her head lolled from side to side, eyes half-closed.

Memories crowded against Red's skull. *Her mother, the day Red and Gamma found her slumped over the side of the bathtub, pills scattered like seeds around her. Gamma, unconscious on the floor when Red came downstairs for breakfast one morning.*

Red couldn't move, couldn't breathe.

Jackson followed the paramedics as they loaded Celine into the ambulance. He had a coat halfway up one arm. As they got her settled, he spun, his eyes searching the front of the house. Nicole stepped out onto the porch, followed by a fourth paramedic. Neither of them saw

Red standing near the garden gate. Nicole looked like a robot. Her movements were jerky.

"Nic, I'm going with them," Jackson called across the driveway.

Her eyes jumped to him. "Of course. We'll meet you there."

"Stay here," he said, then saw Red. His expression twisted, like it hurt him to look at her. "I'll call when I know something," he said to Nicole. Then he climbed into the ambulance with his wife.

Red wanted to run after them, but she couldn't make her feet move. Her hair whipped around her face in a frenzy. She clenched her fists, held her breath.

The fourth paramedic shut the back doors with a sharp *clatch*, then got into the front seat. A siren *bwoop bwooped* as the vehicle turned down the driveway and picked up speed toward the dirt road.

Red watched it until the twinkling lights were snuffed out by the gathering night. When she looked back at the house, the porch was empty and the front door closed.

She was alone.

Chapter
33

An hour later, the phone rang. Red crept into the kitchen and found Nicole leaning against the counter, listening intently.

"Okay. How long?"

Silence.

"What do you need?"

A longer silence. She lifted her head, saw Red.

"I see. No, that's fine. Uh-huh. Okay. Where—?"

Red watched her riffle through a stack of papers on the desk at the end of the counter. She pulled out a business card.

"Yup, I got it. That's fine, Dad, really. No, don't worry. It's okay." She pressed her palm into her eye, listening. "Just try not to worry. Keep us posted? Yeah. Okay. I love you."

The phone beeped when she hung up. Silence crowded into the space left behind. Nicole let out a long breath and rolled her neck.

"Celine's in surgery," she said to the floor. "They're removing her gallbladder and appendix."

Red shifted her weight between her feet.

Nicole pressed her fingers into her eyes again, then turned and finally looked at Red. "She'll be okay, Red. I'm sure she'll be fine." Her expression was stony, unreadable.

Noah had stopped crying a while ago. The house was silent now, except for periodic gusts of wind against the windows. Red's head ached from the effort of keeping the storm inside her skin.

"The boys are in bed," Nicole said. She was leaning on the counter, her fingers gripping the edge of it. "Red—" Her voice broke. She cleared her throat. "I need to know what happened. In the barn."

Red tried to swallow, but her mouth felt like sand.

When she didn't answer, Nicole said, "I don't . . . I can't quite wrap my head around what I saw when I came in."

Red frowned. She couldn't explain it. Even if she wanted to, it wouldn't make sense to Nicole. *It was the wind. I lost control of it. I didn't mean to. I didn't know you were there.*

Of all the words tumbling through Red's mind, only the last set came out. The wrong set. "I didn't know you were there."

Nicole's eyes were the sun. Enormous, scorching, furious. "You didn't know I was there?" Her voice got louder, higher with each word. "You're telling me, what, exactly? If I hadn't been there, you'd have hit my children with that rake?"

The earth seemed to shift under Red's feet. *The rake?* Nicole was upset about the rake? She tried to make sense of it, tried to imagine what Nicole had seen when she'd stepped into the barn. "I—no!" But the words were too small, too quiet in the face of Nicole's fury.

"Were you going to hurt my children?" Nicole came closer.

Red stepped back, stumbled. *No no no!*

Something heavy and black brushed past Red's legs. Gandalf. The dog stood between the girl and the woman, her head high and her tail up. Standing like this, her usual bigness became downright huge. She faced Nicole, angling so that Red was behind the wall of her body.

Anthony was there a second later. "What's going on?" His voice seemed to jolt Nicole out of her rage.

She wilted and covered her face with her hands. When she dropped them, the fire had vanished. "Red has to leave. We need to call her social worker to come pick her up. The number is on the counter."

Chapter
34

Red shut the door to her room, locking even Gandalf out, and sat on her bed. Anger and shame and confusion coiled around her heart. How could Nicole think she'd hurt the boys? She was just trying to get rid of the rat. Hadn't Nicole seen it? That giant, *hissing* rat that probably would have bitten off Noah's fingers the second he got close?

A cold whisper shivered through her. But she *had* hurt them. *Her* wind had knocked them down. She hadn't meant to do it, but it was still her fault.

No matter how hard she tried, she kept losing control. She didn't want to be scary or dangerous. She didn't want to hurt anyone.

She wanted her wind to protect, not hurt. Like her

mother's had once done for Red. *Before*. Before the pills turned her into something Red didn't recognize.

But Red's wind wasn't like that. It had always been like her mother's wind *after*. Chaotic. Out of control. Destructive.

If it wasn't for her wind, the boys wouldn't have fallen. Noah wouldn't have gotten hurt; Nicole wouldn't be so angry. And Red wouldn't be waiting for Ms. Anders to come and take her away. Again.

Gandalf whined in the hallway, but Red ignored her and curled up on the bed. Why did her wind have to be bad? Why couldn't she control it?

She thought of the leaves she'd sent flying for the dogs. She thought of Celine hearing her voice in the blizzard. Since coming to the Grooves', she'd been able to control her wind a little. But definitely not enough.

Maybe that can change.

The thought held a shiver of possibility. *Maybe that can change.*

So much had changed since she'd come to the Grooves'. She'd started believing in impossible things again. Her mom had come back. She'd found Tuck. Maybe her wind could change, too. Maybe she could make it good.

Maybe Celine and Jackson wouldn't kick her out if she had better control of it.

But how?

The remaining half of the oak tree outside the bedroom window creaked like an old hinge. Snow was falling now, a million dandelion-seed wishes, glinting and vanishing before they hit the ground. Vaguely, she thought that it was going to be a white Christmas after all.

A social worker arrived two hours later. It wasn't Ms. Anders. A fresh wave of fear crashed over her.

The social worker—Peter Something—said, "Ready to go?"

Red nodded. Anthony was there, but not Nicole. She probably wanted nothing to do with Red now. Gandalf and the other dogs pressed their noses against her legs, and for once didn't yap or jump.

"You're staying with the Klines tonight," Peter said.

She tightened her grip on the strap of her backpack. *Not the Kapules?* The Kapules were the respite family for the Grooves, their Support Friends. If they weren't taking her, that could only mean she wasn't Celine and Jackson's foster kid anymore.

Peter kept talking, but Red didn't hear anything he said. This was it. She was leaving. Nothing else mattered.

The front door blew open, slammed against the wall. Peter and Anthony jumped, and three of the dogs yelped and scurried away. Red closed her eyes as the wind churned through the house. There was no use trying to control it. Her wind would never be good. *She* would never be good.

A cold nose pressed into her palm. She looked down at Gandalf, and the dog licked her fingers. Red's fear deflated a little.

"We better go," Peter said. He approached the door cautiously, like he was afraid it would slam in his face.

Gandalf stayed on the porch, staring after them. The trees lining the driveway bowed as the car passed, and clouds curtained the stars. Peter tuned the radio to Christmas carols, but Red barely heard the music. All she could hear was the angry howl of wind inside her skin.

Chapter
35

BEFORE

She could hear laughter coming from down the hall.
Music, too. It sounded like a party.

Three-year-old Red climbed off the toddler mattress
on the floor of her bedroom and tried to open the door,
but it was locked from the outside. She pulled on the
doorknob and called for her mother.

Her mother didn't come.

She banged her hands against the door. She wanted
to play, too!

Footsteps. The lock jiggled. Red stepped back, excited. Her mother had come. She would take her to the
party!

A man opened the door. Red was so surprised, she

didn't flinch when he picked her up. He smelled sharp and earthy, like dirt and sweat and something sweet.

"What's wrong, girlie?" he said, his face too close to hers.

Red called for her mom, even louder this time.

"You wanna party, too, princess?" He tickled her legs and belly, his fingers so rough they scratched her skin. Red shrieked and pushed against his shoulders. He laughed.

Suddenly, the door blew open, and there was her mother.

"What are you doing to my kid?" she demanded, reaching for Red. Red's cries had turned into choking sobs.

The man dodged Wanda's hands, like Red was a football and this was a game. "We're just getting to know each other!"

"Give her to me, Taps. She's scared!"

He laughed. "Naw! She loves her uncle Taps!"

He sidestepped Wanda and pressed his lips to Red's neck and raspberried her. She screamed, terrified of the loudness and wetness of his lips on her skin.

Out of nowhere, a gale-force wind slammed into Taps, pinning him against the wall. His stringy hair blew back from his face and his eyes watered. He let go of Red, and her mother snatched her from the air before she could fall. Wanda's hair was a wild, writhing creature in the tempest. She held Red close to her body as she leaned in to Taps's face.

"You don't *ever* touch my child! You hear me? Not ever!"

Red dug her fingers into her mother's shirt, tucked her head under her mother's chin.

A second man appeared in the doorway, eyes huge. Wanda stepped back from Taps and the wind died instantly.

"Ricky, you and Taps should go."

Taps slipped down the wall like a stain, and Ricky grabbed him and hauled him to his feet. They hurried from the apartment.

A gentle breeze wound around Red's arms and legs and face, cooling the raw places.

"You're safe now," her mother whispered.

And Red believed it was true.

AFTER

"You can't keep doing this!" Gamma slammed a laundry basket onto the bed. It bounced, clothes erupting from it and scattering onto the floor.

Wanda grabbed Red's arm and lifted her from the bed. "She's *my* kid."

"Yes, she is. But you seem to forget that. You spend every night out. You can't hold a job. Red needs you to *be here*, Wanda! She's five years old. She needs her mother."

"I'm here now, aren't I?" Wanda growled. "Come on, Red. We're leaving."

Her fingers were hurting Red's arm, and she tried to pull away, whining. Wanda half dragged her into the hallway.

"Don't do this, Wanda! Don't take her like this!"

"You just said she needs her mother," Wanda said, turning on Gamma. "So I'm being a mother and taking her home!"

Red twisted out of her grip and tried to run back into the bedroom. Wanda moved to follow her and Gamma stepped between them.

"Not like this," she said.

"Get out of my way, *Mother*."

Gamma lifted her chin. "I'm not letting you take her this time, Wanda. She isn't safe with you. Not like this."

"Red, come on," Wanda barked.

Red clutched Gamma's legs from behind. Wanda's eye twitched. Her hair was stringy and her skin grayish and dull. There were scabs on her arms that she kept picking at with ragged nails.

"Come on," she said again, holding out a hand.

Red shook her head. "I don't want to."

For a moment, her mother didn't move. And then, before Red knew what was happening, a wall of air slammed into both her and Gamma, flattening them. Gamma landed on top of Red, and Red felt something snap. Her mother's wind roared through the room.

"Stop this!" Gamma shouted.

Wanda screamed in rage and then turned and disappeared down the hallway, taking her wind with her. Red heard her footsteps thundering down the stairs, followed by the slam of a door.

Gamma sat up and bundled Red into her arms. She was crying.

"Are you okay, baby girl?"

Red's wrist throbbed and her whole body shook, but her eyes were dry. Gamma let out a strangled gasp when she saw Red's wrist, which was already swelling. But Red didn't feel the pain. All she felt was the heavy understanding that her mother was gone again. And that it was her fault.

Chapter 36

When the phone rang late on Christmas morning, Red was still in bed. She'd said her stomach hurt when Mrs. Kline came to get her for breakfast, and turned down opening presents around the tree. She knew she was ruining the Klines' Christmas. It was better if she just stayed out of the way.

"Red, honey. Mr. Groove is on the phone."

"Jackson?" Red sat up. Jackson was calling her? Here?

Mrs. Kline smiled. "Yes, dear." She held out a yellow cordless phone.

Red took it. The plastic was cool against her ear.

"Hey, kiddo." Jackson's voice was gravelly. "How's my girl?"

Red hesitated, glancing back at Mrs. Kline. She'd been so sure she would never see the Grooves again. Never hear their voices. Or if she did, she was sure they'd be furious, like Nicole had been. But aside from sounding tired, Jackson sounded . . . like Jackson.

Red wanted to say, *I'm sorry*. She wanted to say, *I wasn't going to hurt them*. She wanted to say, *I want to come home*. Instead, she said, "How's Celine?"

"Resting. The surgery went okay. They took out her gallbladder and her appendix."

"Is she gonna be okay?"

"Yeah, she is." His voice snagged on some invisible hook. "She is. They just need to keep her a few more days. She needs some tests."

His voice caught again, and Red frowned. Something was wrong. Something Jackson wasn't saying.

"Are *you* okay?" he asked.

"Why can't I go to my mom's?" The words were sour on her tongue. "Why did you have to send me to the Klines'? I can go to my mom's house!"

Jackson cleared his throat. "Red, you know the judge said your mom isn't ready yet. We—"

"She *is*! She is ready! I don't want to go back into the stupid system again. She's ready enough!"

"Back into—? Red, listen to me. Nicole told me something happened yesterday."

There it was. The reason they didn't want her anymore.

Nicole. Nicole, who saw the wrong thing. Nicole, who didn't let her explain. Nicole, who was their *real* daughter. Red lay down on her side and curled into herself, the phone pressed hard between her face and the pillow.

"She said she lost her temper and was unfair to you. And she was afraid maybe you didn't understand why the social worker had to come."

Red whimpered. She couldn't help it.

"We'll talk about it more later, but I want you to know that the *only* reason you're with the Klines is because Nicole and Anthony aren't certified to take care of you without me or Celine there. And the Kapules are out of town for Christmas. It was just an emergency situation. Okay?"

The Kapules were out of town. Relief washed over her so quickly, she sat up again. How had she forgotten the Kapules were in Hawai'i?

Jackson kept going. "Nicole feels terrible about what happened. Nobody wanted to confuse or upset you. I'm sorry I didn't talk to you myself. Can you forgive us?"

Her throat was as dry and scaly as Tuck's feet. "You're not . . . kicking me out?"

There was a rush of breath in the phone. "No! Oh, Red, *no.* No, we are not kicking you out. We will *never* kick you out. No matter what. This situation was a mess, and I'm sorry. But we're still your home, Red."

They weren't kicking her out. She wanted to laugh

and cry at the same time. Yet she wanted to go back to her mom—didn't she? Was it bad that she suddenly wanted to stay with Celine and Jackson? She closed her eyes. "Okay," she whispered.

"Okay." The phone crackled and she heard the trill of a distant ambulance. "I better get back inside. Will you thank the Klines for hosting you for me?"

Red asked, "How long?"

"I'll pick you up tomorrow, unless something changes here. You'll be okay one more night?"

One more night. Just one. Not all the rest of her nights. Just this one. She could do that.

"Yeah."

"Good girl." There was a smile in his voice.

"Tell Celine—" Her voice vanished. She wanted to say, *I love her.* She wanted to say, *I was so scared.* She said, "I'm glad she's okay."

"I will. I'm glad she's okay, too."

"Jackson?"

"What, honey?"

"Merry Christmas."

He grunted, like the words were a jab in his ribs. Like he'd forgotten it was Christmas at all. "Merry Christmas, Red."

When Jackson arrived to pick her up the next evening, the last storm clouds had cleared, and the air was crisp and bitingly cold. He stepped into the Klines' foyer, his hands tucked deep into his coat pockets, and his shoulders hunched up to his ears.

"Hey, kiddo," he said.

Something in his smile seemed off. Looking closer, she thought maybe his eyes were red, like he'd been crying.

"Well, come along, Red," Mrs. Kline said, waving for her to hurry.

Red swallowed the lump in her throat and picked up her backpack. Jackson's gaze flitted away from hers too quickly.

He offered his hand to Mrs. Kline. "Thank you so much. I hope we didn't disrupt any holiday plans for you."

She waved him away. "Not at all. That's why we're here. You have my number now?"

Jackson nodded. "We do. Thanks."

"You call us anytime. If we can, we will! That's our motto." She smiled at Red. "And you, young lady. Thank you for spending Christmas with us." She pulled Red into a stiff hug.

"Let's get home," Jackson said, holding the door for her.

On the drive back to the farm, Red told him about the Christmas movies they'd watched, and showed him the book Mrs. Kline had given her. He didn't say more about Celine, other than that Nicole and Anthony had helped her to get settled at home. The conversation between them wasn't easy or smooth like it usually was. The warning bells in Red's head clanged. *Something is wrong. Something is wrong.*

When they pulled into the driveway, gravel crunching, Jackson turned off the engine and sat still. The truck *click pop tinked* into silence. Red waited. Finally, he shook himself, chasing the haunted look out of his eyes with a small smile.

"We better get inside."

She wanted to scream at the mystery of it all. She wanted answers and words and understanding. But she also didn't. She also loved the quiet safety of the truck and of not knowing.

Celine was wrapped in a blanket in her rocking chair in the living room. The sight of her sent relief rushing through Red. She'd been half afraid Celine wasn't coming home at all. But the initial relief faded as she looked more closely at her foster mother. Celine's hair was limp and lifeless. Her cheeks were as pale as paper, and she looked thinner, even though it had only been a few days.

But the worst part was her eyes. The green of them was faded and glassy, and her eyelids were swollen.

She'd been crying, too.

Chapter
37

Celine's smile was tired but warm. She squeezed Red's hand and brought it to her face.

"I'd hug you, but moving isn't much fun," she said. "Are you okay?"

Red nodded and shrugged at the same time. "Are you?"

Gandalf came plodding up to Red, pushing her wet nose into her palm. Red scratched Gandalf's ears, but kept her eyes on Celine.

"Sit down, sweetie," Celine said.

She waited until Red was sitting on the couch, shoes off, feet tucked up under her. Gandalf didn't join Red, instead sitting next to Celine and leaning her head against her legs. Celine ran the dog's silky ear through her fingers over and over again.

She took a breath. "There was something strange about my gallbladder and appendix. The doctors were concerned and wanted to do tests. We didn't want to worry you, so we didn't tell you yesterday." She smiled apologetically. "Honestly, I thought the tests would take longer. But right before they discharged me today, the doctor came in with the results." Her voice was steady and low, but emotion thrummed beneath the surface.

"It wasn't good news." Jackson was pacing the room. He ran a hand over his face, then looked at his palms like he was checking to see if he was still there.

"It's cancer," Celine said.

Fear shimmered in the air above Red's skin. *Cancer*. She'd seen cancer before. She knew what it did.

"It's called—" Celine paused, glancing at Jackson. "Well, it's a big name. But it's called PMP for short."

"Pseudomyxoma peritonei," Jackson said.

Celine reached up and caught his hand as he paced, stopping him. She kissed his palm, then tipped her cheek into it. His hand easily covered her whole face. She looked so small and fragile. He drew a slow breath.

Gamma, getting thinner every day. Gamma fading like breath on a window.

Red pressed her fingers into the seam of the couch cushion. "Is it—bad?"

"It's cancer," Celine said, sounding tired. "Cancer is scary no matter what kind it is. But the good news is they caught this one fairly early. The doctor said treatment can be very effective if it's caught early enough." Celine was still working one of Gandalf's ears between her fingers. "I've spent the last few hours reading about it online. Which is a really, really bad idea, by the way. Who knew the internet is all bad news and cat videos?"

Jackson made a sound somewhere between a cough and a laugh and a sob. Celine squeezed his hand again, then looked at Red in that way she had, the way that made Red feel present and important. "Do you want me to tell you more about it right now?"

Red shook her head. Nodded. Shrugged. Nodded again. An anxious breeze was rippling from her skin, but she barely even noticed.

The bruises spreading like tea stains over Gamma's arms. The cold, dry, papery feel of Gamma's skin.

"How about you ask me questions when you're ready. Ask me what you want to know, and I won't tell you more or less. Not until you want me to. Deal?" Celine said.

Red tried to think of a question that could bottle up some of the explosion that was cancer. The pages of the magazines on the coffee table rustled. Gandalf sniffed the air, eyeing Red.

"Will you need chemo?" Red asked.

She and Gamma playing card games during the first chemo sessions, the ones that made Gamma sick, but didn't yet scrape her out completely.

"I'm not sure," Celine said. "It may depend on the course of treatment we decide on. There are so many questions we need to ask. First, we need to find a doctor who specializes in PMP. I'm meeting with an oncologist this week, so I'll know more then."

Gamma sleeping so deeply she didn't wake up, even when Red was crying on the bed next to her.

"What happens with me?"

The last, long beep of Gamma's heart monitor.

"We'll have to talk to Ms. Anders." Jackson moved to the second chair and slumped into it. "I don't know what the procedure is."

Celine nodded. "I'll call her tomorrow."

Gamma gone. Gamma gone, and no one left for Red when her mother forgot to come home.

Red began to tremble. Fingers curled into fists, nails biting into her palms. "So I'm leaving?" Then, hotly, "Even though you promised I can stay? I have to leave again?"

Celine looked surprised. "Oh, Red, no! No, no. That's not what we're saying. We're saying we don't know what happens next, but you are part of it, whatever it is. You're family. We're all in this together."

But Red wasn't listening. She jumped up, and the magazines on the table scuttled back and flapped onto the floor. Her hair was wild against her cheeks. "I want to live with my mom!"

She wanted to say, *At least I know what to do when*

my mom leaves. She wanted to say, *If you leave me, how will I hear the stars?* She wanted to say, *If you leave me, I'll be even more alone than when Gamma left me.* Tears choked her, cut off the words.

"Red—"

"NO!" Red's voice shattered. Her chest heaved. "I don't want to be here anymore! You already sent me away once! I hate it here! I want my MOM!"

And then Celine was crying. Great heaving sobs that made her body shake. She covered her face, apologizing through her fingers in gasps. She wrapped an arm around her middle and groaned, like each sob was ripping her open. Gandalf whined and pawed at her leg, and Jackson rushed to her, kneeling in front of her. He was crying, too.

Red was embarrassed by the openness of their grief. Embarrassed and angry and afraid. She wanted to go to them, to let them wrap their arms around her and pull her into them. But she also wanted to run away. As far away as she could. Away from tears, from cancer, from every broken, impossible feeling funneling through her.

She backed up, bumping into the couch, then spun on her heel and fled.

Chapter 38

No one followed her, and Red was glad. She paused by the back door only long enough to stuff her feet into her rubber boots and then stomped into the night. The ground was pale with snow and moonglow, and the yellow light on the front of the barn drew her in like a breath. She pushed open the door and slipped into the silky, warm darkness. Hooves shuffled and one of the horses chuffed in greeting. A chorus of sleepy clucking rose from the chickens, then fell silent again.

She stood for a long moment in the darkness. Only Tuck's heat lamp glowed fire orange in his stall near the back. Her fingers fumbled against the wall and clicked on a light switch. Instantly, the barn began to sparkle with silent, twirling stars.

Cancer.

Her feet dragged her heavy body forward, past the chickens and the horse stalls. Past Fezzik, who nodded in his customary greeting, and the goats, who blinked at her while Lancelot glared and Merlin looked indifferent. The latch on Tuck's gate closed with a soft *snick* behind her as she stepped into his stall. His head swayed in her direction and he shifted toward her.

She slumped onto the floor, leaning against the wall. The wood was warm from his heat lamp. She picked up a carrot that had fallen out of his food dish. He came close, black eyes glinting like wet stones. Red ran her hand over the dimpled scar.

"Do you remember it?" she asked Tuck. It was a silly question, though. Of course he remembered. Pain never really went away. It scarred over. It dulled. But its shadow always lingered.

"I hate it," she whispered.

Tuck blinked.

"I hate it, Tuck. I hate that your family left you alone. I hate that the first people who found you hurt you." She pressed her palms into her eyes, hiccuping a sob. "I hate it that you finally came here, and Celine and Jackson love you, and then *I* came along and . . . and the wind—" The words tore through her chest. She groaned, curling into herself. "My—wind—hurt you—too."

The tortoise turned in to her. His bowed, scaly knee

knocked into her shins. She shifted her body so he could come closer, and he swung his face toward hers. She sniffled, her breath coming in broken gasps. He lowered his head and nosed her arm.

"I hate that you were lost," she whispered, rubbing his neck. The tortoise sighed so deeply, his whole body sagged toward the floor.

"And now Celine is sick. Bad things keep happening to you, Tuck. Everywhere you go. It isn't fair."

Tuck bobbed his head slowly. His knees and the sharp front edge of his shell pushed against her. She took a deep, shuddering breath and wiped her nose and eyes. Disco-starlight danced around them, brushing over shell and hair and face and scaly feet.

"It's not fair," she repeated.

Sometimes, Red's whole life felt like a heaping serving of *not fair*. Gamma, her mom, the wind . . . And now Celine was sick.

"I was mean to her," she whispered to Tuck.

He blinked.

"I guess that isn't fair either, is it?" She sighed.

It wasn't like Celine got sick on purpose, just to hurt Red. Gamma certainly hadn't.

"I hate cancer, too, Ruby girl," she used to say. "But there's no sense worrying about fair or not fair. All I can do is try to make this world better while I'm here."

Gamma *had* made things better, no matter how sick

she got. Maybe not for the whole world, but for Red. She'd danced broken things into life. She'd shown Red how to believe in the impossible. She'd made Red laugh.

The ache of missing Gamma that always stayed inside Red's heart swelled and throbbed. She traced the pattern of Tuck's shell with her fingers. There wasn't much in her life she had control over. She couldn't bring Gamma back or make Celine's cancer go away.

But she could apologize.

It wasn't a lot, but sometimes an apology made things more bearable.

"I don't ever want it to hurt you again," she said to the tortoise.

Tuck's toenails scratched against the floor. She bit her lip and gently rubbed the J-shaped scar above his eye. He looked at her like, *It still hurts*. Like, *Everyone else forgets*. Like, *I never do*.

"I know," she said. Leaning forward, she rested her cheek against him. Her tears left polished pathways on his shell. "Me too."

Chapter
39

When Red came back into the house a while later, Celine was in the guest room on the main floor, propped up by what looked like a hundred plump pillows. Her lank hair was matted in the back, and strands of silvery blond stuck out at the top. But her eyes were clear, like crying had scrubbed out the dullness left behind by sickness and surgery.

"Where did they go?" Red asked. It had just occurred to her that Nicole, Anthony, and the twins were gone.

Celine patted the bedspread next to her, inviting Red to sit. "They decided to take the boys to a hotel near the airport since they leave early tomorrow. More space for everyone that way."

"Oh." Red heard the whisper behind Celine's words. *More space from her.*

Celine traced the tortoise-shell creases in Red's cheek. "You okay?"

Red bit her lip, nodded.

A moment later, Jackson came in carrying two steaming mugs. "Hot chocolate and tea," he announced, handing one to Celine and the other to Red. His eyes, too, looked clearer. "I thought you'd like a little warm-up."

She took the mug of cocoa. Jackson fetched his own mug and returned, settling into a chair by the bed. They all blew away the steam from their drinks before saying anything.

Celine started: "It's been a rough few days, and I know we're all tired. But we wanted to talk to you first, Red, before the world takes over tomorrow."

Before the world takes over. The words rolled around in her brain and she realized they described her whole life. The world always took over, and nobody ever bothered to talk about things before it did.

Except for Celine and Jackson.

"Nicole told us what happened in the barn." Jackson gazed at the mug hugged between his palms.

Red set her hot chocolate on the nightstand and slid away from Celine, toward the foot of the bed. She pulled her knees up under her chin. A nervous spinning tickled the insides of her skin, but she kept the wind in, where it couldn't hurt anybody.

"We want to hear your side," Celine said.

Jackson looked up. Red's cheeks burned under their steady, quiet gaze. She couldn't tell them the truth. They'd never believe her. She chewed her lip. Pressed her nails into her wrists.

Maybe they will. Celine had followed Red's voice on the wind to find her in the blizzard. Celine had asked the stars to sing. Celine believed in impossible things.

So maybe she'd believe in Red, too.

"Red." Celine reached for her foot, grimacing a little as she leaned forward. "Honey, look at me, please."

It took a moment, but Red finally did.

There was no anger in Celine's expression. Just the steady gaze of, *It's okay*, of, *I see you there*, of, *I am listening.* "Please, Red. Help us understand."

"It was for the rat."

"Rat?"

Red nodded. "The rake. It was for the rat. Not the boys."

She waited for the deep sigh of, *She's lying.* But it didn't come. Sneaking a glance at the Grooves, she saw they were looking at her, not each other. They weren't having a secret conversation with their eyes, like adults so often did when they thought they already knew the answers to their questions. Instead, they were watching her, waiting, listening for *her* answers. Something invisible and heavy lifted from her shoulders.

"There's—there's a rat. In the barn. It was huge. It hissed at me. Noah was trying to touch it, and I got . . . scared. I wanted to make it go away. It's my fault they fell. I shouldn't have let them climb."

The words tumbled from her like lumps of snow from the branches of a blue spruce, relieving her of their weight. "But I didn't mean for it to happen. I promise. I wasn't trying to . . . hurt them. Nic—Nicole said I was. But I wasn't. I only wanted to help. Anthony was trying to call . . . but Jack . . . crying so loud . . . I took . . . to the barn because it was quieter and . . . warm and . . . the chickens."

She was crying now. Great, heaving sobs that snapped her sentences.

And Celine was there. Somehow, without Red noticing it happen, Celine had crawled down to the foot of the bed and wrapped her arms around Red's shoulders. Her nightgown smelled like lavender and minty tea, and the press of her fingers was cool and firm.

"Okay," she whispered into Red's hair. "It's okay."

Red knew she shouldn't squeeze Celine so tight, but she couldn't stop herself. She *needed* her. Needed the crush of Celine's arms. The heat of Celine's breath against her ear. She needed the weight and strength and song of her.

"I'm sorry," she moaned into the flannel against Celine's chest. "I didn't mean it. I don't hate it here. I don't want to leave. I'm sorry, I'm sorry."

"I know, honey."

"I'm sorry."

"Hush now, my girl. That sorry is big enough, you hear me? It's plenty big enough."

Aloha!

This is a picture of Kīlauea, the volcano in Hawai'i. We're visiting my uncle on the Big Island. We went to see his old neighborhood that got destroyed. I wanted to take a spin-eo to show you the lava flow, but Tūtū said it's disrespectful to film someone's loss for entertainment. I told her it's not entertainment, and besides, I was filming the lava, not the loss. She still said no. Oh well.

Mele Kalikimaka! Aloha nui loa,
Marvin

Chapter
40

A few days later, as soon as Celine felt well enough, the
three of them celebrated Christmas together. Jackson
made chicken noodle soup, which was all Celine could
stomach. After dinner, they turned out the lights, except
for the Christmas tree, and lit some candles. Jackson
and Celine took turns reading the Christmas story in
the Bible. Red had never heard it read like that before,
and it was a lot less boring than she expected. It was a
story full of impossible things—angels filling the night
sky, a star that burned bright to announce the birth of a
baby, kings bringing gifts to a child.

They sang songs, too. Hymns that were familiar, like
"Silent Night," and a few she didn't know but learned
as they sang. Jackson played the guitar. Not very well,

but Red didn't mind the missed chords. Even imperfect music made everything feel cozy and close. Finally, they turned the lights back on to open presents.

"Christmas Eve and Christmas Day, all in one evening!" Jackson said, bringing a tray of cinnamon rolls and hot chocolate into the room.

"I'm going to have to pass on the traditional Christmas-morning cinnamon roll," Celine said, wrinkling her nose at the tray. She took the cocoa though. "Best medicine around," she said, winking at Red.

Once all the presents were opened—and there were a *lot*, especially for Red—they let the dogs back into the house. They ran around like maniacs, tearing up wrapping paper that Jackson crushed into balls and threw for them. Gandalf, who was twice as big as the other dogs, would plow her way into the wrapping-paper pile and emerge with bows stuck to her long fur. They hung from her legs and tail like ornaments. Celine and Red sat side by side on the couch, laughing.

It was the best Christmas Red had had since Gamma died. Even if it was a few days late.

The next morning, Red took *Wishtree,* one of the new books she'd gotten, to the stargazing rock. Gandalf followed her, carrying a plastic ball in her mouth. Though there was still a little snow on the ground, the rock itself was dry and even warm in the sunlight. She stretched out across it, Gandalf at her side, and watched the clouds shape-shift across the bright blue sky for a while.

Gandalf finally grew tired of the stillness. She stood and dropped her ball onto Red's face.

Red laughed. "I can take a hint."

She sat up and threw the ball into the field. Gandalf dashed after it, her huge body crashing through the dry grass. She came back a minute later, tiny snowballs clinging to her fur and the pink ball in her mouth. Red threw it again. When Gandalf brought it back the second time, she dropped it next to Red's feet and barked.

"What?"

Red tossed the ball into the field again, but Gandalf just looked at it, then back at Red. She shook her head and sneezed.

"Go get it!"

The dog lumbered after it, not nearly as excited as before. When she brought it back, she held on to it, staring hard at Red.

"You don't want to play anymore?" Red shrugged. "Fine. I'll read my book."

Gandalf pawed at her leg when she sat down. She dropped the ball and sniffed the air, then looked at Red expectantly, tail wagging.

"What are you doing?"

Gandalf sniffed the air again, her nostrils flaring a

little, then sneezed and crouched before Red's feet, tail high. Red laughed and picked up the ball.

"I don't know if I can do it," she said. She glanced at the sky. It was blue and bright and perfect. "I make things stormy, remember?"

Gandalf wuffed.

Red rolled her eyes. "You don't care at all, do you?"

Gandalf eyed the ball, tail wagging.

Red tossed it between her hands. It was one of those plastic balls with holes in it. Thin and light. Perfect for flying.

Gandalf sneezed.

"Fine." Red closed her eyes and concentrated. She opened one eye to peek at Gandalf. The dog's tail was going crazy. Grinning, she took a breath and focused.

A tickling sensation swept across her skin. Her fingers began to tingle. Opening her eyes, she threw the ball, trying with all her might to send a breath of air with it. The ball sailed over the grass before dropping into the snow. Gandalf bounded after it and brought it back.

Red tried again. She thought of the way her mom's wind used to feel, warm and gentle. Like laughter. This time, the ball sailed a little farther. Gandalf returned it with a sneeze.

"I'm *trying*," Red said.

She let the wind skim off her skin, not worrying about trying to control it for a moment. Her hair billowed around her head, and Gandalf's fur flurried. Holding the ball out, she imagined her wind wrapping around it, lifting it, playing with it. She felt the plastic shudder in her fingers. Pulling her arm back, she threw the ball as hard as she could and sent her wind chasing it.

The ball dipped toward the field, then turned suddenly to the sky, carried by an updraft, before falling into the snow again. Gandalf's bark was bellowing and happy as she raced after it. She ran in circles a few times, like she was celebrating Red's success. Red laughed, tugging the ball from Gandalf's teeth when she returned.

With the next throw, she sent the ball skittering just above the grass. Gandalf ran for it at top speed, yapping when it surprised her by soaring back over her head. Red's whole body hummed with excitement. She was doing it! She was controlling her wind!

They played until Red's arm hurt from throwing and her head ached from concentration. The wind made the ball bounce through the air like a skipping stone across water. It rolled the ball over the ground, slowly, then faster as Gandalf chased it. With every throw, Red's wind tried new things, keeping the ball aloft or sending it farther down the field.

When Gandalf brought the ball back for the last time, she dropped it, then flopped onto the ground, panting. Red sat on the stargazing rock and watched Gandalf roll in a patch of snow to cool off. Red looked up and smiled.

The sky was still blue and clear and perfect. There wasn't a storm in sight.

Chapter
41

"She's here!" Red unfastened her seat belt and scrambled out of the car as Wanda's hatchback turned into the parking lot. Wanda's car moved tentatively at first, like Wanda didn't see them, then zoomed toward Celine's car with a roar.

Celine glanced at the dashboard clock, which showed seventeen minutes past the hour, and climbed out of the car without a word. Red waved toward her mom, grinning so widely her jaw hurt. Wanda's car squealed to a stop. She left it running and stepped out.

"Mom!" Red ran to her, wrapping her arms around her waist.

Wanda patted her back. "Hey, you."

Celine held out her hand. "It's nice to see you again, Wanda. How was your New Year's?"

Wanda hesitated before shaking Celine's hand, her lips pulled thin. "Fine, thanks."

"Red's really excited about today." Celine's smile was warm, despite the exhaustion in her eyes. Even though Celine hadn't been feeling well, she'd insisted on driving Red to meet Wanda for their first unsupervised visit. She said she wanted to be there, just in case Red was nervous.

Red looked between the two women. Celine's face was pale and thin. Her hair was a cloud of silvery gold around her head. Wanda's hung down the middle of her back in a dark, thick sheet. She kept running her hand through it, pulling out long strands and balling them up in her fingers before dropping them to the ground. Her eyes shifted constantly, and Red could feel a nervous shiver in the air.

"I've never been to the aquarium," Celine said to Red. "You'll have to tell me all about it when you get home."

"We better go." Wanda glanced at the screen of her phone.

"Of course. See you later, Red," Celine said.

Red hugged Celine, then saw the way her mom's lips tightened. "Bye," she said, pulling away from the embrace.

Once they were in the car, Wanda jabbed at the radio preset buttons, settling on some jangly rock music as they sped out of the parking lot.

"How's work?" Red asked. The woman on the radio growled words Red couldn't understand over a wailing guitar.

Wanda ran a hand through her hair. "It's okay. My boss is kind of a jerk." She blew out a breath and shook her head.

Red pulled on the shoulder of the seat-belt strap to keep it from cutting into her neck. *Clunk clunk clunk.*

"Stop, please. You'll break it."

Red laughed. "I can't break a seat belt by *pulling* on it, Mom. That's the whole point of seat belts."

"Red." Her mother shot her a warning look.

Red's smile faded. "Sorry."

When the growling song finished, Red turned down the radio. She ignored her mother's scowl and talked about the book report she had to finish before school started again next week. She told her about Billie's latest escapades. The goat had somehow broken into the locked back room of the barn, where Jackson stored all the animal food, and had eaten herself into a stupor.

But what she wanted to tell her was that Celine was sick.

She tried to imagine the look on her mom's face when she said the word. *Cancer.*

Maybe this time that word wouldn't scare Wanda away like it had when Gamma got cancer. Maybe this time she'd be there for Red. Maybe she'd realize how much Red needed her to do all the things the judge said so Red could finally come home.

Because now, more than ever, Red needed her mom.

But could she tell her that?

Wanda laughed at the story about Billie, and hope flared in Red's heart. She opened her mouth, but Wanda spoke first.

"Guess who I ran into the other day?" Wanda adjusted the rearview mirror so she could check her lipstick.

"Who?"

"Ricky! Remember?" She squeezed Red's knee, like this news was something Red should be excited about.

Red shifted, tugged on the shoulder strap of her seat belt again. *Clunk.* "You saw Ricky?"

"Crazy, right? It's been ages. He's doing good, too. Really good."

Hope fizzled.

"I thought you said you weren't gonna talk to him anymore."

Wanda made a sound somewhere between a laugh and a scoff. "Why would I say that? He's my friend, Red." She glanced at her. "I'm allowed to have friends."

Red scowled.

"Come on. Don't be like that! This is *our* day." Wanda

241

looked at her with wide, excited eyes. "This is the first time we've gotten to hang out just us two in a long time."

"Three years," Red grumbled.

"Right! *Three years*." Wanda squeezed Red's knee, but Red pushed her hand away.

"Come on, baby. Let's promise each other we'll have fun today. No brooding over silly things," her mother said, jostling her shoulder. "I promise, Red. Today is all about you. Okay?" She gave Red a pouty look. "Please?"

"You *promise* promise?"

Wanda nodded, crossing her finger over her heart.

Finally, Red smiled. Three years was a long time. "Okay." She reached for her mom's hand. "I'm glad you're back."

Wanda squeezed her fingers. Her smile was bright and warm. "Me too. I've missed you."

Chapter 42

"North American Wilderness? Is that where we go?" Wanda asked, looking over the aquarium map.

"Sure," Red said.

They wandered down the hall of the exhibit, the sound of running water and the tangy stink of aquatic animals filling the air. A group of kids walked away from the otter exhibit as Red and Wanda approached, opening a space in front of the glass. Red watched the sleek brown creatures twirling and diving in the green water.

"They're so cute!" She turned, expecting Wanda to be next to her, but she wasn't. "Mom?"

Wanda was sitting on a bench behind her, eyes on her phone. Red called her again. "Mom!"

Wanda looked up, surprised. "Oh, yeah, they're really cute. Just a second."

Red waved her over. "Come look at them! This one is playing with a rubber ring."

Wanda finished typing out a text, then dropped her phone into her bag and came to the glass. She smiled at the playful display. "It looks like a dog toy."

Red nodded, watching the otter let go of the ring and do a quick flip, diving beneath it and snatching it up before it could touch the bottom of the tank. She lifted a hand to the thick glass. The otter hooked the dog toy on his arm and swam a smooth lap, his eyes on her. He shot through the water and launched himself onto the rock next to his buddy. They chattered at each other, then dove in unison and surfaced against the glass, face-to-face with Red.

"Whoa," Wanda said.

Red leaned forward and pressed both of her hands against the cool tank. The otters, too, each lifted a paw.

"That's crazy," Wanda whispered. She put her hand next to Red's. The otters launched themselves backward, spinning flips before disappearing into the murky waters on the other side of the tank.

Red looked at Wanda, who raised her eyebrows.

"Impressive," she said. "Do you speak otter or something?"

Red grinned and shrugged. "Maybe."

Her mother tugged lightly on Red's hair. "I've definitely been away too long then."

"Yeah." Red leaned in to her mother's arm. "Definitely."

They wandered through the desert exhibit next. Wanda peered into each tank, occasionally pointing something out to Red. She moved quickly, especially past the rattlesnake display, as if she didn't trust the glass separating them.

"Why is there a desert in an aquarium, anyway?" Wanda asked, grimacing at a collection of giant tarantulas.

Red shrugged. "It's cool, though." She led the way from the desert hall toward the next exhibit. Wanda's shoes clicked on the path behind her.

The lighting shifted from warm yellow to blue green as they entered the room. An enormous glass tube was before them. Above and all around the tube, an assortment of fish, sharks, and gliding rays meandered through clear blue water. Coral reefs bulged from the sea bottom like colorful, rolling hills, and hundreds of creatures bobbed among the waving fingers of anemone and various corals. The light danced against Wanda's silver shirt and wove strands of gold and blue and green into her hair.

"It's kind of creepy in here, isn't it?" Wanda said.

Red was transfixed by the belly of a spotted fish as it swam overhead.

Wanda tapped her pink nails against the curve of the wall. She looked over her shoulder at Red, her eyes dark and glittering. "Why don't the sharks eat the fish?" she marveled. "If I was stuck in a bowl with a bunch of food, I'd eat it."

Red stepped closer to the wall of the tubular tank. A fish darted through the faint reflection of her face.

"Let's keep moving," Wanda said. She pulled out her phone again, smiled, then typed another text.

Red frowned, but kept walking. She tried to ignore how often her mother looked at her phone. Whenever it vibrated with a new text, Wanda would grin and stop to respond. She barely glanced at the animals in most of the tanks they passed.

"Mom," Red whined. "This is *our* day, remember?"

Wanda sent another text, then put the phone away. "I know. Sorry, sorry. Just a friend."

A quiet *vbbtt* from her purse signaled another text. Red turned her back when Wanda fished the phone out.

"I'll just be a second," Wanda said, stepping away.

Red listened to the *clack* of her mother's shoes fade as she watched a tank fill rapidly with water, the fish inside bobbing back and forth in the current. Irritation rippled from her skin, but Red forced herself to calm down. *No wind. Not here.*

A little boy appeared at Red's side. He pressed his nose against the glass and watched as the fish rocked helplessly back and forth in the deluge. They stared in silence for a moment. The water drained again. The lack of floodwater meant the fish could move a bit more freely, so they drifted around, looking for food stirred up by the tide.

"If I was dem, I'd fly away," the boy said confidently.

Red wanted to say, *Me too*.

"Corin! Hey, don't disappear like that!" The boy's mother came around the corner, her cheeks flushed with worry. "Sorry," she said to Red. "I hope he isn't bothering you."

Red smiled and shook her head. She followed a little ways behind Corin and his mom, into the humid air of the rain-forest exhibit. Birds jabbered overhead and mist clung to the plate-size leaves of the plants and palm trees along the path. The fishy smell wasn't as bad in here. The air was earthier, like wet, rich soil.

As she rounded a corner, sunlight poured into the room through the clear glass ceiling. She squinted against the sudden glare and moved toward a crowd of excited children staring into a tank so large its glass walls almost touched the translucent ceiling.

Red stopped, amazed. Before her, two enormous tigers were swimming in a pool on the other side of the glass, pawing at each other and opening their powerful jaws. There was a rubber ball between them, its surface deeply gouged with teeth and claw marks. They both wrestled the ball, one clutching it, trying to bite it, until it rolled out of reach. The second tiger lunged for it, wrapping both of its front legs around it and somersaulting over the top. The smaller tiger climbed onto a rock and leaped into the water again, front legs outstretched like Superman in flight. His body sent a wave of foamy water over the head of his companion. The children squealed with delight.

Red looked around for her mother, and finally found her across the room. She almost called out, but stopped herself. Wanda was talking to someone.

Red stepped away from the tiger tank so she could get a better view. Her mom was under an archway near the exit, her body cast in shadow. She was speaking to a thin man with a shock of light brown hair and a web of colorful tattoos up both arms. Red's body went cold. *Ricky.*

Wanda touched his arm and smiled. Red clenched her fists and headed toward them. The tall, wide-leafed palm trees along the perimeter of the room rustled and swayed as Red passed.

"Mom."

Wanda jumped, a mix of surprise and embarrassment flashing across her face. "Oh! Red! There you are. Look who it is!"

Ricky's smile was crooked. He pushed his knuckles into Red's shoulder. "Hey, kiddo. Miss your uncle Ricky?"

Red ignored him. "What's he doing here?" she asked her mom.

Wanda frowned. "I told you I ran into him the other day. Now, be polite." She pinched Red's arm gently but firmly. "Ricky's the reason we get to do this today. He works here. He got us the tickets."

Red stepped back, away from both Ricky's shoulder-punch greeting and her mother's *be-polite* pinch. All around them, tree leaves shook and shivered against each other. *Shhhkk shhhkk.*

"You *promised*," Red hissed.

"Don't be rude, Red." Her words were clipped. "Say hello."

Red held her mother's gaze, glaring. Finally, she shifted her angry stare to Ricky. "Hi," she said.

Ricky chuckled. "Someone's getting a jump on being a moody teenager."

"I apologize for my *very rude child*," Wanda said, directing the last words at Red. She rolled her eyes at Ricky like, *She's so dramatic.*

"It's cool. You ladies ready for lunch? I made reservations at the restaurant. We can sit right in front of the mermaid tank." Ricky waggled his eyebrows at Red. Did he think she was a little girl?

"That sounds nice, doesn't it, Red?" Wanda reached to pinch her again.

"Fine," Red said, dodging her mom's fingers.

Ricky ran his hand through his hair as it whipped around on his head. He looked up toward the vents along the wall, frowning like he couldn't understand where the air was coming from. Wanda gave Red a pointed look. Red crossed her arms, trying to hold herself together.

Ricky waved them on. "Let's eat!" He leaned in to Wanda and spoke in a low voice. "We can all get reconnected."

Wanda blushed and giggled. She put her hands on Red's shoulders and steered her toward the exit. "It's just lunch," she said into Red's ear. "Relax."

Chapter
43

The problem with Ricky was that he made Wanda forget. That was what Gamma used to say. *He makes you forget yourself.*

They fought about it a lot. Gamma said Wanda was treating her life like it was something cheap. Wanda yelled that it was *her* life and she could do whatever she wanted with it.

"No," Gamma had said, slamming her palm down on the counter. "No, you can't, Wanda. Not anymore! Not when you have a child."

"She's more yours than mine," Wanda said. "She loves you best, and we both know it."

"I'm *here*. That's the *only* difference between her love for us."

Red shook the memory away and glared at Ricky. She couldn't let her mother forget herself. Not this time. Red needed her now more than ever. Wanda had promised to be there for Red. She'd *promised*. Red needed to remind her of that.

But the only way she could think to do it was to talk about Gamma.

Anxiety fluttered through her. She didn't want to talk about Gamma, about her cancer. She didn't want to remember those weeks and months when Red felt so alone and scared while Gamma got sicker and sicker.

When Gamma was diagnosed, Red's mom left. She just *left*. One day she was there, hearing Gamma's news alongside Red, asking questions about treatment plans and alternative care. And the next day, Red came down for breakfast, and Gamma was at the table, head in her hands. Red knew without asking. She knew without Gamma saying a word.

Her mother was gone.

Wanda came back once. Gamma was on her sixth chemo treatment at that point, and was really tired and weak all the time. She was in a lot of pain, too. Red used to hear her crying at night through the bedroom wall. Crying because she hurt so bad and nothing helped, not even the pills the doctors gave her.

When Wanda came back, she'd lost weight and had dark circles under her eyes. She was jumpy and cranky, snapping at Red for every little thing. She said she wanted to help, that she felt bad for leaving. She said she knew Gamma needed her, and that Red shouldn't have to take care of Gamma alone. Red wanted to believe her, and she could tell Gamma did, too.

But two days later, Wanda and Gamma had a fight. A bad one. That afternoon, Gamma bought Red the impossible notebook, and told her *hard* wasn't the same as *impossible*. The next day, Wanda stole Gamma's bottle of prescription pain meds and vanished again.

Red put down her spoon. The ice cream her mom had ordered her for dessert was much too sweet. Across the table, Wanda was talking to Ricky, her hands moving as she spoke. She didn't even look at Red.

If she reminded her mom about the promises she'd made after Gamma died, if she told her about Celine, would it help? Would it keep Wanda from disappearing, or would it make her run?

Wanda had already broken her promises. But that was before she went to prison, before rehab. She was stronger now, wasn't she? She had a job, she was going to school. She *wanted* to be better. And she was trying to get custody again. She was trying to start over. She was succeeding, too.

As long as she stayed away from Ricky.

Red sat up straighter. "Mom, what kind of cancer did Gamma have?"

Wanda's hands froze in midair. "What?"

Red tried not to squirm. "What kind of cancer did Gamma have?"

Her mother adjusted in her seat so she was facing Red. "She had leukemia."

"Oh, yeah." Red looked at Ricky, who was sitting back a little from Wanda now. "I went to a *lot* of appointments with my gamma."

He raised his eyebrows. "Yeah? Well. You're a good kid."

"My mom couldn't come to any appointments, though. Mostly, it was just me and Gamma. Alone." Red sighed. "It was really hard."

He nodded. "I bet."

Wanda's eyes narrowed. "It was a long time ago," she said.

"Did you know I'm in foster care?" Red kept her attention on Ricky.

"Um. Yeah. Yeah, your mom told me." He picked up a limp fry.

Red nodded. "I had to be, after Mom got arrested." She pushed the ice cream in her bowl around, but didn't eat it. "Foster care really sucks."

Ricky cleared his throat. "Um, yeah. I bet it does."

"The family I'm with now is nice, though. They have a lot of animals."

He glanced at Wanda, shifted in his chair. "Oh yeah?"

Red nodded. "But I'm really happy my mom's back."

"You and me both, kid." He smiled. "Your mom's awesome."

Red bit her lip and set down her spoon. They looked at her crumpled expression and exchanged another glance.

"What's wrong?" Wanda asked.

Red's eyes filled with tears. "It's just . . ."

Her mom leaned forward. "What?"

"My foster . . . Celine has cancer."

Wanda's eyebrows shot straight up and she sat back hard, like Red had pushed her.

Red continued, her voice trembling. "They just found out. And I don't know if they'll be able to take care of me very much longer. But it's okay. You know why?"

". . . Why?" Ricky asked.

Red could feel discomfort breezing from her mother's skin. Wanda pulled her hair over one shoulder, gripping it in her fist to keep it from blowing around her face.

"Because as long as my mom does what the judge says and doesn't take those pills anymore, then I can live with her again. She'll *be there* for me." She shifted her gaze to her mother. "Just like she promised."

For a moment, Red wasn't sure what she saw on Wanda's face. Shame? Sorrow? Humiliation? But then she saw something she did recognize: anger. The air pressure in the room changed, making Red's ears pop, as Wanda plucked her napkin off her lap and dropped it onto her plate.

255

"We better get going," she said, standing. "Thanks for lunch, Ricky."

Ricky stood, too. "Yeah, sure, of course." He rubbed his hands together. "Um. It was good to see you again."

Wanda picked up her purse. "Yeah. You too. Come on, Red."

Red bit back a smile as they wound around tables on their way to the exit. The air in the aquarium lobby blew cold against Red's face. Her mother's wind should have made her nervous, but she didn't care. She'd gotten what she wanted. Wanda couldn't ignore her now.

That was worth any windstorm.

Chapter 44

"What was that, Red?" Wanda slammed her door and jammed the key into the ignition. "Are you *trying* to humiliate me?"

Red's hair blew back from her face as she clicked her seat belt into place. "No."

"Oh, really? *I had to go to foster care after Mom was arrested.*" Her voice was a high, whining imitation of Red's. "*Mom abandoned me when Gamma was dying. Geez, Red!*" She smacked her hands into the steering wheel.

Red's wind pushed against Wanda's, scooping up receipts and discarded papers from the floorboards and plastering them against the windows. "I didn't say that."

"Yeah, you basically did, Red." Her mother shot her a dirty look, then turned away. She took a shuddering breath and suddenly her breezes quieted.

Red could see Wanda's reflection in the window. Her eyes were wide and shiny, like she was about to cry. Red bit her lip. "I'm sorry," she said softly. "I didn't mean that."

Wanda was silent a long time. Then she swiped a knuckle under each eye before turning to her daughter. "Well, it's kind of true, I guess." She twisted the ends of her hair. The expression on her face made her look younger. "I wasn't around really."

Red said nothing.

"I'm sorry I didn't tell you Ricky worked here. I'm sorry I sprung him on you like that."

Red squeezed her fingers together. "It was *our* day, Mom."

Wanda nodded, her lip caught between her teeth. "Yeah. I know. Sorry."

Red's wind calmed, too. They didn't speak. Snow began to fall. The flakes were teeny, tiny hailstones. They shushed against the windshield like sand.

Wanda dragged a hand through her hair. "Why do you hate Ricky so much?"

"He gave you pills."

Her mother pressed her lips together and closed her eyes. "Yeah. He did. But I was messed up before that.

I've been messed up for a long time." Wanda opened her eyes and faced Red. "He's my friend. But if you're gonna get so upset, I won't see him anymore."

"Promise?"

Wanda rolled her eyes and a breeze ruffled Red's hair. "Yes, I *promise*. Geez. I swear, you're too much like Gamma sometimes."

Red was glad.

Wanda started the car. Cold air blasted from the vents and they both aimed the slats away from themselves.

Wanda clicked off the radio and buckled her seat belt. "So . . . does she really have cancer?"

Red nodded.

The car groaned when Wanda put it into gear and released the break. "I'm sorry. You must be scared."

A family crossed the parking lot in front of them. Red watched the three kids. The youngest was in her mother's arms, and a little boy held the father's hand while clutching an otter stuffie. A girl about Red's age walked between them, gesturing as she talked, a wide smile on her face.

"I want to live with you again." The words were quiet, unexpected. But true.

Wanda pulled out of the parking lot as soon as the family was clear. Something in the car's engine rattled like a loose tin can.

"I'm trying, Red. I'm doing what the judge asked."

There was a *but* in her voice. Red could hear it. She looked at her mom and waited.

"It's just—it feels impossible. They know all the mistakes I've made. They know Gamma had to help me a lot when you were little. And then, after she died, I didn't take you to school enough and you had to repeat a year. Plus, my . . . problem. And the arrest. You know. I have a lot to prove, is all."

"It always feels impossible until it's done, Mom."

Wanda laughed and shook her head. Red stared at the twisting metal frames of thrill rides at the Elitch Gardens across the street. The theme park was empty this time of year, and the abandoned red-and-white tower and looping blue roller coaster looked like forgotten toys.

"Can I help?" Red asked.

Wanda smiled. "Maybe. Just tell them how great I am." She winked at Red. Then her smile wavered a little. "And maybe don't mention Ricky? They might not understand."

Red nodded again. She didn't understand either, but her mom had promised. And for now, that was good enough.

Volcanoes are dangerous.

When they erupt, they can bury whole cities. It happened to a place called Pompeii a long time ago. People were killed by hot ash while they were eating or sleeping or just living their lives. There wasn't any warning.

This still happens, even now.

The Fuego volcano erupted in Guatemala, and whole villages just disappeared.

In Hawaii, rivers of lava poured out of Kilauea. Hundreds of homes were destroyed.

It seems impossible to think of volcanoes as a good thing.

But they are still important.

Volcanic soil is full of minerals that help plants and crops grow. The gases that come from volcanoes make up Earth's atmosphere. Volcanoes even create land in the middle of the ocean, like Hawaii.

Sometimes the things that make up our world are scary. Sometimes they hurt us. Sometimes they destroy everything we love.

But that doesn't mean we don't need them.

Chapter 45

"We went to this festival in honor of Pele. She's the goddess of fire. The park where it was held overlooks a huge lava flow that's not active anymore. The whole thing is solid black. It's crazy!"

Marvin hopped from one foot to the other as he spoke, pretending to tiptoe through a field of hot lava. Red tried to picture a solid black landscape, but since the one she was currently looking at was white with snow, it was hard to imagine.

"Mom and Tūtū were excited because they knew some of the dancers. They used to be their students, and now they're competing and dancing professionally. During the show, some of them grabbed Tūtū's hand and made her go up onstage to dance. Everyone was cheering. It was really cool."

"I wish I could have seen that," Red said. She still hadn't seen Mrs. Kapule dance since her storm had interrupted their lū'au back in November. Marvin had shown her videos online, though, and she thought hula was beautiful.

"It was cool. Look out!" He leaped from one mound of snow to another, absorbed in his own game.

Red focused her attention on a clump of soggy leaves sticking out of the snow and sent a current of air in their direction, trying to bury them. A few sparkling flakes danced and shimmered over the brown leaves. She'd been practicing with her wind in the weeks since Christmas, trying to control it, to make it playful and gentle. Or at least not dangerous. It was the middle of January, but she hadn't made much progress. Whenever she was upset, her wind would ripple and shiver from her skin like always.

She frowned, giving up on burying the leaves. "Did you see all your cousins?"

Marvin had a lot of cousins. So many cousins, in fact, that he hadn't even met some of them. It had become a joke between them, since Red didn't know if she had any cousins at all.

He stopped jumping. "Not even close. Oh, but I did

meet my new second cousin. Wait. First cousin once re-moved?" His face scrunched up in thought. "Maybe third cousin? Is there such a thing as a third cousin?"

Red shrugged. "I didn't even know *first cousin once removed* was a thing."

"Maybe it's my second cousin. Anyway, someone I'm related to has a new baby. His name is Nolan, and he's super squishy and cute."

They were in the Kapules' backyard, both bundled in thick coats and scarves. Red was staying with them for the weekend while Jackson and Celine visited a cancer treatment hospital in Texas. According to Jackson's research, one of its doctors was the leading specialist in the type of cancer Celine had.

"Do your grandparents still want to move back there?" Red asked, pushing away her anxiety about Celine.

Marvin's dimples appeared just above the zipped-up collar of his coat. "Nope! Well, maybe a little. But I showed them the video I made, and Tūtū hugged me really hard and started crying and said she loves me even more than she loves the ocean. And that woman *loves* the ocean!"

The snow around Marvin's feet was crushed from all his pacing and hopping. They were trying to build a snowman, but the snow wasn't sticking together very well. Red pulled her glove back on, then scooped another handful onto the base of their snowman pile. They'd given up trying to make three snowballs and stacking them. The snow just crumbled like dry sand every time. Now they were building a mound and hoping to chisel out features later.

Marvin stepped back and examined their snow pile. "It doesn't look like a snowman."

"Nope."

"It kind of looks like Luke Skywalker's house on Tatooine. Except dirtier." Marvin turned to her, his eyes wide with some brilliant idea. "Hey! We *could* make it Luke Skywalker's house on Tatooine!"

Red laughed. "I don't know what that is."

"Holy bananas, Red. We have *got* to level up your *Star Wars* game this weekend."

While Marvin gave her instructions on how to make the snowman into a more accurate depiction of Luke Skywalker's ancestral home, as he described it, Red was coming up with an idea of her own. During her last therapy session, she'd asked Dr. Teddy if there was something she could do to help convince the judge that Wanda was ready to have custody again. He told her that some kids wrote a letter saying what they wanted. He said the judge always took the kid's opinion into consideration. Wanda's next court appearance was at the end of February. That gave Red six weeks to figure out what she wanted to say.

What if, instead of a letter, Red did something even

bigger? Like a video. Marvin would help her, she knew. It would be so much better than a letter. Marvin's video had convinced his grandparents not to move back to Hawai'i, so maybe Red's video would convince a judge that she should move back in with her mom. The sooner the better, too.

Celine would be having surgery and starting treatment soon, and Red remembered how awful Gamma's treatment had been. How she'd been sick for days, and too weak to do anything. Once, she'd slept on the bathroom floor for three days because she was too weak to get into bed after throwing up so much. Red had brought her blankets and towels, food and water. Gamma kept apologizing, saying Red was too young to have to take care of a sick old lady. But nobody else was there to do it.

Remembering Gamma's treatment filled her with dread. Even though she liked living with Celine and Jackson, she knew the last thing they needed was to worry about a foster kid while Celine was sick.

No. Red had to live with her mom.

"Maybe we could make the ice caves on Hoth, too!" Marvin's voice sliced through her thoughts. "I mean, we couldn't make a real one. There's not enough snow. But we can do a miniature, like the Tatooine house. We could make replicas of *tons* of things. And then we could take a spin-eo of the whole landscape!" He started jumping up and down. "I LOVE THAT YOU'RE HERE FOR A WHOLE WEEKEND!"

Laughing, she scooped some snow and lobbed it at him, hitting him in the shoulder. He froze, his expression stunned, then started chasing her, throwing handfuls of snow that disintegrated in midair. For the next few hours, all thoughts of cancer or videos or court dates were buried by laughter in the snowy desert of Tatooine.

Chapter 46

Marvin stood by the whiteboard hanging on his bedroom wall. He'd already drawn a neat table with three columns in blue dry-erase marker. In each column, he'd started listing tasks.

Pre-Production	Production	Post-Production
script	shooting	editing
location scouting		music
storyboard		preview/final cut

"The first thing we need to do," he said, "is decide what story you're trying to tell."

Red tossed his pineapple pillow into the air and caught it. "I just want to live with my mom," she said.

He waved a hand. "The whole point of making a film is to tell a story. You want your audience to experience *eeemooootion*." As he spoke, he uncapped a green marker and wrote *EMOTION*. "Emotion is what motivates a response."

Red rolled her eyes. "That film class is getting to you. You sound like a teacher."

He beamed. "Thanks!"

"Maybe we can do something like your *Kitchen Kahuna* videos?"

Marvin put his fists on his hips and paced. "*Kitchen Kahuna* is awesome," he said. "But I don't think that format is right for you. You need something with a narrative." He wrote *NARRATIVE* on the board under *EMOTION*. "It's kind of like a journey. Every good story starts in one place and ends somewhere else."

Picking at a loose thread on Marvin's comforter, Red stared at the whiteboard, her face screwed up in thought. He waited, bouncing up and down on his toes.

"I guess . . ." She paused. "I guess I want to tell the judge how good my mom is doing compared to before?"

Marvin thought for a moment, his fingers tapping his chin. Then he shook his head. "I think you need to *show*, not tell. That way the judge feels something." He grabbed his laptop and sat down on the bed next to her. "Have you ever seen those videos of, like, puppies that are really sad or sick, and by the end of the video they're cute and happy and ready for their *fur-ever homes*?"

"I guess."

"And when you see the happy puppy, you feel happy, right?"

She shrugged.

His eyebrows arched up into the middle of his forehead. "*Why?* Why are you happy for the puppy?"

"Because it's happy?"

"No. Watch." He clicked a video.

They watched as rescuers pulled tiny, shivering dogs out of a well. The camera rotated around the puppies as they sat, wide-eyed on a towel in a car. They were skinny, and so covered in mud and sores that it was hard to tell what color they were. As the video went on, they were treated by a vet and got big bowls of food. Red smiled when they were shown slipping and sliding around on a wood floor, tugging on toys and tumbling on a dog bed. The video was only about a minute long, but by the end, the skinny, half-drowned puppies had grown into healthy, romping dogs.

"See?" Marvin said when it was over.

"I guess," she said again, thinking. "By the end, I'm happy for the puppies because I see how much better it is for them now."

"Right!" Marvin closed the laptop, smiling. "You saw the journey. You remember how sad they were, and that makes you feel happy about where they are now. And it makes you want to give money to the organization that goes around saving puppies from wells, right?"

"Yeah."

"So we gotta show the judge *your* journey. We have to show them how sad you are without your mom, and how much better it is with her."

"Okay. That makes sense."

He stood and returned the laptop to his desk, then picked up another dry-erase marker. "Let's brainstorm."

For the next hour, they listed different ideas for Red's story. Most of Marvin's had something to do with *Star Wars*, which Red rejected. But none of her ideas felt right, either.

"You could do a montage of pictures, maybe," Marvin said. "Show some of you when you were a baby? When your mom wasn't sick?"

Red shook her head. "I don't really have any pictures."

"None?"

She tossed the pineapple pillow into the air and caught it again. "Foster kids don't really get to take that stuff with them. Especially when the cops take you away in the middle of the night."

"That happened to you?"

She hugged the pillow and shrugged, feeling awkward all of a sudden. "It's not a big deal."

He stared at her for a second, then became preoccupied with the marker in his hands. "I don't know. I'd be scared if that happened to me."

Something squirmy wrapped itself around her heart. She *had* been scared. Really scared.

"Yeah," she said, her voice quiet.

Marvin turned back to the whiteboard and drew a line through the *photographs* idea. "Okay. Well, you could tell stories about your mom. About good things she's done."

Red considered this. "I guess I could talk about the time she took me swimming."

Marvin nodded for her to go on.

"I was six, I think. It was a really hot summer, and Gamma didn't have air-conditioning. One day, Mom said she wasn't going to sit around and melt like a Popsicle! So we walked down the street to a hotel that had a pool.

"The gate was locked, so Mom climbed up on this big planter thing. She got all scratched up by the tree that was in it. But she hopped the fence and let me in, and we swam all day. She even taught me how to dive to the bottom of the deep end."

Marvin looked impressed. "That's cool! I don't think my mom would ever climb a hotel fence. She'd probably say it's against the rules."

Red frowned. "Really?" She hadn't thought about that. What if it *was* against the rules? Telling a judge that her mom had broken the law probably wasn't the best idea. "Maybe it's not that great a story."

Marvin sighed. "Coming up with good ideas is hard."

"Really hard," she agreed, tossing the pineapple again.

His dimples appeared and he threw his arms up in exaggerated defeat. "It's *impossible!*"

Red froze, eyes wide. Marvin made a face.

"What?" he asked.

An excited ripple of air bubbled up inside of her, pushing the pineapple pillow out of her hands.

She grinned. "I have an idea!"

Chapter
47

"What are you working on?" Celine asked, pulling out a chair across the table from Red.

Red finished writing her sentence in the notebook. "Something for my mom."

For the last two days, Red had spent every spare minute looking up information that would prove all the impossible things she and Gamma hadn't been able to finish. Ever since talking to Celine about the notebook, Red had been trying to add things to it. But now she wanted to finish it as soon as possible. Marvin had said they could make the movie like a documentary, showing that all kinds of impossible things came true when people believed and worked hard enough.

"It'll be *so* inspiring," he'd said. "We can use really good music in the background, too. Maybe the *Star Wars* theme song! That always gets people."

For the end, Red planned to show her mom the finished notebook, and Marvin would film Wanda's reaction. Red would remind her that there was a difference between *hard* and *impossible*, and Red knew her mom would say how she believed that nothing was impossible now. Then she and Red would hug and cry. Marvin said everyone who watched it would definitely cry. Probably the judge would cry, too.

It was going to be perfect.

A brisk, excited breeze ruffled her hair and shivered down her spine. The notebook's pages flapped and the cover lifted, but Red pressed her palm against it.

Celine lifted an eyebrow. "What's on your mind, kiddo?"

While Celine and Jackson were in Texas, they had video-called Red at the Kapules' every day. They even sent her a spin-eo of Celine's hospital room, much to Marvin's delight. Red had gotten to see Celine's doctor, who promised her he'd be taking good care of Celine, should she choose to do her treatment there. Though the trip was a serious one, it seemed to have gone well. Both Celine and Jackson had been in better spirits since they'd gotten home.

Red took a breath. She hoped what she was about to

say wasn't going to make Celine sad again. "I—I want to make a video. To tell the judge why I should live with my mom again."

Celine folded her hands on the table and cleared her throat. "Okay."

Red hurried on. "It's not that I don't like living with you and Jackson! I do! It's just . . ." She paused and lifted a shoulder.

Celine brushed the back of Red's hand with her fingers. "You don't have to explain yourself to me. She's your mom, and you love her. I know that. And I know that wanting to be with her doesn't mean you don't love us."

Red nodded and shrugged at the same time.

"What can I do to help?" Celine asked.

Red opened the notebook and slid it toward Celine. "I want to talk about impossible things in the video. I want to say that there's a difference between hard and impossible, and that maybe it has been hard for my mom, but it isn't impossible for her to take care of me."

Celine nodded, but there was something in her expression that Red couldn't quite identify. "I think that's a really good idea."

"Thanks. Can you think of something for this one?" Red took the notebook, turning to a page near the back.

Celine read Gamma's writing. "*Impossible: seeing something invisible.*" She sat back, her lips pressed together in thought. After a moment, she stood up. "I might have an idea."

Red followed her out of the kitchen and into the library. Celine browsed one of the bookshelves, standing on her tiptoes to pull a book off the top shelf.

"This might be a little hard to read, but I can help you find the right part," she said, handing it to Red.

Red turned the book over in her hands. It was a book about stars, and had a bunch of glossy pictures.

"You could talk about how sometimes the stars are invisible."

"Like when it's cloudy?"

"Actually, I was thinking that they're invisible during the day. The stars are always there, always watching over us." Celine waved a hand toward the sky. "We just can't see them when it's light. When darkness closes in, though, the stars shine brightest."

Red felt a familiar tickle on her skin. "It's perfect. Thanks!"

Celine tucked a piece of Red's hair behind her ear. "You're welcome. Are you going to show the notebook to your mom?"

Red thumbed the pages of the book and nodded. "Marvin is going to film it when I do."

"Really?"

"Yeah. We're gonna put her reaction in my video for the judge."

A shadow crossed Celine's face, but she said, "Well, you should be very proud, Red."

The two of them went back into the kitchen. Celine made a cup of tea as Red looked through the star book. There were a ton of amazing pictures, but also a *lot* of big words. She'd definitely need to google them. Setting the book aside, Red watched Celine pour hot water into a mug.

"Hey," Red said suddenly. "You don't rub your neck anymore. You used to, a lot."

"You're right. The pain isn't there anymore." Celine pressed her fingers into the curve of her neck and shoulder, like she was checking to make sure it was true. "My doctor said it was something called *referred pain*. I thought my neck hurt, but really, it was my sick gallbladder."

"That's kind of weird."

Celine laughed. "Yeah, I guess so. Pain is funny that way. Sometimes it tricks us into thinking one thing is wrong, when really it's something else."

Red frowned. "What if pain never goes away?" she asked.

Her foster mother shook her head. "It doesn't always. There are a lot of people who feel pain every day. It takes a lot of courage to face pain like that. But courage can reveal beauty."

"Gamma was in pain for a long time," Red said, her voice wobbly. "And then she died. It wasn't beautiful."

Celine's face reflected Red's sadness. "I'm sorry you had to watch your grandma suffer so much. I bet she was glad you were with her, though. You took care of her. You made her feel loved."

Red picked at the edges of the notebook. "I danced for her," she said. The memory came sparking to mind, like a candle that wasn't quite blown out. "Gamma used to do this thing where she'd try to dance things into life if they were broken. She said the world always showed love by dancing. Like how trees move or birds fly together in huge flocks. She said if something was broken, she wanted to show it as much love as she could, so she'd dance."

Celine smiled. "Now I *know* I would have liked your gamma."

Red nodded. "I mostly danced when she was sleeping. But once she woke up and saw me. When I looked at her, she was watching me and crying." Her voice broke and she frowned. "So I guess that wasn't good, actually."

"Oh, sweetie," Celine said, coming toward her. "It was. It was wonderful. Your grandmother saw you dancing, and she knew how much you loved her."

"But she was crying."

Celine considered her next words. "Sometimes crying isn't sad," she said. "Sometimes it's how we respond to something we think is beautiful."

"There's my girls!" Jackson's voice boomed as he came

in through the back door. Snow swirled around him. He took off his *I Like Big Mutts* baseball hat. "Red, you'll never believe what I just saw in the barn."

Red raised her eyebrows. "What?"

"A possum."

Celine laughed. "A possum? Really?"

Jackson nodded, grinning. "Yup! It was huge." He held his palms about eighteen inches apart. "And it *hissed* at me! Red, I bet you anything it's what you saw and thought was a rat. Especially if you've never seen one before."

Celine made a face. "Did you get rid of it?"

"I'll have to get a trap so I can relocate him. Or her. I need to search the barn to make sure there aren't babies hiding somewhere."

He planted a kiss on Celine's cheek and tugged lightly on Red's hair. He smelled like animals and sweat and cut wood. "What are you two doing?"

"Just talking," Celine said.

"Did you tell Red your good news?" he asked.

Red looked at Celine. "Good news?"

Celine lowered herself into a chair, her hands wrapped around her tea mug. "Well, the doctor in Texas called today. They've scheduled my surgery."

Red looked between their faces, suddenly uneasy.

Celine's expression was guarded. "It's at the end of February. In Houston."

Chapter
48

Jackson came downstairs, the dogs trailing him, and knocked on the doorframe of the library. Red was at the computer. She'd been working on the impossible notebook, but had gotten distracted trying to figure out if foster kids were allowed to go with their foster family to another state if their foster parent was having surgery there.

There wasn't an easy answer. Especially since Celine said she'd be in the Texas hospital for at least six weeks.

"Hey, kiddo. I'm going to take you to meet your mom today. Celine isn't feeling well."

It was early February, and today was Red's third unsupervised visit with her mom. Last time, they'd gone to a skating rink that was set up in downtown Denver, and discovered that neither of them was very good at ice skating. After bruising their tailbones a few too many times, they'd gotten coffee and walked around the 16th Street Mall. Red had wanted cocoa, but her mom convinced her to get a mocha instead, saying it was more grown-up. She didn't like how bitter the coffee tasted, though, and eventually threw it out.

As Red and Jackson waited now for Wanda to arrive at the Park-n-Ride, Jackson asked, "Is the plan still to see a movie?"

"I think so." Red looked at the clock. Her mom was late. Again.

"How's your movie coming?" he asked.

Red shifted in her seat. Her stomach had been hurting all morning. "Okay. I'm almost done finding impossible things, and we've filmed a few scenes already. I'm gonna ask Mom if our next visit can be somewhere Marvin can come and film."

"Does she know about the video?"

"Kind of. I told her I was working on something for the judge. I'll tell her more today."

Jackson seemed lost in thought for a moment, then looked like he wanted to speak, but Wanda's car zipped into the parking lot. The two of them climbed out of Jackson's truck and waved. A sudden, biting wind stung Red's face, and she jammed her hands deep into her coat pockets.

"Hey there," Jackson said, bending at the waist to look into Wanda's car window.

Wanda barely smiled. She was always uncomfortable around Jackson. The wind tangled her hair around her face. "Hi."

Red climbed into the passenger side. She had to push a few fast-food wrappers and some mail onto the floor before she could sit down.

"Still planning to go to a movie at the mall?" Jackson asked.

Wanda barely looked at him. "Mm-hmm."

Jackson angled his head, trying to catch Wanda's eye. "No other stops?"

Wanda sighed. "I know the rules. She's my kid, okay?"

Jackson held up a hand. "I'm just making sure we're on the same page," he said. "I have my cell if you need me." He bent lower so he could see Red. "Have a nice time, kiddo."

He knocked on the top of the car before turning away.

They were barely out of the parking lot when Wanda's phone twanged. A twirly discomfort stirred in Red.

Wanda glanced at the screen, then answered. "Hey. What's up?" She listened, rolled her eyes, then giggled and glanced at Red. "I'm with my kid right now."

A pause.

"No . . ." Another giggle. "No!"

A longer pause. Wanda sighed. "Adam . . ."

Who was Adam? Red eyed her mother, the splotches of color in her cheeks, her low, whispery laugh. Suspicion sank its needle-sharp teeth into her brain.

"I said I'm with my kid." But Wanda's tone was warmer, less insistent. She glanced at Red questioningly. Adam said something and she laughed again. The question on her face evaporated. "Okay . . . yes, okay. Yeah, I'll meet you. But fast, okay? We have plans. I'll just stop by your place." Another giggle. "Right. Okay. Bye."

She dropped the phone into the cup holder and it clattered against used stir sticks and coins and tubes of lip gloss.

"We're not going to a movie?" Red asked.

Wanda rolled her eyes. "Don't have a cow. I just have to make a stop."

Red glowered at her. "I'm not having a cow!"

"A friend needs me to stop by real quick," Wanda said. "Don't sigh like that, Red. I'll be *quick*. And we won't miss the movie. Maybe the previews, but that's it."

Red squeezed her fists tighter. "Why can't you go later?"

"I said it would be quick, okay?" Wanda snapped.

"Okay."

The silence felt papery and dangerous, like a hornets' nest. Red was afraid to poke too hard.

Outside, the clouds began to darken.

The car bumped down Colfax Avenue, which had so many potholes in the winter that it was impossible to avoid them. Strings of bright plastic beads dangling from the rearview mirror clacked against the windshield. Wanda clicked a lighter into flame under a cigarette that wobbled between her lips.

She caught Red looking. "What?"

Red shrugged.

"I smoke, Red. It's a bad habit—whatever. If you're gonna hang out with me in *my* car," she emphasized, as if Red had a choice, "do me a favor and don't judge."

"I wasn't!"

Wanda cracked the window and blew smoke into the sky. She tapped her fingers against the steering wheel, eager for the light to change to green.

How had this day suddenly gone so wrong? The last time the two of them were together, they'd had fun. They'd laughed and talked about Wanda's job and her classes. It felt like they were friends.

Red wanted that feeling back.

"How are your classes going?" she asked.

Wanda shrugged, tapped her cigarette through the cracked window. The air roared as they picked up speed.

"How's work?" she tried next.

Her mom rolled her eyes. "It's fine, Red."

They turned down a narrow street and pulled to a stop in front of a brick apartment building. There was a plastic bag caught in the bare branches of the bushes lining the apartment wall, and a pair of shoes hanging by their laces swayed and bounced from the power lines.

"I'll be quick," Wanda said, putting the car in park.

Red didn't want to stay in the cloud of cigarette smoke. "Can I come?"

Wanda stiffened, then smiled warmly. "Baby, it'll just be a minute. You're a big girl. You can stay here for a few minutes, right?"

Red wanted to scream. She wanted to grab Wanda's long hair and tie it to the steering wheel. She wanted to go to a movie and pretend everything was okay.

She did not want to be left alone in a car with trash under her feet and cigarette smoke burning her eyes.

But Wanda didn't wait for an answer. She gave Red another false, bright smile, said, "Good girl. Be back soon!" and slipped out of the car, taking the keys with her. The car alarm chirped a high-pitched *whoop whoop* as she disappeared around the corner of the building.

Chapter
49

The cooling engine clicked and popped. Traffic whizzed down the busy street, and Red could hear muffled shouting from somewhere in the building. The pulse of a bass line blared from behind another closed window.

Even though the air inside the car was cool, sweat prickled along the back of her neck. The numbers on a small dashboard clock marched on in their steady, slow parade. She closed her eyes, ignoring their progress. A gust of wind rocked the car, startling her.

No. She wouldn't let the wind get out of control. Not anymore.

She took a deep breath and focused on making her wind good. Fingers tingling, she directed a steady stream of air toward a piece of paper on the floor near her feet. It shuddered and scooted away. Frowning, she concentrated. The paper flipped once, twice. Suddenly, it blew back, flattening against the floorboard. It was no use. Red growled and crossed her arms.

A man wearing a stained dark green coat walked by. His eyes were yellow where they were supposed to be white, and he moved like he was made of mismatched gears and loose parts. She looked away when he caught her eye.

She watched the clock, but could feel the man watching her.

Ten minutes. Fifteen.

Her stomach cramped a sharp, stabbing cramp. She tried to curl up in the seat, but it was a little too small to be comfortable. The sun was making her head ache, too.

Twenty minutes.

She unbuckled her seat belt and turned around, peering through the back windshield. No sign of Wanda. The man in the green coat was sitting on a low brick wall by the front entrance to the building, rolling some kind of cigarette. He looked up at her and smiled.

She ducked down in her seat, angling herself so she could see his reflection in the side mirror. He looked toward the car for another few seconds, then back to his cigarette.

Twenty-two minutes.

How could her mom do this to her? They were supposed to be at the movie already, but there was still no sign of Wanda. A shiver of wind rose from her skin like heat. There was no turning this gust into anything gentle or good. The air circled through the car, rustling papers and crinkling garbage. Red squeezed her eyes shut, took a slow breath, but another stab of pain in her stomach sent more wind spinning from her.

An envelope plastered itself to her face. She yanked it off and glared at it. It was addressed to her mom and had bright red letters across the front that said, *Overdue Notice*. More papers whipped into the air, and she let out a frustrated growl.

A knock on the window made her yelp. She shoved the envelope into her pocket in a panic. The man was bending low, peering at her through the glass.

"You okay in there?" His voice was muffled, and his hooded eyes took in the twirling papers.

"I'm fine!" she said.

He stared at her, and Red held her breath, trying to rein in the storm. Finally, he shrugged and ambled away, taking a long drag on his cigarette. Tears of relief flooded her vision, quickly followed by resurgent anger. *Where was her mother?* She started to climb into the back seat so she could see the building's entrance better.

"Ouch!" She yanked her hand back. A line of blood oozed across the bottom of her palm. She examined the spot where she'd put her hand and saw a glimmer of metal. Carefully, she moved aside an old T-shirt and some papers. A crumpled soda can was on the seat, its sharp, torn edge catching sunlight.

The wound stung. She pressed her hands together and looked at the clock again. Wanda had been gone for fifty minutes. A quick search of the storage pockets in both doors for a clean tissue or napkin proved fruitless. Pulling open the glove box, she pawed through receipts and half-empty cigarette boxes. Her fingers closed around something small and plastic and familiar. She froze, a numbing disbelief flooding her, and pulled out a baggie of white pills.

No.

Her mom wouldn't do that. Not again. She was getting better! She wanted Red back. No. No. *No.*

Rage and frustration boiled over like lava and she kicked the glove box closed. A storm cloud of swirling papers rustled around her, but she didn't care. She stared at the baggie, then crushed it in her fist. How could her mother do this to her? She'd *promised*! Didn't she know Red needed her? *Really* needed her? Her court date was just three weeks away. Celine's surgery was soon after that.

"This is stupid."

A piercing alarm sliced the air when she opened her door. She clambered out of the car and slammed the door, moving away from it before anyone could see her. The man in the green coat was gone, at least.

The lobby of the apartment building smelled like garbage. It was a long, bare room with stained linoleum flooring, yellowing walls, and a single, graffitied elevator. A door opposite the entry was marked STAIRS. Alarms louder than the continuing squeal of Wanda's car rang in Red's head.

"No way," she said, shaking her head at the dim stairwell. She'd seen places like this before, and she wasn't about to start wandering around the halls.

With the wind cold on her face, she marched down the sidewalk, glowering at the few people she passed. Walking loosened the cramping in her stomach, but she still felt nauseated. Finally, she found a gas station. Ignoring the clerk, she made a beeline for the bathroom. It smelled like sewage and gasoline.

She ran her hand under water. Blood swirled in pink whirlpools down the drain. Once she had cleaned herself up, she stood and gazed at her reflection. She looked and felt like a used tissue. The mirror tilted a little to one side as a wave of dizziness crashed into her. She leaned over the sink and gagged, but nothing came up.

What was wrong with her?

Suddenly, she remembered she had to pee. She pulled down her pants and sat on the toilet.

Panic brought a gust of wind from her that was so fierce the door rattled.

There was more blood. It had stained her underwear and soaked the crotch of her pants.

Trembling, she reached for the toilet paper dispenser, only to find it empty. A little sob escaped her throat, and more wind shook the door.

I have to calm down. She couldn't lose control of her storms. Not in a gas station bathroom. She took a slow breath, counting backward from ten.

It's just my period. She knew about periods. One of the group homes she'd stayed in once had had a poster about the menstrual cycle on the bathroom wall, and the house mother had made a big deal about showing all the girls where pads and tampons were stored.

Back then, getting her period seemed like something that was way too far in the future to worry about. She was just a kid. But now she was almost twelve. She was growing up. Whether she was ready to or not.

But Red had felt like a grown-up for too long already. She was tired of it. All she wanted was to be a regular kid going to the movies with her mom. She didn't want a period. She didn't want to find pills in her mom's glovebox. She didn't want secrets and excuses and broken promises.

She repeated her breathing exercise two more times, until her wind stopped rattling the door and she didn't feel as panicked. Breathing hadn't relieved her cramping stomach or the urge to cry, though.

She opened a little cabinet by the toilet, but it didn't have any toilet paper, only cleaning supplies that obviously hadn't been used recently. Sniffling, she grabbed a wad of paper towels instead.

Nothing about this day was going right.

Suddenly, she wanted Celine. Celine would know what to do, what to say. She wouldn't embarrass Red or make her talk about things she didn't want to talk about. Red wanted to go home and let Celine make her hot chocolate so she could forget about all of this.

But Celine wasn't *home*. Her mother was.

Wasn't she?

Red washed her hands again, and stared at her reflection in the dirty mirror. *Mom is my home*, she thought, over and over. *She is, she is, she is.*

She had to be.

Chapter
50

The gas station clerk was a pimply-faced teenager with shoulder-length dishwater-blond hair and thick black plugs in his earlobes. His faded T-shirt was covered by a flimsy red vest with stains under the armpits.

"You okay, kid?"

She wished people would stop asking her that.

Still, she didn't need him calling the police to report a bloody kid in his store, so she smiled and said, "Yeah, I'm okay. Do you have a Band-Aid? I cut my hand." She held up her palm to show him the wound.

He was easily satisfied, the worried look in his eyes switching back to the autopilot of boredom. "Sure."

She secured two strips across the cut and crumpled

the wrappers. He watched her and raised a questioning eyebrow when she didn't move.

"Need to call someone or something?"

Chewing her lip, she stared at the phone on the counter. Its beige handle was gray with grime and there was a blackened piece of chewing gum stuck to the lower corner.

Don't be a baby, she told herself. She didn't need Celine to come save her. She was fine.

She was.

Sniffling, she shook her head. "No thanks." She hurried from the store and out into the cold air. The sun had been buried by ash-gray clouds that churned restlessly in the sky. The temperature had dropped by several degrees, too. Red ignored the weather and walked, head down, in the direction of her mother's car.

Calling Celine would only get her mom in trouble, anyway. She didn't want that. Even though Wanda had left her alone in the car for almost an hour. Even though they'd missed the movie. Even though she'd found a baggie with pills . . .

Back when Red was little, Gamma used to say, *Don't jump to conclusions.*

When Wanda's mood swings got so wild that she'd sometimes be up for days at a time, Gamma said, *Don't jump to conclusions.*

When Gamma's own medications started disappearing from their bottles like water down a drain, she said, *Don't jump to conclusions.*

It wasn't until Wanda got arrested the first time, and Red found Gamma crying over a basket of laundry, that Gamma said, *I should have jumped, Red. Maybe it wouldn't have gotten this bad if I'd let myself jump to conclusions.*

Red wondered what Gamma would say now. Would she warn Red not to jump to conclusions? Or would she say the baggie was exactly what Red was afraid of?

No. Mom promised. The thought was the safety railing on a rickety carnival ride, and she clung to it with everything she had.

She shivered. Her jacket was tied around her waist to cover the bloodstain on her jeans. She'd examined herself from every angle in the bathroom mirror and didn't think the spot could be seen, but she wasn't going to take any chances. Her thin sweater wasn't exactly warm, so she moved quickly, almost jogging. Her stomach cramped and she hoped the wad of paper towels in her underwear wouldn't slip down her pant leg.

Plastic crinkled in her jean pocket. Instead of throwing the pills down the toilet, like she'd wanted to, Red had decided to keep them. She would ask her mother about them. Give her a chance to explain. They were probably a mistake. Maybe they were just aspirin.

Rounding the corner, she saw Wanda leaning against the hood of her now-quiet car, her phone pressed to her ear. Her mother's back was to her as she approached, her cascade of dark hair hanging thick and heavy. At the sound of Red's slapping footsteps, Wanda turned. Her face sagged with relief and she hung up the phone.

"Oh my God, Red. Where *were* you?"

"I'm sorry. I—"

"Sorry? *I almost called the police!*" Wanda threw her phone through the open car window. It bounced off the seat and clattered onto the floor. "I've been out here for fifteen minutes looking for you! Do you know what would have happened if I'd called the cops?"

Red felt hot and cold all at once. She hugged her stomach and shook her head.

"Take a guess! How would it look if I lost my kid during one of these unsupervised visits, huh? I guarantee you, these would be *over*. For good. Is that what you want?"

Red's heart broke. A cavern, dark and deep, opened up between its pieces. "No."

When Wanda spoke again, her voice was softer, though still brittle. "Are you okay?"

Red's hand stung and her stomach ached. Her cheeks were raw with cold, and there was a dull throbbing in the back of her head. But the worst pain had nothing to do with her body.

"Where did you go?" Red whispered.

Her mother's eyes narrowed. "What?"

"Where did you go? You were gone forever! We missed the movie!"

Shame tripped across Wanda's face so fast Red almost didn't see it. "I told you, a friend needed my help."

"You said it would be a few minutes. I waited for an hour!" Air rippled from her body, fevered and frenzied. She didn't even try to pull it back.

Wanda rolled her eyes. "Don't be such a baby, Red. I wasn't gone that long."

Red stomped forward and pulled the plastic baggie out of her pocket. She held it up between them. "I'm. Not. A. Baby. *Babies* don't know when their moms are *lying*."

Wanda's brown eyes widened and her cheeks flushed scarlet. "Where did you—" She stopped, her lips clamping together. Taking a step back, she shook her head. "I don't know what you're talking about."

Anger seethed from Red, and Wanda was almost knocked off-balance as it gusted. "I'm not stupid, Mom."

Wanda reached for the baggie. "Red, I—"

Red dropped her arm, closing the baggie in her fist again, and glared. "Mom."

"It's nothing, Red! It's not what you think." Her gaze flicked between Red's fist and face. "It's just for my migraines. You know I get migraines. I need them for that. That's all."

"*I* need you, Mom." As soon as the words were out, the anger that had been coursing through Red's body vanished. She suddenly felt as fragile as fresh snow. With one step, Wanda could flatten her.

Her mother stared at her, her face hard and unreadable. Then the current shifted between them, wrapping them both in warm tendrils of air. Red felt it against her cheek, gentle. Like *before*. Tears filled her eyes.

Wanda stepped closer. "You're right, baby. You're right. I'm sorry." She opened her arms. Red hesitated, and then fell into them. With her chin pressed against the top of Red's head, Wanda whispered, "I keep messing this up."

Pulling back, Wanda tucked Red's hair behind her ear. Her eyes gleamed with tears and she shook her head. "This feels impossible."

Red wasn't sure if she meant beating her addiction or taking care of her daughter. She opened her palm. They both stared at the crumpled baggie. With her other hand, the one with the bloodstained Band-Aids, Red hooked her mom's fingers.

"It's like Gamma used to say. It always *seems* impossible . . ." she said, then waited.

Wanda let out a little breath and closed her eyes. "Until it's done," she whispered.

Finally, Wanda took the baggie and walked it to a trash can by the side of the apartment building, her other hand still holding on to Red's.

Dying of a broken heart

People say it's impossible to die from a broken
heart. They say we never get more than we
can handle and that pain always heals.
　　But they're wrong.
　　There's a disease called broken heart syndrome.
Sometimes when a person is really, really sad
or hurt or even happy, their heart can stop
working. The blood vessels swell and sometimes
even burst.
　　Most of the time, people don't die.
　　Most of the time, people recover from broken
heart syndrome and are just fine.
　　But sometimes...
　　sometimes they don't.

Chapter 51

The days were starting to get away from Red. Between school and homework, looking up impossible things with Celine, and worrying about her mom, almost three weeks had flown by, and Red still hadn't told her mom about the video.

"My mom's court date is in *four days*, Marvin. Four days!" she sighed into the phone.

"You're seeing her tomorrow, though, right?" Marvin asked. Red heard the clank of dishes in the background.

She flopped onto her bed. Gandalf jumped up onto the foot of it, jostling her. "Yes. But I haven't asked her if you can come."

"You don't really need me. I mean, you could just set up a camera and film it that way."

"I guess."

"You totally can. Just come over and get my camera tonight. I'll show you how to use it."

Red kicked her heels against the bed. "What if my video's not good enough? What if the judge doesn't listen to me? What if I have to stay a foster kid forever?"

There was a particularly loud clatter of plates being stacked on a counter. "What if aliens invade tomorrow?"

She rolled her eyes. "I'm serious!"

"Me too!" He mumbled something to his mom, and the background got quieter, like he'd gone to another room. "Look, Red, I know you want to live with your mom again, and I really think the judge will let you. But if you can't . . . well, is that so bad?"

"I can't stay here, Marvin."

"Why not?" he asked. "Celine and Jackson totally love you. Plus, if you stayed, then we'd still get to see each other every day. That's pretty cool, right?"

Marvin didn't understand. He hadn't ever been taken away from his family. He couldn't know what it was like to miss them. Plus, he'd never seen anyone go through cancer before. He didn't know how scary it was.

Still, she didn't want to hurt his feelings.

"Yeah," she said. "That'd be cool."

He brightened. "Good. See? It'll be okay. Anyway, I'm sure the judge will love your video. Come get the camera and then film your mom tomorrow. I'll edit it for you on Sunday night, and you'll have it on time for court Tuesday."

She smiled. "Okay. I'll ask Celine if I can come over."

Red hung up and hurried downstairs. Her foster mother was sitting in the chair by the library window, wrapped in her favorite sweater and staring out at the darkening sky.

"Can I go to Marvin's?"

Gandalf pushed past her into the room and nuzzled Celine's legs. "It's a little late, hon," Celine said, scratching the dog's ears.

Red glanced at the clock. "It's only six forty-five. Please? It'll be quick. I just need to pick up Marvin's camera. And learn how to use it."

Celine rested her head against the back of the chair. "I don't want to drive right now, sweetie. I really don't feel well."

"I can walk!"

"It's already dark, Red. I don't want you walking."

"Can't Jackson drive me?" She made her face pouty. "Please? I really need to go."

Celine sighed. Gandalf whined softly and lifted a paw to Celine's thigh. "Red . . ."

Red gave Celine the biggest, saddest, most pleading eyes she could. "*Please?* It's really important! It's for my court video."

303

Celine pinched the bridge of her nose. "Jackson's in the barn. Go ask him to drive you."

Marvin only had a thousand instructions for her to follow on how to use the camera. Red nodded as he talked, showing her all the buttons and explaining the best way to frame a shot, but she knew she wouldn't remember it all. By the time she wandered back into the Kapules' living room to tell Jackson she was ready to go, her head was buzzing.

As they pulled into their driveway again, Jackson ruffled Red's hair.

"I'm proud of you, kiddo," he said.

She grinned, swatting his hand away. "Why?"

He put the car into park in front of their house and turned to face her. "For making this video. Sometimes it takes a lot of courage to tell the truth about what you want."

Red was glad it was too dark for Jackson to see her face. The truth was, she didn't know what she wanted anymore. Even though her mom kept promising she was okay, Red couldn't forget that little baggie of pills. But she also couldn't forget what cancer had done to Gamma. She couldn't watch that happen to Celine, too.

Gandalf greeted them at the front door with a loud, urgent bark. Jackson frowned when she wouldn't let him pet her.

"What's wrong?" he asked the dog.

The other dogs were there, too, equally anxious. Jackson eyed them, then called for Celine. Her voice answered weakly from upstairs. Jackson took the steps two at a time, Red right behind him, her heart thundering.

They found Celine in her bathroom. She was on the floor, her back against the bathtub. Her face was white and gleaming with sweat. Red could smell that she'd been sick.

Celine cringed when Jackson touched her shoulder.

"What happened?" he asked.

She shook her head. "I'm okay."

He pressed his hand to her face. "You aren't. You're burning up."

Red's entire body trembled as he took Celine's pulse. *Gamma sleeping on the bathroom floor after chemo. Gamma's face as white as the side of the bathtub.*

"We're taking you to the ER," Jackson said.

"I'm fine," Celine argued feebly.

"You're not." He turned to Red. "Call the Kapules. Tell them we're going to the hospital. Ask Mr. Kapule to take care of the animals. Then meet us in the car."

Red nodded, too scared to speak. She hurried from the room, dodging the anxious dogs, and did as she was told. Marvin's mom assured her that Mr. Kapule would be right over.

Celine got sick twice during the car ride. Red leaned forward and held her hair back as she vomited into a bucket Jackson had brought along, just in case. Her skin was hot under Red's fingers.

They didn't have to wait long when they got to the hospital. The minute Jackson told the nurse about Celine's cancer and how sick she was, they rushed her through the double doors to somewhere Red didn't want to follow. Instead, she stayed in the waiting area even when the nurse came to escort Jackson to wherever Celine was a while later. Red didn't want to go. She couldn't. She couldn't see Celine hooked up to machines. She couldn't listen to the sharp *bleep* of another heart monitor, knowing that each chirp might be counting down to a last, long wail.

Chapter
52

By the time Jackson and Red pulled into the driveway again many hours later, the eastern horizon was the deep burning crimson of near-dawn.

Jackson turned off the car and dragged a hand across his face. "Thank you." His voice was as dry as sand.

Red's eyes ached with exhaustion, and she could barely keep them open. "What for?"

He squeezed her knee gently. "I'm so glad you were with me tonight." His dark eyes were bloodshot from lack of sleep. "I know it was scary, but you were really brave."

She looked away.

Inside, Gandalf and the other dogs wuffed and pressed their noses into Jackson's legs and licked Red's arms.

Red jumped when Mr. Kapule stood up in the dark living room. She hadn't seen him sleeping in Jackson's recliner.

"Kai," Jackson said. "Thank you."

"How is she?" Mr. Kapule asked.

"Stable. Resting. It's an infection, so she's on major antibiotics. They'll run more tests tomorrow."

Mr. Kapule and Jackson hugged in that back-slapping way men sometimes did, and Mr. Kapule squeezed Red's shoulder before he left.

Red's dreams were chaotic and tense. When she woke, Mrs. Kapule was in the kitchen, making something that smelled both sweet and spicy.

"Good morning, Red." Mrs. Kapule gave her a hug and kissed the top of her head. "How are you feeling?"

Red looked around, confused. "What time is it? Where's Jackson? Is Celine okay?"

Mrs. Kapule shushed her. "Celine is okay. Don't worry. Jackson is with her at the hospital."

"What time is it?" Red asked again. She sank her fingers into the soft fur of Gandalf's ears. The other dogs were barking and chasing one another in the backyard.

"It's almost three."

"But my mom! I was supposed to see her."

Mrs. Kapule looked apologetic. "Jackson had Ms. Anders cancel. I'm sorry, Red. He thought you might be too tired today."

Red rubbed her eyes, the initial panic draining away. She really was tired.

"I just got off the phone with Marvin. His grandfather is bringing him over soon." Mrs. Kapule gently guided Red toward the table and pulled out a chair for her. "Do you want breakfast? Or something more like lunch?"

"Can I have oatmeal?"

Mrs. Kapule smiled. "Of course you can."

An hour later, Red and Marvin were in the barn, visiting Tuck. All around them, bits of straw rustled and skittered across the barn floor. Red's wind had been stirring ever since she woke up, and no matter what she did, it wouldn't quit. She'd hoped being with Tuck would help. The tortoise usually made her feel steady again. But so far, no luck.

Marvin hopped off the stack of hay bales and offered Tuck a limp piece of lettuce. "So . . . do you still want to finish the video?"

Tears flooded Red's eyes. Sighing, she dropped her head back against Tuck's shell. "I don't think there's time," she confessed. "My visit with Mom today was canceled. The hearing is in three days."

Marvin shook his head. "We could change the ending. Instead of filming you giving the notebook to your mom, we could just film the notebook. Keep it simple. And you can talk about what you want."

A shaft of golden light angled into the barn through

one of the high windows, bathing the beams of the ceiling in warm color behind Marvin's head. His brow was furrowed and he gazed at her with serious eyes. Even his dimples were gone.

"I don't know." Red's head ached and worry still knotted in her stomach. "The whole thing just seems dumb now."

"No way," he said. "It's a good video, Red. *Really* good. Even if the end is different than how you pictured it, I think the judge will really like it."

She sighed. "Everything feels impossible." Tears of exhaustion burned her eyes.

Marvin set a hand on her shoulder. "It always *seems* impossible," he said.

He nudged her gently until she gave him a small smile and said, "Until it's done."

When they went back into the house a few hours later, Jackson was home and sitting at the kitchen table with Mrs. Kapule and Mr. Makani, Marvin's grandfather.

"There's my girl," Jackson said. He held out an arm and Red stepped into it, wrapping her own arm around his neck in a hug. "What are you two up to out there?"

"Just finishing a project," Marvin answered. He took a handful of popcorn from the bowl on the table.

"How's Celine?" Red asked.

Jackson's head bobbed in a slow nod. "Better. She's on

IV antibiotics, and she's still tired. But the fever is gone. She misses you." He gave her another little squeeze.

"Will this be a setback? For her surgery?" Mrs. Kapule asked.

"I'm supposed to update her doctor in Texas tomorrow, but I'm guessing her surgery will be delayed."

Marvin's grandfather took a sip from his mug of tea. "Will she need chemo?"

"During surgery, they'll remove any organs they can that the cancer has touched. Then they'll do a chemo wash, which is basically what it sounds like. They rinse the inside of her entire abdomen and all her remaining organs with a liquid chemo. She only gets that one dose of chemo, which is good. It's different than other cancer treatments that way. But it's a major surgery, and the recovery is long and hard."

As Jackson spoke, Red lowered herself into a chair. Limerick, Frodo, and Brontë sniffed her shoes under the table, and Gandalf stuck her enormous head in Red's lap. She barely noticed. The idea of Celine's insides being removed or washed down with chemo—which Gamma always called poison—made her stomach turn.

Mrs. Kapule wiped her eyes, and Mr. Makani reached over and took her hand.

"This is all so unbelievable," she said.

Jackson nodded. "I'm still reeling. Cee is handling it

all so well, but . . ." His voice broke and he shook his head.

The urge to run rose up in Red.

Jackson cleared his throat and rubbed his eyes. "They said she'll probably have all the same side effects of common chemotherapy. Hair loss, nausea. All that."

Red bit her lip so hard she tasted blood. Sweat trickled between her shoulder blades and down her back, and her heart started hammering against her ribs.

Gamma crying as her hair fell out in chunks. The endless days of nausea, and the way her eyes sank deeper into her head. Her papery skin covered in an angry rash.

"Red?"

Jackson's voice startled her. She opened her eyes and realized they were all staring at her.

"Are you okay, kiddo?"

She shook her head, then nodded. The chair squealed when she stood up, making the dogs jump. "I'm going for a walk," she said.

Jackson frowned. "Want company?"

"No. No, I'm okay."

She turned from their concerned faces and headed for the door, Gandalf at her heels.

Chapter 53

Darkness had fallen in earnest, and Red was glad she still had a small flashlight in her coat pocket for barn chores. When she dug it out, something crinkled against her fingers. She pulled out a crumpled envelope. Shining the light on it as she walked, she saw her mother's name and address. It was the envelope that had blown into her face when she was in Wanda's car a few weeks ago. She didn't even remember putting it in her pocket.

Gandalf trotted along beside her. The farther they got from the house, the slower Red's heart beat. Cold air made her lungs ache, but at least she could breathe again.

Her feet took her to the stargazing rock without her even thinking about it. She stretched out across the rock's smooth face under the black velvet sky. With her head on Gandalf's warm flank, Red stared up at the heavens. The stars were so bright, they looked alive. Icy-blue, canary-yellow, even pinkish stars glinted down at her. She closed her eyes and listened for their music.

But all she heard was the wind rustling the grass.

It was Celine who made the stars sing, not Red.

She wanted everything to go back to the way it was that first night she and Celine had come to the stargazing rock. She wanted star-music and the smell of snow and the comfort of Celine's warm, steady presence next to her. She wanted the cancer in Celine's belly to disappear without leaving any scars.

"It's not fair," she whispered.

The stars didn't respond.

"It's not fair!" she said more loudly.

Still, the stars said nothing.

"You were supposed to take care of her!" Her voice rose, stretched thin. "You're supposed to protect her!"

Gandalf lifted her head. The tears were back, sliding down the sides of Red's face. A sob built in her chest, breaking out of her in a strangled gasp.

"She needs you!" she cried. "She *needs* you!"

Overhead, a single star trembled, then broke free from the dark. Red watched it fall in a long, smooth arc.

She imagined reaching out and plucking it like a jewel from the sky, carrying it to Celine. It would sing, and Red would dance, and together they'd make the cancer vanish.

As her eyes adjusted, she saw that dark, empty scar across the sky again. It was strange, but she felt like she understood those starless spots. Like they were made by something familiar, something that swirled through her own heart.

The sky-scar curved over Pleiades, Celine's favorite constellation. The Seven Sisters of Pleiades winked down at her like old friends.

Red sat up. She couldn't look at it anymore—the silent sky with its shadow of sadness. She needed someone to tell her it was going to be okay.

She needed a mother.

Jackson was alone in the kitchen when she got inside. He was in a clean shirt and smelled like he'd taken a shower. The fresh spice of his soap tickled her nose when he offered her a cup of hot chocolate.

"Have a good walk?" he asked.

She nodded and blew into her mug. "Is it okay for me to call my mom?"

He glanced at the clock on the stove. "It's almost nine."

"I just want to talk to her. I miss her."

His smile was wistful. "I can understand that. Sure, kiddo. You can go into the library if you want."

She gave him an appreciative smile. Taking her cocoa

and the cordless phone, she went into Celine's library and settled on the chair by the window.

Wanda picked up after the first ring. Her hello was high and singsongy.

"Mom?"

Her mother laughed a weird, delirious laugh. "Red!" She laughed again.

Every last pebble of hope in Red's heart tumbled away in a landslide. "Are you okay?"

"Me? I'm great, baby. I'm greaaat." She stretched out the second *great* like taffy.

Ice sliced through Red's veins.

"Why do you sound weird?" Red asked. *Please, no. Not again. Not* now*!*

"Weird? I don't sound weird!" Her mom giggled. "You kinda do, though. Hey, what time is it? You should be in bed, young lady!"

Hot, angry tears spilled down Red's cheeks, dripping off her chin. *No no no no no.* How could she do this? She'd promised!

"Mom." Red lowered her voice and hoped Jackson wasn't listening at the door. "What did you do?"

Something clinked and clanged in the background on Wanda's end of the phone. "Nothing. Relax!"

She wanted to scream, *You promised!* She wanted to rage and cry. "Mom, your court date is this Tuesday!"

Wanda sighed, then giggled again. She couldn't seem

to stop giggling. "It's no big deal." Her words slurred together. "I didna do anything *bad*, Red. I jus' took something for my *migraines*." A snorting laugh bubbled through her sinuses.

Red closed her eyes. Her hair was whipping against her face and snarling around the phone. The whole library started to rattle, softly but urgently. Wanda giggled again, the sound hollow and tinny and far away.

"You promised," Red whispered.

Her mother was laughing at something or someone in the background. "Gotta go, Red. Night night, baby cakes! *Mwah mwah mwah!*"

The line went dead.

get on with my life.
But living without something I need this much? It's
impossible.

In 1945, a farmer chopped off the head of
one of his chickens. He didn't do a very good
job though. Because the chicken didn't die!
They called him Mike the Headless Chicken,
and he lived for two whole years after losing
his head. He even traveled the United States
and got really famous. People paid twenty-
five cents to see him walking around, pecking
at the ground like a normal chicken—except
he didn't have a beak or a face or eyes or a
head!

Mike the Headless Chicken lived the life of
a celebrity, which was a whole lot better than
being someone's dinner.

So maybe, sometimes, living without
something—even something you really need—isn't
the end. Maybe it's the beginning of something
better.

Chapter
54

"Something on your mind?" Jackson asked.

She stared out the window of his truck. The sky was thick with moody gray clouds, and the weeds along the side of the road whipped back and forth in the wind.

"I'm fine."

"You sure? You've been quiet the past few days." He nudged her gently with his elbow. "I'm a good listener."

"No. It's okay." She couldn't bring herself to look at him.

He sighed, but didn't ask her any more questions as they pulled into the Kapules' driveway to pick up Marvin. When Marvin climbed into the truck, Red slid over on the bench seat so she was between the two of them. Jackson was as solid as a mountain against her left arm, and she wanted to lean in to him and put her head on his shoulder.

But she couldn't. If she did, she might start crying. And if she started crying, she'd end up telling him what she was planning to do.

They were halfway to school before she noticed how quiet Marvin was being. He had his head against the window, and his hands were limp fish in his lap.

"You okay?" she asked.

The truck whistled around them. He shrugged. "Yeah."

When they pulled up to the school, Jackson smiled sadly at the two of them.

"Well, we're a cheerful bunch today, aren't we?" He reached over Red's head and ruffled Marvin's hair, then dropped his arm around her shoulders and gave her a quick hug. "Mrs. Kapule is taking you to their house when she picks you up after school. I'm planning to stay at the hospital with Celine all day, but will come get you around seven. Okay?"

She nodded, afraid her voice would betray her.

Jackson kissed the top of her head, and she started to scoot out of the truck.

"Red?"

She paused and looked at him. An anxious breeze pressed against her skin, wanting out, but she held it back.

His gaze was steady. "I love you, kiddo."

Red smiled tightly and slid out of the truck, slamming the door before Jackson could see her heart, shattered into ten thousand pieces.

When Jackson was gone, Red grabbed Marvin's arm and dragged him around the side of the school, behind a clump of evergreens.

"Holy bananas!" he complained, twisting his arm out of her fingers. The look he gave her was so un-Marvin that she almost laughed.

"What's wrong?" she asked.

She expected him to deny anything was wrong, like he had in the truck. But instead, his eyes darted away from hers and he kicked the ground.

"I . . ." He sniffed and wiped his nose with his sleeve. "I'm sorry, Red. I messed up."

"What are you talking about?"

"I was working on your video last night. I wanted it to be perfect. But I—I lost it somehow. I deleted the file. My dad helped me look for it for, like, *hours*, but it's gone." A tear escaped his eye and glistened on his dark lashes before dropping down his cheek.

"Oh."

"I'm really, really sorry!" His voice trembled. "I didn't do it on purpose, Red. I *swear!*"

"I know." She shrugged. "It's okay. Really."

He sniffed again and gave her a dubious look. "You're not mad?"

She shook her head. She was plenty mad, just not at Marvin.

"What are you gonna do? For the judge?"

The sound of her mother's wild laughter rang in her ears and she shook her head again. "I don't know."

"I'll help you. If you want my help, I mean."

She bit her lip, glancing over her shoulder. Mrs. Ward, the fourth-grade teacher, was on Kiss-n-Drop duty, but had her back to them. "I do need help, actually. I need you to cover for me."

"Huh?" He rubbed away his tears with his palms.

"I need you to tell Ms. Bell I'm . . . I don't know. Visiting Celine in the hospital or something."

"Why?" he asked, eyes narrowing.

"Because I—I need to see my mom." There. She'd said it. The trees shivered, and they both hunched their shoulders against the cold. Tiny snowflakes started to fall at an angle.

"Aren't you gonna see her tomorrow?"

Desperation started spinning in Red's chest. She was running out of time. The only bus to Denver was leaving in fifteen minutes. She'd have to run to make it to the bus stop.

"I need to see her *today*. She's—I—I just need to see her."

His eyes searched hers, then his lips turned down in a determined frown. "Okay. As your best friend, I will uphold the Best Friend Code and cover for you."

Red wrapped her arms around his neck. He grunted in surprise, but hugged her back. Hard.

"Will you write me an email? Or letters? I know you like real letters." His voice was muffled in her hair.

She pulled away. "I'm not going *forever*, Marvin. I'll be back by the time school is out."

"I mean, when you go live with her again."

This surprised her. "Oh."

"You have to promise. I don't want to lose my best friend, Red." His voice cracked.

She kicked at the frosty dirt. "You're not losing me, Marvin. I promise."

He grinned. Dimples and all. "Good."

The bell rang. Red jumped and stepped closer to the trees. Marvin started toward the school. She stayed in the shadows to wait until the coast was clear. Suddenly, Marvin turned and ran back to her.

"Red!" he whispered, ducking under a tree branch.

"What?"

"You're my best friend," he said. "So don't make this weird."

"Make *what* weird?"

He gently grabbed the sides of her face and touched his forehead to hers. For a moment, their breath mingled between them in a wisp of cloud. "*Aloha nui loa.*"

Then he was gone.

Chapter
55

Snow was falling harder when Red got off the bus. She tucked her hands under her armpits and slumped into the wind. A man at the bus stop watched her from behind a beard so thick and matted that she could barely see his eyes. She kept her head down and hurried past.

After she'd gotten off the phone with her mom on Saturday night, she sat and stared at nothing for a long time. Then her eyes landed on the little jar of change Celine kept on one of the bookshelves, and she knew what she had to do.

She used Celine's computer to look up the address on the envelope she'd taken from her mom's car. Then she looked up the bus route. Her mom's place was a short walk from a bus stop. Just ten blocks.

Easy.

Her pocket was heavy with the handful of change she had left for the return ride. The bus had taken much longer than she'd planned, though. When the Grooves drove into Denver, it usually took less than an hour, but the bus had made a lot of stops on the way. It had sat for so long at one stop, Red worried she'd gotten on the wrong bus entirely. Now it was just after noon, and a wintry darkness was settling over the city. Long slate clouds hid the sun.

About five blocks from her mom's, Red froze, mouth open in disbelief.

The hospital—Celine's hospital—was staring down at her. She had had no idea it was so close to her mom's apartment. Because of the snow, there weren't many people on the streets, so Red kept her head down and picked up her pace, hoping Jackson and Celine wouldn't look out a window and see her.

She kept walking, past a car dealership that was out of business. Its empty parking lot spread down one long block like a huge, gaping wound. The buildings on either side of it looked closed, too, with boarded windows and metal gates over the doors. It seemed like nothing was alive on these blocks.

A streetlamp blinked on overhead. Wind moaned through the pine trees above her. She shivered and picked up her pace.

Finally, she saw Wanda's car parked under a blue spruce in front of a beige-brick apartment building. Relief trilled through her, then vanished into the fist of anxiety in her chest. Shaking the snow from her hair, she climbed the metal stairs and knocked on her mother's door. Even with it closed, Red could smell cigarette smoke and hear tinny TV voices.

Footsteps. A quick, dry cough. The door opened. Wanda was barefoot, in leggings and an orange Broncos sweatshirt. Her hair was tangled and plum circles cradled her eyes. It took her a moment to recognize Red.

"What are you doing here?" The coldness of her mother's greeting stung more than the snow.

"I wanted to check on you," Red said.

Wanda crossed her arms. "Check on me? Why?"

"You sounded weird on the phone the other night."

Her mother looked confused. "The phone?" The wind picked up, whipping Wanda's hair back. "Hurry up and come in. I'm freezing."

Red followed Wanda inside, her heart sinking with each step. The living room was chaos. Dirty dishes, discarded cups. Clothes slung over the back of the couch. There was a haze of smoke glowing in the light of the television. Wanda draped herself onto the couch and reached for a can of soda, slurped, and swallowed.

Red's skin prickled.

"Well, sit down or something. You're making me nervous."

Red obeyed. She slipped off her backpack, relocated a stack of mail from a chair, and sat, pulling her knees up under her chin. Wanda was constant motion. Her fingers picked at hangnails on her thumbs. Her feet wiggled. Even her eyes were restless, darting around the room, bouncing off Red, off the TV, off anything they landed on.

Red swallowed a lump of thunderclouds in her throat. "What are you watching?"

"*Wife Wars*."

"Oh."

Red suddenly missed Gamma with such ferocity her teeth ached.

"Should I sell tickets?"

Red blinked. "What?"

Wanda still wasn't looking at her. "You're staring at me. Should I sell tickets to my face or something?"

"No. Sorry."

How could her mother let herself get like this again? She'd been doing well! She had a job, she'd been following the rules—mostly.

Wanda dug a piece of candy out of a bag on the coffee table. The crinkle of the wrapper filled the space between them. Heat was building in Red's chest. She chewed her lip, biting it hard enough to make her eyes water.

"I—I'm worried about you," she said.

"I'm fine, Red."

Red looked around the room. "Aren't you afraid they'll see?"

"Afraid who will see what?"

"This!" She gestured to the mess. "Aren't you afraid they'll do a home visit and see how bad it looks?"

Her mom rolled her eyes. "Relax, Red. Nobody is coming."

"What about tomorrow?"

"What about it?" Wanda took another slurp from the can of soda.

Frustration boiled over and Red jumped to her feet. "*Your court date!*" she hollered. "Don't you even *care*?"

Wanda stared at her and Red saw something in her expression—a fragility that made her pulse quicken with hope. For an instant, her mother wasn't this woman on the couch with sweat stains on the neck of her shirt and a tremor in her hands. Instead, she was the mother who climbed the fence of a hotel pool on a blistering-hot summer day. She was the mother who taught Red to stand close to the movie theater screen as the end credits scrolled and throw her hands into the air, looking up at the rising stream of words. *We're falling!* That mother giggled, and Red squealed with glee.

She saw, in that moment, the mother she always wanted.

Wanda cleared her throat. Her face hardened again. "Hey, do you want pizza? I want pizza." She stood, wiping her hands on her leggings, and walked into the kitchen. The windows rattled, pellets of snow tinking against the glass.

Red pursued her. "Did you hear me? Court is *tomorrow*, Mom."

Wanda batted her words away with a wrist flick. "I want olives on it. No arguments."

"Mom!"

"How about veggie? Vegetables are so much healthier than meat."

"Mom, *listen to me!*"

Wanda stopped. Turned. Folded her arms. Red folded hers as well and stood her ground.

"What do you expect me to say, Red? Of *course* I remember that court is tomorrow. My whole *life* revolves around court dates and social workers and freaking *rules!*"

"Only until the judge lets us live together again."

Wanda laughed a hard, cold laugh. "You *really* think that's gonna happen? You really think a judge is gonna look at me"—she gestured to her disheveled outfit—"a woman whose *own mother* took her kid away because I couldn't keep my act together, and think I am a qualified parent? You think any judge in their right mind believes for one second that I'll hold a job and stay in line and drive my kid to soccer practice and go to PTA meetings? It's *impossible*, Red!"

Red shook her head. "No! It always seems—"

Wanda roared, and a hot gust knocked Red backward. "Aaaghh! If you say that stupid Gamma quote *one more time*, Red, I *swear*, I'll lose it!" She stomped toward her and stood so close, Red could smell her stale breath. "Sometimes things seem impossible because *they are*. They just *are*! The sooner you figure that out, the better off you'll be!"

Wanda turned away and grabbed her purse off the counter. She dug through it, then shoved it aside in frustration. "Where is my phone?"

Red closed her eyes, clenching her fists to hold back her storm. She tried to remember the mother whose wind kept her kite aloft. The mother who helped her dance sleepy polar bears into life. The one who loved her *infinity plus one*.

"I just want my mom." Her voice was small and fragile.

Wanda paused, closed her eyes. Then she started shuffling papers and magazines again. "*I* just want my phone."

Tears filled Red's eyes, but she didn't want Wanda to see them. She spun around and ran to the bathroom, slamming the thin door as hard as she could. A little framed picture of a butterfly fell off the wall and clattered behind the sink. She kicked the door, then the side of the tub. Her frustration billowed from her skin, lifting her hair and shivering against the shower curtain. Outside, the wind growled and the sky churned. The clouds were as angry and bruised as the girl in the bathroom.

Chapter
56

A buzzing sound made Red jump. She knelt and peered behind the sink, moving the fallen butterfly picture. Wedged between the sink pedestal and the wall was her mom's phone. Its screen cast a little rectangle of light against the floor. She pulled it out and read the text.

MESSAGE FROM RICKY: U coming over??

Red sank to the edge of the tub and stared at the phone. Her mother's promises tumbled, one after another, onto the floor around her feet.

She stood and opened the mirrored cabinet above the sink, knowing full well what she'd find.

More broken promises.

One by one, she took the pill bottles from the cabinet, read the labels, opened them. The pills stared up at her. How could something so small do so much damage?

Wind sliced through Red's heart. It wanted to explode from her chest. It wanted to rattle the whole world, obliterate the stars. It wanted to consume every happy memory, every good thing.

And Red wanted to let it.

Her mom—the mom whose breezes comforted her, cooled her raw skin, made her feel protected, safe—that mom was gone. It was like she'd swallowed so many pills that they'd swallowed her.

A heavy, cold sense of understanding pressed against Red's heart. It was time to jump to conclusions.

U coming over??

Red wanted to throw the phone into the toilet and flush Ricky out of her mother's life forever. But Ricky wasn't the problem. Not really.

Slowly, she tipped each bottle over the sink. The pills fell like pebbles, snickering against the sink's stained surface. White ovals. Little round yellow ones. Pills as thick as Red's pinkie. She turned on the faucet and let the water wash them all down the open drain.

Red picked up her mom's phone again.

She thought of Gamma, and the notebook that was

now filled with possibilities. She thought of Celine's words the night they'd searched for Tuck. *Love can do impossible things.*

She hoped that was true. Because what she needed to do now felt like the most impossible thing in the world.

Chapter
57

"I found your phone."

Wanda was lifting the pillows off her bed, searching. Dropping them, she snatched the phone from Red's hand, eyes glued to the screen as she walked back into the kitchen.

"Mom?"

Wanda didn't look at her. "What?"

"I'm sorry."

"What for?" she asked, her tone impatient.

"I'm sorry for making you mad. About court and stuff."

Wanda sighed and leaned against the counter, pulling her tangled hair around one side of her head. "Whatever. It's fine." She bit her lip, then continued. "I'm sorry, too.

For what it's worth. I know you expect a lot from me. It just—sometimes, you expect too much."

The branches of the giant spruce outside the window began to tap on the glass. Snow streaked sideways under the light across the street as the sky continued to darken with thick, ash-gray clouds.

"No, I don't," Red said.

Wanda huffed a humorless laugh. "News flash, Red. *Everybody* expects too much. That's how the world works! We go around expecting things from each other, and when we don't get them, we whine about it."

Something metallic banged outside, and they both jumped. Wanda peered out the window, frowning. A trash can had fallen over and been pushed into the street by the wind. As she turned back to Red, Wanda's frown deepened. She examined Red's face, her eyes narrowed with suspicion.

"What's going on?" she asked.

Red began to shake. Wanda came forward a few steps, her head cocked slightly to one side.

"Red? Did you do something?"

Red said nothing.

"You're hiding something, aren't you?" She pointed out the window, toward the whipping branches of the blue spruce, like that told her everything she needed to know.

Nervous whispers lighted from Red's skin, dancing

in her hair and around her ankles. Red pulled in a slow breath and set an empty pill bottle on the counter.

"I called Ms. Anders," she said.

Wanda's eyes locked on the bottle. The air suddenly went thick and dangerously still, pressing down on Red so heavily her knees almost buckled.

"You *what*?"

Red's mouth gaped. Her own storm, the one she'd been struggling to keep inside, pulsed and throbbed against her ribs.

"I called Ms. Anders."

Wanda's mass of solid air lifted, and Red's own wind came rushing out of her as she coughed. It scooped up bits of trash like dead leaves. Dishes vibrated in the sink. Lights flickered.

Wanda looked around wildly. "Are you insane? I didn't invite you over here, Red! You just showed up! And now you called your *social worker*? Do you realize what you've done?"

She stormed past Red into the living room and yanked back the thrashing curtains. The street outside was deserted and quickly being buried in drifting snow.

Wanda turned to face her again. "Do you *want* me to get busted? You realize they'll never consider giving me custody now, right? I could go to jail again! Is that what you wanted?"

Red shook her head. Her eyes burned and her whole

337

body ached with the effort of keeping her tornado inside. "No! I don't want you to get in trouble!"

"Well, that's what's gonna happen. I hope you're happy!"

"I'm not!" Red sobbed.

Her mother crossed to her again, her face inches from Red's. "Congratulations, Red. You're officially gonna be a foster kid forever."

Wanda stepped back, her fingers gripping her dirty hair. A chair squealed dully across the kitchen floor and paper flew like confetti through the air. The television rocked on top of its table, threatening to topple forward. A clap of thunder shook the entire apartment building. The tornado pounded against Red's ribs. She whimpered.

Wanda looked at the angry, churning room, then back at Red. "I don't have to stay here for this."

"Wait!" Red chased her toward the door, but her mom shook her off.

Red stood for a moment, paralyzed by the mess she'd made of things. This wasn't what she wanted! She didn't want her mom to go to jail again, or to get in trouble at all. The only thing she wanted was for her mom to be okay, for them *both* to be okay.

Red spun around and dashed across the room, picking up her backpack. *The notebook*. If she could show it to her, get her to understand . . .

Slinging her backpack over her shoulder, she followed her mother, running out into the storm. But when she got down into the parking lot, her mother charged back toward her.

"Look what you did!" she screamed, gesturing behind her.

A tree branch as long as a dining table had fallen onto Wanda's car. The windshield was a spiderweb of glass. "How could you do this to me?" Wanda shrieked. "Do you hate me? Is that it?"

Red scrabbled for the notebook in her backpack. She held it out for her mother. "I don't hate you! Look, I proved almost everything!"

Wanda barely glanced at the notebook. "What are you talking about?"

"All the impossible things, Mom! I proved everything Gamma wrote. And—" Red turned to the page where she'd taped in the pieces of her mother's letter. "I tried to prove everything you wrote, too."

Red held out the notebook. If only her mom could believe, then together they could prove the last three impossible things: *Being a good daughter. Staying sober. Being a mom.*

Wanda pushed the notebook aside and started to turn away. Red grabbed her arm.

"Look! You wrote to Gamma. You said you didn't believe in impossible things. See?" She held the notebook out, but Wanda took half a step back. Red pointed to the words Wanda had written.

"You said it was impossible to live without something you really needed. You said you couldn't be two things at once." She gripped the notebook in both hands, holding it up to her mom's face. "You said you couldn't get back the things you lost. Look, Mom! *Look!*"

Wanda was staring at the notebook now, at the tatters of her own words.

Red came closer, shouting over the storm. "I know you think you're alone. I saw you tear up that letter and blow it away. But you aren't alone, Mom. You have me! I found the pieces of your letter. And I put them here."

She turned the pages, holding them down in the wind. Snow bit into her cheeks like needles, but she ignored it. Her mother stared at the notebook, her face expressionless.

"Gamma wrote down a bunch of things people thought were impossible," Red continued. "She wrote them all down, and then we started finding out how they *weren't* impossible. She said there's a difference between *hard* and *impossible*, and she wanted me to know it. She wanted me to remind you!"

Wanda touched the notebook. Her fingers were trembling.

"There wasn't time to finish them all. Not with

Gamma. But I did it, Mom. I found answers to everything she wrote. For you."

Her mom's eyes narrowed.

"You've just gotta believe, Mom. If you believe it, then the things you wrote won't be impossible anymore." She turned back to the taped bits of paper and pointed.

"See these last three? These are the ones you have to help me prove. I can't do it without you." Red stepped closer, pointing to the largest scrap on the page. "You said being a mom is impossible. But it's not. It's hard, maybe. But I'll be good, Mom. I swear. I'll be so good and easy! I'll be the best kid ever!"

There were tears on Red's cheeks, cold and stinging. "We can do it! We can prove all of your impossible things, too. I know it!"

For a long moment, Wanda stared at the page. The wind was tearing at the edges of the taped papers. But Red wasn't looking at the notebook. Her eyes were locked on her mother's face. Silently, she begged her mom to look at her, to *see* her.

Wanda swatted the notebook aside and it sailed into the snow.

"No!" Red lunged after it, but her mom yanked her back.

"You're just like your grandmother!" Wanda shouted, her face too close to Red's. "But she was wrong about a lot of things, Red. She was wrong about me. And you are, too."

Red shook her head. "No . . ."

She released Red's arm. "You are. It doesn't matter how many things you write down in your stupid notebook. It's time to grow up, Red. It's time to learn that sometimes hard and impossible *are* the same."

She turned, shoulders bowed into the wind, and walked away.

"Mom!"

Red screamed and screamed, but Wanda never looked back. Red watched her disappear into the storm.

Then she opened
her heart and let
the tornado
out.

Chapter
58

It was as if the sun had set, even though it was still mid-afternoon. The darkness of the tornado was somehow absolute, a sponge soaking up every glint of daylight. It snaked down from the clouds, winding through a wall of snowflakes until its hungry lips kissed the pavement.

Movement and chaos.

Roar and rush.

Anger and fury and heartbreak.

Red stood in the middle of the street, looking east, watching her tornado gobble up brick and pavement. Bare trees were pulled from the ground, roots and all, and swept up into the sky. Streetlamps, too, their bulbs flickering, then popping into darkness, tiny fireworks against churning clouds. Sirens wailed as asphalt peeled from the ground. And everywhere, snow—swirling, shifting, slicing.

Around her, the world quaked in the face of her tornado. She'd thought it would hurt to let it out. She'd been afraid of it, of the damage it could do, of its power. But now she stood before it and felt nothing at all.

All the pain inside Red was poured into the wind, leaving her numb.

Gamma dying. Oldest Boy pinching her arm, the hiss of his voice in her ear. The fosters before The Mom, whose names she couldn't even remember, faces she couldn't see.

The tornado was so hungry that it sucked it all up, everything she feared and hated, everything she had never even realized she felt.

Tuck disappearing into the night. The cancer chewing through Celine's belly. Celine sitting limply on the bathroom floor.

Celine.

The image of her foster mother's face broke through the numbness, and she stumbled back. She saw her tornado tearing down the street, away from her.

Straight toward the hospital.

Red lurched to her feet, then stumbled again. Broken asphalt tore the skin of her knees, even through her jeans. She looked up at the vortex. The twisting cloud had swollen. It gorged itself on the street and empty buildings before her, growing in fury and speed. The

hospital was blocks away. There was so much fuel between here and there.

It will kill them.

The thought rocketed her forward. *My tornado will
kill them!*

Ignoring the pain in her knees, Red ran toward the
funnel cloud. Debris from gnarled cars and buildings
careened toward her head, but she ducked and dodged,
chasing after the wind. She tried to lasso it in her mind,
but it was out of her control now. She couldn't pull it
back no matter how hard she tried.

A tree crashed in front of her, and she scrambled over
it, the branches tearing at her face. There was no catching up! She screamed in desperation.

A car horn bellowed, long and insistent. Red turned
toward the sound. The horn pounded out a quick rhythm,
and Red finally found the source. A black sedan was at
the corner half a block behind her. She could see a tiny
angel swinging wildly from the rearview mirror.

She ran, leaping over the chewed remains of the
street. Ms. Anders opened the passenger-side door from
the driver's seat. "Hurry!"

Red climbed inside. Shutting the door was like turning
down the volume on a too-loud TV. Ms. Anders yanked
the wheel to the left, spinning the car in a tight circle.

"Is this yours?" she asked Red.

Red was too stunned by the question to form an answer.

"*Is it?*" her caseworker asked, looking at her. The car bounced over a curb as she took a turn.

"Y-yes. How did you know?"

Ms. Anders looked grim. "I've wondered. Colorado is never so windy as when you've got trouble brewing."

"I have to go back! I have to stop it!" Panic overtook Red's temporary shock. "It's headed for the hospital!"

The engine roared. "Red—"

"CELINE AND JACKSON ARE THERE!"

Ms. Anders shook her head, but it didn't look like a no. Not really.

"You can stop it?" she asked.

"I have to!"

Red's elbow cracked against the car door as Ms. Anders took another sharp turn. They were heading back into the storm down another street, one that ran parallel to the road her tornado was eating up.

The caseworker muttered as she floored the gas. "You better not be out of whatever magic you got in you, baby girl."

The tornado was carving its mark into the asphalt and abandoned businesses of Wanda's neighborhood. Red couldn't see it, but she could feel it. All she saw were the dark, vicious clouds above her, and the outlines of old brick houses along the street they were driving. Yellow light from streetlamps illuminated the car in quick flashes as Ms. Anders raced through the neighborhood.

People stood outside their homes, looking up into the flurry of snowflakes. They could no doubt hear it, but who would possibly believe that a tornado had touched down in Denver on a February afternoon?

Get back inside, Red thought. Her heart lurched and twisted, the tether between it and her tornado growing tighter the closer she got.

"Go past it!" she said. "I can't pull it back. I have to get in front!"

Ms. Anders didn't question her. She started praying out loud as her car barreled through another intersection.

"Oh, please don't let anyone be coming!" She scrunched her shoulders toward her ears until they were through the intersection, then blew out a string of, *Thank you thank you thank you.*

The invisible line in Red's heart snapped taut. "Here!" she screamed. "Turn here!"

Ms. Anders—God bless her—didn't hesitate. Tires squealed as they turned. The headlights of cars fleeing the twister blinded Red for a moment. But she knew they were close. The trees were frenzied. Ms. Anders braked hard, pulling to the side of the road at the north corner of the street.

"Go on, Red! I'll be right here if you need me!" Ms. Anders shouted. Red wanted to hug her. Instead, she got out and ran as fast as she could toward the storm.

Chapter
59

She didn't have a plan. She had no idea how to stop the sky from turning her world to dust. But she had to try.

The wind almost lifted her off the ground as she ran. She skidded to a stop in the middle of Colfax Avenue, the hospital half a block behind her. Aside from Ms. Anders's sedan, there were no other cars. Red didn't see anything other than the churning mass of cloud and snow and wind.

Her heart beat wildly. It felt like an invisible rope was squeezing it, prying it through her ribs toward the tornado. She knew the storm had come from inside of her, but now it felt like the storm was pulling *her* into *it*.

"No!" she said, gritting her teeth. She dug her heels into the street. "You can't have me or them!"

She stared down the sky as it reached for her. In it, she could see and feel and taste her anger. It throbbed like a heartbeat. *I'm yours*, the tornado hissed.

Snow blurred beneath the flickering streetlights.

I'm yours. It sizzled and crackled.

Red was puny compared to the vortex. What could she possibly do to stop it?

"I don't need you! I don't want you anymore!"

The wind seemed to laugh.

Asphalt shuddered beneath her feet and darkness closed in around her, as thick and dangerous as the black lava of a volcano. *You belong to me*, the wind shrieked.

"I don't." She clenched her fists. "*I don't!*"

But the wind was hungry. It pulled her toward its dark mouth.

"No! I'm not yours!"

Her voice shattered. She wasn't strong enough. How could she be? She was just one girl. A child. A child whose mother had walked away. Despair overcame her, flooding the open wound the tornado had left in her heart. The storm's rage roared in her ears and she fell to her knees.

Then, behind the howling, Red heard a faint, clear chime. Like the voice of a bell, soft and sweet. She looked up, ears straining. There it was again! A bright, warm ringing. The song of a violin. The trill of a flute.

Red knew that sound.

Standing, she searched the sky.

And she saw them.

Pleiades. The Seven Sisters shone down on her, their light cutting a near-perfect circle through the roiling black clouds. The air immediately around her warmed. She leaned in to listen. The stars spun their song around the wind. Their music was warm and rich and full. Fuller even than Beethoven's symphonies.

And Red understood.

She had been wrong about Gamma. The notebook wasn't Gamma's way of reminding Red to take care of her mom. The notebook was Gamma's way of reminding Red to take care of herself.

Her mother was broken. She knew that. Red was broken, too. Everybody was. But Red believed something that her mother didn't: being broken didn't make happiness impossible. Harder, sometimes. But not impossible.

Red knew something else now, too. Brokenness wasn't the end.

It could be the start of something better.

"Love can do impossible things," she whispered.

The star-song crescendoed in response.

Tears streaming down her face, Red lifted her arms above her head and started to dance.

She twirled and hopped and glided. Dipped and

waltzed and spun. She danced for Gamma, for Celine and Jackson and Ms. Anders and Marvin and Gandalf and Tuck. For her mother. The music of the stars ribboned around her, illuminating her as she danced the whole world—*her* whole world—into life.

Chapter
60

The flashing lights of police cars and fire trucks bounced off the brick exterior of the hospital and the jagged glass of broken windows across the street. People milled around, taking pictures on their phones.

The worst damage had been done to the abandoned car dealership. Its building was a pile of rubble, and the street had been torn up for several blocks. Trees lay across it like an enormous game of pick-up-sticks. A fire hydrant was still spewing a jet of water into the air.

The news said they were lucky—the freak storm hadn't hit in a very populated area. Red didn't feel lucky. She felt sick.

But things could have been a lot worse.

Ms. Anders had brought her up to Celine's hospital

room shortly after the storm fell silent and told her to stay put. Red watched the activity from the window while Celine slept. She could see two police officers talking with Ms. Anders by the open back end of an ambulance, taking notes and shaking their heads, as if they couldn't believe what they were hearing. If Ms. Anders was telling them the truth—the whole, real, gigantic truth—then Red couldn't blame them for disbelieving.

"There's my girl."

Red startled and turned. Celine was propped up in her bed, blinking sleep from her eyes. She held up a hand and Red walked to her and took it.

"Pretty crazy out there, isn't it?" Celine said.

A lump in Red's throat made it difficult to swallow. She nodded. Lights from the emergency vehicles lit the room in rotations of red, blue, white.

"Did I ever tell you," Celine said, squeezing Red's hand, "about the night the stars fell?"

"No." Red lowered herself onto the bed.

Celine's hair caught the colors of the flashing lights in its web, illuminating her. Her eyes were as bright as moonlight. Even the pale curve of her cheek flushed pink.

Suddenly, Red felt certain that no matter what came—no matter how bad the surgery was, no matter how much cancer they scooped out and washed away with chemo—that Celine would be okay.

She had to be.

"It was the night my son died." Celine paused, and silence hung there between them, as full as the silence after a symphony.

After a while, Celine continued. "I spent my whole life looking up at the stars. They were, I thought, my friends. Their song lived inside of everything I knew. But the night my son . . . that night, everything changed for me. I was so angry. I felt abandoned. By God, by my own faith, by the stars." She took a deep breath. "I left the hospital and drove. I didn't know where I was going. Just drove and drove until I ran out of city light. I was probably halfway to Kansas when I finally pulled over. It was summer. The sky was black as ink. And the stars. They were so big.

"I got out of my car and started walking. I even climbed over a barbed-wire fence without realizing it. Tore a hole in my jeans. I went out into this field. Rage and grief were bottled up inside of me, like every drop of blood was angry. I wanted to explode."

Celine's eyes had gone glassy with the memory. Red didn't move.

"And so I did. I screamed and cried and yelled. I looked up at the stars and sent all my rage and pain at them like a fire hose. I blasted them." She sniffed and shook her head, the tiniest of smiles on her lips. Red stared at that smile, wondering how it could possibly exist.

"You remember when you first arrived," Celine said,

"that day Jackson power-washed the side of the barn? The jet of water from the compressor blasted away all the muck and peeled off the stains?"

Red nodded.

"Well, that's kind of what I did to the stars that night. The stream of my grief just pummeled them right out of the sky. I watched them snap off the black like leaves off a tree, and they tumbled down all around me. They fell like sparkling rain into the field, fading into darkness where they landed."

"What did you do?"

"I stopped. I had to. I saw those stars falling, one by one, and I knew I'd black out the sky with my rage. I could have taken down the whole universe, Red, I assure you. I was that mad.

"But as I stood in that glittering star-storm, I suddenly realized that I would never hear the stars sing again if I let my anger destroy them. I was hurting so deeply. But my love for the stars, for their music, saved me."

Red thought of the gnarled street just outside the window. "You weren't sad anymore?"

Celine shook her head. "Oh, no. I was sad. My rage was spent, but my grief wasn't. Grief isn't like anger. Anger can burn out. It can be released. But grief is something that becomes a part of you. And you either grow comfortable with it and learn how to live your life in a new way, or you get stuck in it, and it destroys you."

"Did the stars come back?" Red asked.

Celine sighed. "No. They were gone. Anger tends to leave a scar. Even in the sky."

Red's anger had left a scar down Colfax Avenue. And in her own heart as well.

"Thank you," Red said a moment later.

"What for?"

"You sent Pleiades to sing for me."

Celine smiled. "The music was already inside you, Red. All I did was teach you to listen." She brushed her fingers across Red's cheek. "I'm proud of you."

"Why?" Red asked, voice cracking.

"You did something amazing today."

Red wiped her nose with the back of her hand. "The tornado?"

"No." Celine sat up more and looked toward the window. "Although that *was* amazing. I mean, calling Ms. Anders. Telling her where you were."

Red looked up at her, surprised. "How—?"

"Ms. Anders called us the second she got off the phone with you. We were frantic when we found out you didn't go to school, and had already been in contact with her."

"I'm sorry," Red said, shame flooding her. "I shouldn't have run off like that."

Celine shook her head. "No. You shouldn't have. But I understand why you did, I think."

"You do?"

"You love your mom," she said. "And sometimes love makes us break rules, doesn't it?"

Tears blurred her vision, and Red blinked, letting them slip down her cheeks. Celine pulled her onto the bed next to her, wrapping her arms around Red's shoulders.

When she finally found her voice again, Red asked the question that scared her most. "Who's gonna take care of me?"

A surprised laugh bubbled from Celine's chest and she lifted Red's chin to look into her eyes. "Red! Oh, my girl! *We're* going to take care of you! You hear me? We aren't going anywhere. Not without you."

Chapter
61

When Red walked with Celine and Jackson into court the next day, she was surprised to see that her mother was there. Ms. Anders and Wanda each stood with a different lawyer near the front of the small room.

Ms. Anders came over to the three of them and spoke in a hushed voice. "I'm glad you all could make it. How are you feeling?" she asked Celine.

Celine nodded. "Okay. I told them I wouldn't miss today." She squeezed Red's hand.

The caseworker explained what would happen once the judge came in. Red mostly didn't hear her. Her eyes kept landing on Wanda, who stood with her back to Red and her head down.

"I gave your letter to the judge already, Red," Ms. Anders said.

The night before, while still at the hospital, Red had written to tell the judge what she wanted. She said how much she loved her mom, how she wanted her mom to get better and be okay. She said that being in foster care was really hard, and that what she wanted most in the world was to be part of a family. A real family.

And then she said that she wanted to live with Celine and Jackson.

I used to think it was impossible to love strangers as much as I love my mom, she wrote. *But now I know that, with love, nothing is impossible.*

Ms. Anders told them to sit in the chairs behind her. They did, standing again when the judge came in a few minutes later. As the judge spoke—addressing the lawyers, mostly—Red kept her eyes on her hands. Her heart thundered against her ribs, even though she knew how the proceeding would turn out. Ms. Anders had already told her: Wanda had failed to meet the judge's expectations, so there was very little chance the judge would decide Red should live with her again. Plus, the judge had Red's letter, and Ms. Anders promised that what Red wanted would be taken into consideration.

Still, Red was nervous.

The judge finished talking and shuffled papers.

"Your Honor," the lawyer next to Wanda said. "Before you make your decision, my client would like to make a statement."

When the judge gave her permission, Wanda stood. Red stared at the back of her mother's head. Her hair was in a braid that slid from side to side a little as she moved.

"Your Honor." Wanda stopped, cleared her throat. "I'm pretty sure we all know what you're going to say about me today. And it's true. I haven't done very well lately."

She cleared her throat again. "The truth is, Your Honor, I haven't done well in a long time. I had my daughter when I was nineteen. I was already on the road to addiction, even then."

Red's hands began to shake and she clasped them in her lap.

"My mom took care of Red for a lot of years. I was just too sick and too young." She paused, looked down. "And too selfish."

Celine's hand covered both of Red's.

"She gave me a lot of chances, my mom. Probably too many. But I kept failing her. And failing my daughter."

Wanda took a deep breath.

"I love my daughter." Suddenly she turned and looked right into Red's eyes. "I love her infinity plus one." They held each other's gaze for a moment, then she turned back to the judge. "But I haven't loved her well. I want to be a good mom to her. I really do." Her voice broke, and she looked down, clearing her throat a third time.

Celine sucked in a small breath, and Red glanced at her. Her eyes were wide and her face pale. Her other hand clutched Jackson's, and he, too, was staring at Wanda with an intense look on his face. Red couldn't tell if he was scared or angry. Or both.

"I haven't done very much right by her, and I know that. But I want to do right by her now," Wanda said. She lifted her chin and squared her shoulders, then said, "I want to give up my parental rights. I want Red to be adopted by a family who can love her better than I can."

Wanda turned and looked at the three of them. "And I think that family is sitting with her right now."

Her mother held her eye for the briefest moment, and the air between them warmed and shimmered. It brushed Red's cheek in a whisper like, *I'm sorry*, like, *I love you*, like, *Infinity plus one*.

Red dipped her chin in a nod. *Me too.*

Celine made a noise next to her, and the shimmer of air vanished. Wanda faced the judge, and Red turned to Celine. Her foster mother was crying silent streams of tears, like she had been the night she told Red about Roan. But this time, she was smiling, too.

Happy and sad, Red thought. *Two things at once.*

She understood what it meant for Wanda to give up her rights, just like she understood what it meant when she told the judge she wanted to live with Celine and Jackson.

It meant she and her mom were family. But also that they were not.

It seemed impossible, but it had to be done. Her mother loved her, but she couldn't take care of her. The knowledge of this was a small, sharp pain in Red's chest. And some pain, she knew, never went away.

Red didn't hear a word that was said after her mother's statement. She could only stare at her mother's braid as she leaned in to Celine, Celine's arm tight around her shoulders.

They all stood when the judge left. Celine and Jackson hugged her and then each other. Celine was still crying, but Red felt too hollow to cry. She wasn't sad exactly, but she also wasn't happy. It would come, she knew. Both the sadness and the happiness. Grief and joy. Like two separate tornadoes under the wings of her heart.

She needed them both to fly.

Ms. Anders hugged her.

"You're a brave girl, Ruby Byrd," she said, squeezing her extra hard.

With a glance at Celine, Red broke away from the Grooves and Ms. Anders, winding around the chairs on her way to Wanda. Her mother chewed her lower lip, her gaze flitting nervously about as Red approached. They stood staring at each other's feet in silence.

"I have something for you," Wanda said after a moment. She knelt and riffled through her purse, pulling out the green notebook. One of the corners was crumpled, and its pages were wobbly with water stains. She held it out, her expression apologetic.

"I read it." She gave Red a small smile. "You really did prove them all."

Red hesitated, then took it. She went to the table where Wanda and her lawyer had been sitting and picked up a pen. Opening the notebook, she wrote one last entry, then turned to Wanda again.

"You keep it," she said, handing it back.

Wanda took it, looking both bewildered and disappointed. Red wrapped her arms around her mother's waist.

"That way you won't forget," she said.

As Red followed Celine and Jackson out of the courtroom, she looked over her shoulder. Wanda stood where Red had left her, the notebook open in her hands.

You say

Being a mom is impossible.

But you love me infinity plus one. And that's what being a mom is all about.

Chapter
62

Two weeks later, on a perfectly still evening that smelled like snow and starlight, the Kapules brought over dinner, and they all celebrated Red's twelfth birthday in the barn. Marvin made a pineapple stir-fry, and Mrs. Kapule brought an enormous chocolate cake with raspberry-cream frosting. Marvin's grandparents hugged Red and kissed her cheeks, wishing her a happy birthday.

The barn was decorated with strings of Christmas lights that filled it with a warm glow. Celine had made party hats for all the animals, even tiny ones for the chickens. The goats ate theirs, but Fezzik kept nodding, like he was showing his off.

Everyone sat on bales of hay, except Red. She sat leaning up against Tuck. Marvin plopped down next to her, surprising the tortoise. Tuck's glittery party hat slipped down over the front of his face when he tried to pull his head into his shell, making everyone laugh.

After dinner, Jackson slipped into the back room of the barn and returned carrying a box with holes cut out of the lid. Inside, Red found two black-and-white kittens.

"Every petting zoo needs a couple of cats," Jackson said.

"To keep the rats away." Celine winked at her.

"And possums!" Jackson laughed.

Red cuddled the kittens under her chin. "They're perfect."

"They were Nicole's idea," Jackson said.

Nicole had called from Seattle the day after the custody hearing. She and Red talked for a long time. Before they hung up, Nicole apologized for her behavior on Christmas Eve. She told Red that she'd been really scared, but that didn't excuse the awful things she'd said. Red forgave her. She knew what it was like to be scared, and how sometimes scared and angry felt like the same thing.

The kittens were passed around the circle. Gandalf and the other dogs sniffed them eagerly, jumping back when one of the cats swiped at their noses. Marvin's grandparents gave Red a stack of books from her favorite bookstore in Denver, and Mrs. Kapule gave her a handmade coupon for hula lessons.

"I hear you are a dancer," she said, eyes glittering. "And hula *is* the language of the heart."

Red hugged her. "Thank you!"

Marvin gave her a small journal. The cover was adorned with stars that seemed to twinkle in the light. Inside, he'd written a quote:

It's kind of fun to do the impossible. —Walt Disney

"Since you lost your other notebook," he said.

Red grinned at him. "*Mahalo.*"

"I've got one more gift for you, Red," Celine said, handing her a rolled-up piece of paper tied with a green ribbon.

Red tugged the ribbon off and unrolled the page. It was a petition for adoption.

"When we started the process of becoming foster parents," Celine explained, "we were licensed as foster to adopt."

"From the very beginning, we told Ms. Anders we wanted to adopt you, if we could," Jackson said.

Red held the paper on the flats of her palms, afraid to wrinkle it.

"I told you that we wanted whatever was best for you," Celine said, reaching for Red. "So when you said you wanted to live with your mom, we respected that.

We love you, and we've always wanted you to be ours. But more than that, we wanted you to be happy. We want that still."

"We're hoping," Jackson said, his smile as wide as the sky, "that you'll give us permission to adopt you now."

"But what about your cancer?" Red couldn't stop the words from tumbling out. Celine's new surgery date was in two weeks.

Celine's face crumpled a little. "Oh, Red. I am going to fight the cancer, and I have the best doctors on my side. But cancer or no cancer, *you* have my heart. I chose you—I *loved* you—the moment I saw you, and nothing will *ever* change that."

A little sob burst from Red's lips. She jumped up and wrapped her arms around Celine's neck. Celine hugged her back, and Jackson enfolded them both.

Red would never forget what losing Gamma had been like. It was a sadness that would stay with her forever. Watching Celine go through surgery and chemotherapy and everything else would be hard. Red knew that. But it would be impossible—for both of them—if they didn't have each other.

Red sobbed, "I want you to adopt me! I really, really do."

A minute later, Marvin stood and wrapped his arms

around the three of them, too. Red laughed through her tears as Jackson included him in the embrace.

"Get in here, guys!" Marvin said over his shoulder. His parents and grandparents stood, wiping their eyes, and followed his orders.

When the hugging and crying and laughing finally stopped, Red sat next to Celine on a hay bale, unwilling to break away for even a moment. She looked around the barn at the people and dogs and kittens and tortoise, and wanted to laugh and cry all over again. Marvin's grandfather picked up his 'ukulele and started strumming a song. Marvin and Tūtū played with the kittens, dangling one of Marvin's shoelaces in front of them.

"Can I tell you something else I want?" Red whispered to Celine.

Celine tucked Red's hair behind her ear. "Of course."

Red picked up the petition to adopt. It felt heavier than paper in her hands. It felt like hope. Like the beginning of something better. But there was still one more thing she needed to let go.

"I think, from now on, I want to go by my real name. Ruby."

Celine's smile was brighter than all the stars in the universe. "You've always been more of a Ruby to me, anyway," she said.

Celine pulled her in for another hug. Ruby snuggled

close and tight. Celine's breath tickled her cheek, like the whisper of star-music.

Ruby smiled as something warm and gentle swirled around her heart. It was a breeze brimming with new promise.

She hoped this time it was here to stay.

ACKNOWLEDGMENTS

There was a time when publishing a book seemed impossible to me, and had I been alone on this journey, it would have been. Thankfully, there have been many, many people along the way who've helped give this book—and my dreams—life.

First, my parents. Mom, Dad, you taught me how to dream in the first place, and never even suggested I major in something practical that had more potential to pay the bills than Creative Writing. Thank you for believing in me, for loving me so fiercely, and for instilling a love of storytelling in me through generous trees, little houses on big prairies, and of course, dragons. I love you, infinity plus one.

This story was inspired by my aunt, uncle, and cousin—

but my entire family has left their mark on both this book and my heart. To all of you in the Padgett, Lackey, and Olson clans: I hope you spot some of the little familial "Easter eggs" I've hidden in these pages! And I hope you know how much I love you.

My life would be poorer indeed without the support of some amazing teachers over the years. Mrs. Bell, my second grade teacher, and the first person outside of my family to call me a writer. Faye Padgett (aka Nana), Joann Berrian, Rose Dunphey, Jennifer Maier, Debra Dean, and Luke Reinsma—you all challenged and empowered me with your passion and your exacting expectations. Thank you.

Critique Partners Extraordinaire, Laurel Klein and Cora Martin—you put the Super in Sloth, and I could not have done this without you. "Thank you" doesn't go far enough, but nonetheless—thank you.

A whole host of relationships have shaped this story, as well. From conversations about everything from cancer to goat behavior, Star Wars viewings to social media guidance, hundreds of cups of (decaf!) coffee, early reads and cover reveals, and countless texts and gifs, I owe a huge debt of gratitude to: Christopher Aaby, Christine and Omair Akhtar, Amanda Annis, Shawna Avanessian, Danielle Behr, Courtney Carbone, Amy Dufault, Donna and Lonnie Funk, Sophia Funk, Alyssa Hollingsworth, Tracey and Shawn Hurley, Gary Jansen, Katrina

Lackey, Stacey Lee, Aimee Lucido, Steve Martyn, Betsy and Brandon Neale, Kevin Neuner, Renee Nyen, Kate O'Shaughnessy, Danielle Parish, Parker Peevyhouse, Lisa Ramée, Lisa Raulie, Stephanie Richard, Karalee Sartin, John Schumacher, Jenny Stafford, Anne-Marie Strohman, Noah Tatro, Jen Wilson, and Kristi Wright.

Catherine Toth Fox, thank you for your invaluable insights into Hawaiian culture, and for your generous support along the way. Katherine Applegate, whose kindness in word and deed has meant more than I can express. Also thanks to Middle Grade Lunch Break (KidLitCraft.com), Novel Nineteens, Kepler's Books, Hicklebee's Children's Bookstore, Sparkles and Lace Boutique (you know you deserve to be mentioned!), and SCBWI—especially SCBWI/SF-South.

Of course, none of this would have been a reality without my incredible agent/dragon/unicorn, Elena Giovinazzo. Querying you seemed like the most impossible thing of all, and yet, here we are. Thank you for taking a chance on me that day, and for every single day since. Thanks to Dana Spector, film agent and book-enthusiast, whose kindness won me over from day one. My warmest thanks to all of the Pips, as well. Holly, Larissa, Ashley, Sara—the world is a better, more colorful, more story-ful place because of each of you!

Jen Besser—editor, champion, therapist, and cheerleader with the best taste in blush pink couches (and books)—it is such an honor to work with you and to call you a friend. Thank you for believing in Red and Tuck. And me.

To the entire Macmillan and Roaring Brook Press team—you are wizards, all. Luisa Beguiristain for, well, everything. Elizabeth H. Clark and Sarah J. Coleman (InkyMole) for my stunning, stunning cover. Mandy Veloso and Nancy Elgin in managing editorial. Chandra Wohleber, the most amazing copyeditor of all time. The incredibly kind, brilliant, and enthusiastic folks in marketing and publicity: Molly Ellis, Allison Verost, Morgan Rath, and Katie Quinn—without you, this story would be nothing but a whisper in a windstorm. Lucy Del Priore and Katie Halata, thank you for sharing my love of librarians and wonderful books! My thanks also to the team at Macmillan Audio, Guy Oldfield and Dakota Cohen, and to the magic voice herself, Samantha Desz. If I've left anyone off this list, my sincerest apologies. I've been overwhelmed with gratitude for the whole amazing Macmillan (and extended) family!

To the enthusiastic booksellers, librarians, and book lovers I've met in real life and online—thank you so much for your support for this little book. You've made me laugh and cry with wonder and gratitude, and I hope I get to meet and hug each and every one of you someday.

Animals play an important role in this book because they have played an important role in my own life. For the writing of this book, my pup Guido was either at my feet or on the chair behind me with each word. He's not in these pages by name, but he's all over the story in spirit.

And finally—but mostly. My love and constant support, Brandon. I couldn't have done this without you. You're *my* star-music and I thank God for this journey we're on together. Here's to all the adventures yet to come. I love you.

Shawna Avanessian

Dear friend,

After I published <u>All the Impossible Things</u>, many people asked me why I wrote it. I told them that it is a story inspired by my real family: My aunt and uncle became foster parents, much like Celine and Jackson, and they eventually fostered and adopted my youngest cousin. I told people that I remembered how it feels to be a kid with really BIG emotions, so turning Red's emotions into storms made sense to me.

These things are true, but none of them are really an answer as to why I wrote this book.

When asked why they write, many authors say they feel like they <u>need</u> to write, much like a person needs to breathe air. They say they have something important to express, or that they write as an act of resistance, or that they tell the stories they needed as a child.

These are such wonderful reasons to write—but they aren't my reasons. I love telling stories, yet for a long time, I honestly didn't know why.

Then, one day, I heard someone say, "Stories are healing."

My friend—there are very few moments in life that I'd call "lightning-bolt moments." Those instances when something deeply true is revealed to you and you know you'll never think of things the same way again. This is how I felt in that moment.

Because stories <u>are</u> healing. They have been healing me since I was a child. Reading them, writing them, listening to them—a story in any form has the power to heal us. And suddenly, I knew exactly why I wrote <u>All the Impossible Things</u>, and why I write stories at all.

I write because I want my reader—I want <u>you</u>—to feel seen. I want you to know that you are so valuable, so important, so <u>necessary</u> to this world. You, just as you are, <u>matter</u>. The things you've been through, the things you've done, the big emotions you feel, where you've been, who you call family, what you do or do not believe—nothing can diminish the truth: You. Matter. And I am incredibly glad you are here.

Stories are healing. I also believe that stories are magical. When an author writes a story, they build a bridge to a world that they hope someone will visit someday. When you read a book, you walk across that bridge. You visit that world. There, you meet the author, and from that moment on, you have a friend. Even if you never meet in person, even if you never communicate beyond the world of that single book, you have a friend.

Thank you for being my friend. Thank you for meeting me in the pages of <u>All the Impossible Things</u>. I wrote this story with the deep hope that someone would want to meet me here, and you came. I am so very grateful.

I hope you will continue to find your way into many, many stories, and I hope that each one will remind you just how beloved you are.

Your friend, always,
Lindsay

GOFISH

QUESTIONS FOR THE AUTHOR

LINDSAY LACKEY

What were your favorite books as a kid?
I read pretty much anything I could get my hands on as a kid. The earliest books I remember reading and loving were by Shel Silverstein: *The Giving Tree* and his hilarious poetry in *Where the Sidewalk Ends*. Some of my favorite series were Nancy Drew and the Baby-Sitters Club books. I also loved the Little House on the Prairie series by Laura Ingalls Wilder. When I was in sixth grade, I got hooked on adult thrillers by Mary Higgins Clark. I loved how exciting they were without being too scary! (I hate scary books and movies!)

What inspired you to write *All the Impossible Things*?
I first got the idea for the story when my aunt and uncle in real life decided to become foster parents. They had grown children and even a grandchild, but instead of spending their "empty nester" years traveling the world, they decided to open their home to children who needed a safe place to live. I loved that! Celine and

Jackson Groove in the book are based a lot on my aunt and uncle.

A few years after they started fostering, they ended up adopting a little girl. I was very careful to make Red different than my cousin because I didn't want anyone to think it was a story *about* my cousin. There are some things that are similar between the two of them, but mostly Red is a figment of my imagination.

The animals at the Groovy Petting Zoo have strong literary names, from Gandalf to Frodo to the loveable turtle named Tuck Everlasting. What books or characters have informed your writing?
So many! When I was a toddler, I loved Shel Silverstein's *The Giving Tree* so much, I had it perfectly memorized—page turns and all. My dad read *The Hobbit* and *Watership Down* to me when I was much too young to comprehend them in many ways, but was still able to understand what they meant: Magic was real.

This novel is sprinkled with magic alongside the ordinary. Do you believe in impossible things?
I do—with my whole heart. I've been a witness to many impossible things, and I've experienced them myself. One of which was publishing this book! What I believe in more than anything, though, is love. Celine tells Red that "love can do impossible things," and that is something I've seen over and over again in my own life. I hope that, at the very least, readers will come to believe in the impossible power of love through Red's story.

READER DISCUSSION QUESTIONS

1. Red's emotions affect the weather around her, making things stormy when she's upset. Have you ever felt big emotions like Red's? What did you feel and why? How did you respond when you felt that way?

2. Red is in foster care, which means she has to live with families that are not her own. Have you ever known someone who was in foster care? How do you think you would feel if you were in Red's situation? What kind of friend would you want to have if you were like Red?

3. Tuck Everlasting is a 400-pound tortoise that lives at the home of Celine and Jackson Groove, Red's newest foster family. Red feels a special bond with Tuck. Why do you think Red connects so well with Tuck? Have you ever felt a special friendship with an animal?

4. When Red first meets Marvin Kapule, her neighbor and classmate, she is not very nice to him. What do you think Red was feeling when they first met? How does Red behave toward Marvin during their class party? Why do you think she does this?

5. Marvin's family is very different than Red's experience of a family. Have you ever met someone who has lived a very different life than you? What do you think Red learns about family from Marvin and his parents?

6. When Red learns that her mother was released from prison early, she's very upset. Why do you think this news made her feel this way? How would you feel if you were in Red's situation?

7. After a storm that is caused by Red's big emotions, her friend Tuck Everlasting goes missing. How do you think Red feels about this? Have you ever done something when you were upset that hurt somebody else in some way? How did that make you feel? What did you do to try to fix things?

8. Red's mother, Wanda, struggles with an addiction to pills that makes it very hard for her to take care of Red. How did it make you feel to read about their relationship? What would you do if you were in Red's situation?

9. When Red first meets Jackson's daughter, Nicole, she is nervous that Nicole won't like her. Have you ever been nervous about meeting new people? Why do you think Red is worried Nicole won't want to be her sister? Do you think there is something Red could have done differently so that she didn't feel so nervous?

10. Red learns that "love can do impossible things." Do you think this is true? What things feel impossible to Red in the story? How does love help her do these impossible things? What things in your own life feel impossible? How can you overcome all these impossible things?

For additional resources, visit LindsayLackey.com.